praise for *holly's inbox:*

'This book sucks you into Holly's wonderful, chaotic world. Funny, captivating, and completely addictive.'

—Jill Mansell

'Very funny... [Denham] creates a warm, comedic heroine who slowly grows a backbone. There's a marvelous twist at the end.'

—*Romantic Times*

'Riveting. Holly is the e-Bridget Jones.'

—*New York Post*

'This book is a winner from first page to last.'

—The Romance Studio

'What a hoot. I started this book on a Sunday morning and by evening I had finished it. I couldn't put it down.'

—Cheryl's Book Nook

'Unbelievably, compulsively readable... often funny, sometimes poignant.'

—Bookfoolery and Babble

'Fantastic, heartwarming, and a truly novel stylistic approach. You'll love it.'

—Cuckleburr Times

'It's hilarious, it's completely addictive, and I totally recommend it!'

—WJXB-FM, Knoxville, Tennessee

'Email-tastic! ****'

—*OK!* magazine

Holly's inbox:
Scandal in the City

HOLLY DENHAM

sourcebooks
casablanca

Published by Sourcebooks Casablanca, an imprint of Sourcebooks, Inc.
P.O. Box 4410, Naperville, Illinois 60567-4410
(630) 961-3900
FAX: (630) 961-2168
www.sourcebooks.com

Originally published in 2008 by Headline Review, an imprint of Headline Publishing Group.

Library of Congress Cataloging-in-Publication Data

Denham, Holly.
  Holly's inbox : scandal in the city / Holly Denham.
      p. cm.
  Originally published: London : Headline Review, 2008.
  1. Receptionists—Fiction. 2. Electronic mail messages—Fiction. 3. Chick lit. I. Title.
  PR6104.E566H65 2010
  823'.92—dc22

                              2010017247

        Printed and bound in the United States of America
             VP 10 9 8 7 6 5 4 3 2 1

Subject: PLAN FOR 2008

From: Holly
To: Holly

Whatever you do, Holly, you must remember:

1) Do not let Mum's career suggestions wind you up (she means well)

2) Do not get insecure/jealous with Toby. Stay fun and breezy at all times

3) Do not end up doing other people's work, just because you can't say no

4) Stay away from work witches, company bullies and people who hang around the reception desk telling you their problems then get your email address and email you their problems, then arrange to meet you for lunch each day to give you more of their problems, even though they never ask you a thing about yours—which happen to be worse, talking of which:

5) Stop keeping the bills in the freezer—they know you are still there, even if they can't see you now, and they are waiting for you…

6) Keep away from your strange upstairs neighbour

7) Oh and stop getting ridiculously drunk with people from work (it isn't pretty)

Wish me luck!

Holly Denham, Receptionist, DKHuerst, 50 Cabot Square, Canary Wharf, London

month 1

week 1

tuesday

Subject: Something seriously wrong at this company

From: Holly
To: Jason

No, it's definitely not right.

Holly Denham, Receptionist, DK Huerst, 50 Cabot Square, Canary Wharf, London

From: Jason
To: Holly

You're not lost again, are you?

Jason Granger, Reception Manager, LHS Hotels, London, W1V 6TT

From: Holly
To: Jason

No, although I'm not saying it won't happen again, I can't get used to this building—it's huge and 40 floors exactly the same is just silly.

From: Jason
To: Holly

Has the office merger finished yet?

From: Holly
To: Jason

No, we've still got more DK staff coming, grrrrr.

From: Jason
To: Holly

Change is good Holly, we accept change. Deep breaths, remember—mice and cheese.

From: Holly
To: Jason

Stop saying mice and cheese, it's not helpful, got to go.

From: Jason
To: Holly

Wait, tell me what's so suspicious???

Subject: Meeting

From: Richard Mosley
To: Holly

Dear Holly

Thank you for attending today's meeting, we will keep you updated with any developments.

Yours sincerely

Richard Mosley

Head of Facilities, DK Huerst, 50 Cabot Square, Canary Wharf, London

Subject: Psssst

From: Holly
To: Jason

They're keeping me updated with any developments.

From: Jason
To: Holly

Who are?

From: Holly
To: Jason

Facilities.

From: Jason
To: Holly

So what's so suspicious?

From: Holly
To: Jason

They are, management, HR, the Head of Facilities, the whole lot.

From: Jason
To: Holly

So it's a conspiracy?

From: Holly
To: Jason

Yes.

From: Jason
To: Holly

Involving everyone in the bank?

From: Holly
To: Jason

Possibly.

Subject: RECEPTION DESK ALLOCATION FOR COMING MONTH

From: Richard Mosley
To: Holly, Trisha & Claire

The Bank's Front-of-House Services operate best with the team laid out as below.

Holly and Trisha on the main hall ground floor desk, meeting all staff, clients and anyone else entering the building, with the security staff obviously by the main door. Once you've checked any clients arriving at DK Huerst for meetings, keep them sitting in the waiting area opposite you until Claire is ready to great them upstairs. I don't want Claire's smaller reception area there becoming so full that clients aren't able to sit down.

30th Floor Hospitality Suite: Claire

Ground Floor Main Entrance: Trisha & Holly

We will be employing another receptionist shortly to sit with Claire on the hospitality floor, and of course Marie Lopez will be coming over from the old DK building to merge with us in the coming weeks. She will operate as a lone switchboard operator in the basement.

Subject: That last email

From: Trisha
To: Holly

Wouldn't be in her shoes.

Patricia Gillot, Senior Receptionist, DK Huerst, 50 Cabot Square, Canary Wharf

From: Holly
To: Trisha

Who's that?

From: Trisha
To: Holly

Marie Lopez, sitting down there in the basement all alone, with no sunlight.

From: Holly
To: Trisha

I think she's in the basement at the moment anyway.

From: Trisha
To: Holly

She won't complain then. They should go in, smack her over the head, drag her out and wake her up downstairs pretending nothing's happened. Hey, why is that man staring at you?

From: Holly
To: Trisha

Who?

From: Trisha
To: Holly

That man in the corner. Keeps looking at you over his paper?

From: Holly
To: Trisha

No idea, I don't like his eyes though.

From: Trisha
To: Holly

Shifty.

From: Holly
To: Trisha

Very shifty, and alarmingly bushy.

From: Trisha
To: Holly

Would you go to bed with a man like that?

From: Holly
To: Trisha

If he shaved them and didn't stare at me like that.

From: Trisha
To: Holly

What about if he stared at you like this…

From: Holly
To: Trisha

HOW DID YOU DO THAT??

From: Trisha
To: Holly

Don't know, look I can make em disappear and all.

From: Holly
To: Trisha

TRISHA that's revolting.

Subject: I'm still confused...

From: Jason
To: Holly

It's a conspiracy because they gave you a verbal warning??

From: Holly
To: Jason

No, it's a conspiracy because they didn't give me a verbal warning.

From: Jason
To: Holly

It's a double bluff?? Is that what you think?

From: Holly
To: Jason

I've just heard they've brought the CEO into it all now. Should be meeting him this week so I think this is just the calm before a storm, could be about to be sacked. There's definitely something fishy going on.

From: Jason
To: Holly

A fishy storm you think?!

From: Holly
To: Jason

Are you taking the Pee, Jason?

From: Jason
To: Holly

No? What happened at your works do on Friday?

From: Holly
To: Jason

I met the catering manager, the one Toby knows, the one I thought I'd hate.

From: Jason
To: Holly

But you ended up liking her.

From: Holly
To: Jason

You think you're so smart (but yes, she's nice).

Subject: Last Friday night

From: Holly
To: Tanya Mason

Dear Tanya

Really enjoyed meeting you on Friday.

Hope I didn't embarrass myself too much—I remember cornering you for quite some time and declaring my undying love for your apple strudels.

Kindest regards

Holly

Subject: Greetings from Spain

From: Mum
To: Holly

Holly

I've been going back through your old school books and remembered how good you always were at art. They're running all kinds of exciting evening courses these days, some very near you in Maida Vale. What do you think?

From: Holly
To: Mum

About what?

From: Mum
To: Holly

These art courses? Your father is making some extra cash out here selling paintings to the locals. Every penny helps.

From: Holly
To: Mum

I know it does, Mum, but Dad's very good.

From: Mum
To: Holly

Well, you just need a bit of positive thinking.

From: Holly
To: Mum

I don't want to paint mum

From: Mum
To: Holly

What about if you become pregnant? What with Toby not doing so well these days with his credit house thing, you need to start saving.

From: Holly
To: Mum

He's in banking, Mum, just like James was.

From: Mum
To: Holly

I know he is and we're told these bankers are so smart but they gave mortgages to people in caravans and these people had no jobs, no careers or any kind of way of paying the money back, then everyone's so surprised when it went wrong. I could have told them.

From: Holly
To: Mum

That happened in America, Mum, Toby didn't lend them the money. I'm really busy here, can I go now?

From: Mum
To: Holly

Of course, can I just ask one thing?

From: Holly
To: Mum

Yes.

From: Mum
To: Holly

Are you pregnant?

From: Holly
To: Mum

No.

From: Mum
To: Holly

Are you engaged yet?

From: Holly
To: Mum

No.

From: Mum
To: Holly

OK, well there's no pressure. You take your time darling, I'll send dad your love. And think about another career path. You can't be a receptionist all your life, can you?

Subject: Problem with scheduler

From: Richard Mosley
To: Holly

Dear Holly

We have discovered some discrepancies with the scheduler. Items like champagne and wine which were booked in by one of the reception team onto the system, weren't actually ordered by anyone. When you have a moment will you give me a call and let me know how you think this could have happened?

Kind regards

Richard

Subject: Mystery solved

From: Holly
To: Jason

They think I've been fiddling the company.

From: Jason
To: Holly

Are you sure?

From: Holly
To: Jason

Think so, this will be interesting.

wednesday

Subject: Board Room Booking

From: William Duncan
To: Holly

I'm meeting the Dutch Prime Minister this afternoon and I need the board room. I emailed through to the Bookings email, but they said no. Can you sort this for me please.

Will

William Duncan, VP Corporate Finance, DK Huerst, 50 Cabot Square, Canary Wharf, London

From: Holly
To: William Duncan

Are you really?

Holly

From: William Duncan
To: Holly

No, not really, but I want the board room.

From: Holly
To: William Duncan

Sorry, Will, but that room is already taken for that slot, would you like us to find you a similar-sized room?

Regards

Holly

Subject: Answers???

From: Holly
To: Jason

Are you going to help me work out what's going on here or not?

From: Jason
To: Holly

I will if you give me more information. I'm trying to read between the lines, but there aren't enough of them.

From: Holly
To: Jason

Had another call from HR, they just kept asking me loads of strange questions.

From: Jason
To: Holly

Maybe they're recruiting for MI5??

Subject: Hi Honey

From: Holly
To: Toby

What time are you back tonight?

From: Toby
To: Holly

Not till late, sorry sweetie.
Toby Williams, VP Corporate Finance, DK Huerst, 50 Cabot Square, Canary Wharf, London

From: Holly
To: Toby

On my own again. You'll come home one night to find me sitting in a corner talking to my imaginary friends.

From: Toby
To: Holly

Sorry it's been going on for a while, but this is a big deal.

From: Holly
To: Toby

Can't you work on smaller deals, or no deals at all and just stay at home and wait for me? It's been going on for years and years now.

From: Toby
To: Holly

I know it seems that way, but it really hasn't.

x

From: Holly
To: Toby

Years and years and years and years and years and years.

From: Toby
To: Holly

Sweetie.

From: Holly
To: Toby

Years and years and years and years and years and years and I'm not listening to you until you come back earlier it's not fair so there I'm sulking yes I am.

From: Toby
To: Holly

Have you finished?

From: Holly
To: Toby

I think so. You want me to leave you any dinner?

From: Toby
To: Holly

No, I'll get something on the way home.

x

Subject: REMINDER

From: Holly
To: Holly

Meal for ONE :(poor me.

Subject: From Mr Fraser your friendly upstairs neighbour

From: Frank Fraser
To: Holly

Holly
Found a mouse today.

From: Holly
To: Frank Fraser

Did you, Frank? I'm sorry to hear that.

From: Frank Fraser
To: Holly

He was sitting on top of my dustbin watching me so I hit him with a saucepan, flattened him.

From: Holly
To: Frank Fraser

Thank you for letting me know, Frank.

Subject: SOS

From: Holly
To: Jason

Are you around tonight? Toby's working late, thought we could do something?

From: Jason
To: Holly

Sorry, can't, I'm supervising the late shift—we've got a big party of rich Arabs staying here.

Subject: REMINDER

From: Holly
To: Holly

Meal for ONE :(poor me

Wine

Atonement

About a Boy

Subject: Important clients coming

From: Holly
To: Claire

About to put the lot for the boardroom in the lift now.

From: Claire
To: Holly

No no, it's occupied. Hold on to them, Holly, while I find us another room.

Receptionist, DK Huerst,50 Cabot Square, Canary Wharf, London

From: Holly
To: Claire

How is it occupied?

From: Claire
To: Holly

I don't know, but it is and when I asked to speak to the host, someone came to the door and told me they were holding a séance for the late president George Washington.

From: Holly
To: Claire

Did he now?

From: Claire
To: Holly

He said if I had any respect for the dead at all to leave them in peace.
I didn't even know he'd died.

thursday

Subject: Your email

From: Tanya Mason
To: Holly

Dear Holly
Thank you for your kind email, you were very funny on Friday,
very entertaining. Did you manage to get home alright?
Tanya Mason
Catering Manager, DK Huerst, 50 Cabot Square, Canary Wharf, London

From: Holly
To: Tanya Mason

Yes thanks, Tanya I did get home OK. Hope I didn't embarrass
myself too much!
Regards
Holly

From: Tanya Mason
To: Holly

No you didn't at all, you were very complimentary on my cooking,
although I did try and point out that I was the Catering Manager
and not a Chef, but you weren't having it. But a good time had by all.
Tanya

From: Holly
To: Tanya Mason

Sorry about that. We should just make a drunken assault on the West
End next time—let me know when you're free and I'll be there.
Holly

Subject: Morning

From: Jason
To: Holly

Need to know right now if you are coming out to play tonight for
fun and frolics (organizing the hotel rota).

From: Holly
To: Jason

I'll check with Toby now. Also that Tanya just emailed, I might
have found a new party friend.

From: Jason
To: Holly

Will I like her?

From: Holly
To: Jason

Think you will, she even has one of those walks you've been trying
to teach me for the past ten years.

From: Jason
To: Holly

Great, but can she do it without holding the wall and looking like
she's about to pee herself?

From: Holly
To: Jason

Yes.

From: Jason
To: Holly

What about entrances? Can she glide down steps without doing it on her bum? If so don't worry about tonight, I'll call her instead.

From: Holly
To: Jason

Jump off a tall building. Also I just spoke to Toby and I can't make it anyway. Sorry, he's finishing early… And we're racing home for pizza and sex.

From: Jason
To: Holly

Great, lucky thing, give him one for me.

From: Holly
To: Jason

Will do.

From: Jason
To: Holly

On second thoughts, tell him to go cut his hair first, and have a shave.

From: Holly
To: Jason

OK.

From: Jason
To: Holly

Long hair was good in the 80s, it's no longer the 80s.

From: Holly
To: Jason

It's not long and I'm sure he doesn't want sex with you anyway.

From: Jason
To: Holly

Bet he does.

Subject: Clarification needed

From: Holly
To: Toby

Do you want to have sex with Jason?

From: Toby
To: Holly

Sorry???????

Subject: Sex with Toby

From: Holly
To: Jason

You're wrong, he said he couldn't think of anything worse than sex with you. Where's Aisha today anyway?

From: Jason
To: Holly

Busy, making a tower out of pens and paper clips.

Subject: More Attention Needed

From: Natasha Springer
To: Holly

Dear Receptionist

Regarding yesterday's total mess when I specifically booked the boardroom. Can you ensure you book the room I reserve; I thought that was what you did down there????? I want the correct room next time, I'm sure it's not difficult to follow simple instructions or have I missed something here??

Regards

Natasha

Natasha Springer, Head of Commodities Trading, DK Huerst, 50 Cabot Square, Canary Wharf, London

From: Holly
To: Natasha Springer

Hi Natasha

I did book the boardroom for you yesterday, however another important meeting overran.

I'm really sorry to have put you in this situation, Natasha. I will ensure you never go through this again.

Regards

Holly

Subject: Your boardroom séance

From: Holly
To: William Duncan

You got me in trouble just now by using the boardroom when I told you it was booked. Please try and make our lives easier in reception by sticking to the rules.

Holly

From: William Duncan
To: Holly

Sorry about that, who did I upset then?

From: Holly
To: William Duncan

Natasha Springer.

From: William Duncan
To: Holly

Sh*t, what did you say?

From: Holly
To: William Duncan

Didn't mention your name, just that someone had an important meeting.

From: William Duncan
To: Holly

Thanks for that, so remind me again why you won't have dinner with me?

From: Holly
To: William Duncan

You're an incredible womanizer and I am married.

From: William Duncan
To: Holly

Neither statements are true. I am single, totally honest and completely in love with you, and you have a boyfriend, who's never around, always in France and one day will probably stay there.

From: Holly
To: William Duncan

Do you know anything about women at all??

From: William Duncan
To: Holly

No.

Subject: I messed up

From: Holly
To: Trisha

Just upset someone called Natasha Springer. What's she like—have you heard of her?

From: Trisha
To: Holly

No, name rings a bell, I'll find out.

Subject: Meeting Request

From: HR Administrator
To: Holly

For attendance on Friday 7th March at 11am, Meeting Room 23.

Regards

Human Resources

DK Huerst, 50 Cabot Square, Canary Wharf, London

Subject: Being called up again

From: Holly
To: Trisha

This is beginning to be a nightmare, I've another meeting tomorrow?? What's that about now????

From: Trisha
To: Holly

Don't know, maybe this is when they sack you?

From: Holly
To: Trisha

Thanks, Trish.

Subject: Lover?

From: Holly
To: Toby

Are you busy?

From: Toby
To: Holly

Yes.

From: Holly
To: Toby

Just wanted to know if you'd heard of Natasha Springer?

From: Toby
To: Holly

Attractive, head of commodities, very good at trading. Sorry, swamped again, also don't have a go but I've got to cancel plans tonight, got to stay on here. We'll have a great weekend together, I promise.

xxx

From: Holly
To: Toby

OK, I might go to the cinema tonight with Jason then.

From: Toby
To: Holly

I'll be back before you I imagine. See you after the cinema around 11pm?

Subject: HEEEEEELPPPP!

From: Holly
To: Jason

NO SEX NO TOBY POOR HOLLY!!! Can I still come with you please? Please don't say it's too late.

xxxx

Subject: From Spain

From: Elizabeth on Tour
To: Holly

Wish me luck!

From: Holly
To: Elizabeth on Tour

Good luck, Granny.

Subject: Too Late

From: Jason
To: Holly

I'm working in the hotel.

From: Holly
To: Jason

Oh, OK.

From: Jason
To: Holly

Sorry, Holly.

From: Holly
To: Jason

That's alright, I'll get a DVD in.
X

From: Jason
To: Holly

Then at 7pm I'm leaving, picking you up and taking you clubbing with me and Aisha to G.A.Y!!!!! Bought you a ticket so no queuing, you lucky thing, you are my official date!!!!

xxxxxx

From: Holly
To: Jason

I love you, have I ever told you that? OH YAY!!!

From: Jason
To: Holly

Yes you have.

From: Holly
To: Jason

Also told Toby I was going to the cinema, so probably shouldn't do a huge one.

From: Jason
To: Holly

Oh OK, just two glasses of wine then.

From: Holly
To: Jason

Just two… and don't let any of your friends ask me if I'm a man this time.

From: Jason
To: Holly

Then don't wear so much make up.

From: Holly
To: Jason

prrrrrrrrrrrrrrrrrrt

Subject: From England

From: Holly
To: Elizabeth on Tour

By the way, what's the luck for?

From: Elizabeth on Tour
To: Holly

Holly

You are a ninny, I'm going on my trip today, I did tell you about this last week. Are you OK dear?

Granny

From: Holly
To: Elizabeth on Tour

I'm fine, have lots of fun, hope it rains for you.

xxxx

From: Elizabeth on Tour
To: Holly

Oh that would be lovely, wouldn't it. I'm taking cheddar and pickle sandwiches and I've got treacle tart, how naughty of me.

Love Granny

From: Holly
To: Elizabeth on Tour

Very naughty, I wish I was there with you.

Love you

Holly

Subject: RE accounting for our previous big night out...

From: Tickie
To: Holly

Hi sweetie

Don't mean to bring it up, but have you got that £200 you owe me?

From: Holly
To: Tickie

Sorry, of course, Tickie, I'll pop a cheque in the post.

x

Subject: REMINDER

From: Holly
To: Holly

HOLLY REMEMBER FOR FUTURE!!!! When friends who you can't afford to see drunkenly insist you come out to play… and you say you have no money… and they tell you they'll pay for everything… they will never remember in the morning, YOU DIMWIT!!

friday

Subject: Not so good.

From: Holly
To: Jason; Aisha

Anyone know what time we left the club?

From: Aisha
To: Holly; Jason

Aisha was a good girl, she cares about her job at HLS. She went home before either of you and got here early this morning. Tell her, Jason, how early I was for work today.

Receptionist, LHS Hotels, London W1V 6TT

From: Jason
To: Holly; Aisha

Aisha, firstly, you're working for LHS, not HLS, secondly from your erratic behaviour, I think you probably have not been to bed yet.

From: Aisha
To: Holly; Jason

Shame on you!

Little me races to get here early, all spic and span, to have you pick on me. Well, I never!

From: Jason
To: Holly; Aisha

See what I have to put up with, Holly? So what did Toby say when you got in?

From: Holly
To: Jason; Aisha

He was asleep. Talking of which, you've seen *Juno*, what's it like?

From: Jason
To: Holly; Aisha

Tell him the opening scene was hilarious but you don't want to say too much because you'll ruin it for him.

Subject: Charlie's Newsletter

FROM Charlie
TO Holly; Mum; Alice

Dear Family

Having discovered that Dutch musical taste doesn't stretch to thrash-metal played by strippers on cellos, I have spent the remainder of our tour budget on plane tickets for Tatiana, Tina and Therese to bring Sextalica to the Norwegians. Also found a monkey who pretends to play bass. Adds to the spectacle. Let's hope the Scandis have more class.

Charlie.

Subject: My Brother

From: Holly
To: Rubber Ron

If you're going to write something from Charlie's email address, couldn't you write something a little less ridiculous?

From: Rubber Ron
To: Holly

I'm just writing exactly what he wants me to write, I really am. I couldn't make this up.
Sorry, Holly.

Subject: Your mum called while you were on a break.

From: Trisha
To: Holly

So I'll deal with this lot, you've got to call her back. It's about your granny and your mum didn't sound very happy, so good luck.

Subject: SCHEDULE OF PAYMENTS

From: SouthernDebtManagementLtd
To: Holly

Reference No: 730809

Dear Ms Holly Denham

We have still not received a reply from our letter dated 17th January

We are still awaiting your payments for:

November £638.50

December £620

January £620

Unfortunately if you do not call our office today we will have to proceed with further action against you.

Debt Recovery Department

Subject: Should have run away with Granny

From: Holly
To: Trisha

Would have been fun. Better than going for this meeting with HR, I'm really nervous.

From: Trisha
To: Holly

Stand your ground and if they start laying into you for anything just take notes or something.

From: Holly
To: Trisha

Thanks Trisha,

I suppose if things go wrong I could always get a job somewhere where they actually let you talk to the person sitting next to you??? Imagine that?

From: Trisha
To: Holly

Not sure I'd want you with your bad breath in my ear hole all day.

From: Holly
To: Trisha

I do not have bad breath!!!

Stop trying to make me feel more nervous. By the way have you seen what our star guest has been up to now?

From: Trisha
To: Holly

You mean grumpy jaws by the last couch?

From: Holly
To: Trisha

She's moved every magazine and newspaper to another part of the reception, in less than ten minutes.

Right I'm off.

From: Trisha
To: Holly

Hold on, let me have a fag first. I'll straighten up them mags on the way back, and growl at her when I pass.

From: Holly
To: Trisha

OK, but quick and it won't count unless she turns her head, then I better leave because I can't be late.

Subject: Granny

From: Mum
To: Holly

Dear Holly
I'm sorry I got so angry with you. I understand you didn't realise, but I think sometimes you encourage her.
Mum

From: Holly
To: Mum

That's unfair, you really can't blame me for this. Is she OK? Where is she?

From: Mum
To: Holly

She's asleep upstairs. The home won't take her back as they say she's too difficult to manage, so we've organized her own room upstairs. It'll be like her own little flat.
Mum

From: Holly
To: Mum

Good. She'll be much happier with you. She always hated eating either paella and wanted 'proper' bacon. I thought you'd put her address on a card in her pocket or something?

From: Mum
To: Holly

I put addresses everywhere, on her walking stick, her sunglasses. She's taken them all off. I even stitched an address into your granny's handkerchief but she threw it away. I love Mum, but she's hard work.

From: Holly
To: Mum

Where did they find her?

From: Mum
To: Holly

Sitting in a bar, surrounded by men of course, smiling away.

From: Holly
To: Mum

Will you give her a hug from me when she wakes?

xxx

Subject: URGENT

From: Holly
To: Jason

Just had my meeting with all the bosses. Call me Jason quick.

Subject: Cinema

From: Toby
To: Holly

How was the film, sugar?

From: Holly
To: Toby

Brilliant, the opening scene was hilarious but I won't ruin any of it for you. How was your night? What time did you manage to get to sleep, you poor working thing?

From: Toby
To: Holly

About 11, I think.

From: Holly
To: Toby

You fancy dinner after work tonight? We could have pasta in the Cochonet?

From: Toby
To: Holly

Sounds good, you on ground floor reception today?

From: Holly
To: Toby

Always. Pick me up on your way out.

Subject: Holly Holly Holly

From: Jason
To: Holly

From: Jason Jason Jason (I got your repeated bubbling message).
Tell me then??

From: Holly
To: Jason

I went to the HR meeting…

From: Jason
To: Holly

And?

From: Holly
To: Jason

Guess…

From: Jason
To: Holly

You were given a warning?

v

From: Holly
To: Jason

Guess again.

From: Jason
To: Holly

Don't tell me you were sacked on the spot?

From: Holly
To: Jason

Keep guessing.

From: Jason
To: Holly

You were dressed up like a French nun and made to parade around their office with a bucket on your head?

From: Holly
To: Jason

Really?

From: Jason
To: Holly

While Richard played "knees up mother brown"…

From: Holly
To: Jason

?

From: Jason
To: Holly

On a ukulele, dressed as Officer Dibble…

From: Holly
To: Jason

?

From: Jason
To: Holly

From *Top Cat*?

From: Holly
To: Jason

OK, you can stop guessing... They're discussing a supervisory position for me...

From: Jason
To: Holly

NO? Doing what?

From: Holly
To: Jason

As DK Huerst Front of House Manager of the whole bank...

From: Jason
To: Holly

You have got to be joking! Why you?

From: Holly
To: Jason

Because they are looking for someone 'organised, client focused, professional, and, above all, mature'. While they were telling me I was stifling a fit of giggles while trying not to pee myself.

From: Jason
To: Holly

Always the lady. Do they really mean this?

From: Holly
To: Jason

Yes they do and you shouldn't be so surprised! (Having said that, imagine, me in charge of a team???) Also they're employing another receptionist next week I think.

From: Jason
To: Holly

So you would be in charge of Trisha?

From: Holly
To: Jason

Yes, and I know :(that's not so good.

From: Jason
To: Holly

She's been there for twenty years, you've been there for just a year??

From: Holly
To: Jason

I realize this, Jason.

From: Jason
To: Holly

And she's your friend, you sit next to every day? Poor Trisha.

From: Holly
To: Jason

Stop it, don't make me feel bad, it hasn't happened yet anyway.

From: Jason
To: Holly

She will kill you.

From: Holly
To: Jason

No, she won't.

From: Jason
To: Holly

She will drag you out in front of the whole bank and drown you in the fountain.

From: Holly
To: Jason

She won't, because I lied to her, I told her I'd been given a verbal warning.

From: Jason
To: Holly

You will have to tell her the truth at some stage.

From: Holly
To: Jason

But will I?

From: Jason
To: Holly

Yes, Holly, you will.
Unless you think you could somehow manage Trisha without her actually knowing you're in charge of her?

From: Holly
To: Jason

Is that possible?

From: Jason
To: Holly

No, Holly, it isn't. You have to tell her the truth. Have you told Toby yet?

From: Holly
To: Jason

No, and I'm not going to unless I get it, then I'll be telling him every five minutes. He might even respect me then, you never know????

From: Jason
To: Holly

He does already. x

Subject: Last night

From: Toby
To: Holly

By the way, what time did you get in then?

From: Holly
To: Toby

Not sure, didn't check, think it was before 12.

Subject: Caught

From: Holly
To: Jason

Shit, I think Toby's just rumbled me, but he's playing some kind of game.

From: Jason
To: Holly

Damn the games.

From: Holly
To: Jason

Damn those blasted games.

week 2
monday

Subject: Nightmares

From: Holly
To: Jason

Had a nightmare last night, I'd fallen overboard on Toby's dad's boat, and there were all these fish…

From: Jason
To: Holly

And sharks?

From: Holly
To: Jason

No just fish, horrible slimy fish and they were everywhere.

From: Jason
To: Holly

You'll have to get over this phobia if you're going to heaven.

From: Holly
To: Jason

Why?

From: Jason
To: Holly

Fish have to go to heaven and you don't think God's going to fill the sky with water, so they'll be swimming around in the air won't they, all around your face.

Subject: Help

From: Holly
To: Toby

Fish don't go to heaven do they???

From: Toby
To: Holly

What?

Subject: Nightmares

From: Holly
To: Jason

I asked Toby and he says you're wrong, and you should shave your beard off.

From: Jason
To: Holly

Aisha said yesterday I looked like an upside down version of Tin Tin.

From: Holly
To: Jason

Possibly, who's Tin Tin?

From: Jason
To: Holly

Someone who looks like an upside down version of me. OK, tomorrow I'm back to my Timberlake look.

From: Holly
To: Jason

Didn't know you had a Timberlake look?

From: Jason
To: Holly

Go wash your mouth out!

Subject: Your meeting

From: Trisha
To: Holly

So you got a verbal warning. That's not fair, you OK about it?

From: Holly
To: Trisha

No, but onwards and upwards. What's the diary like, busy?

From: Trisha
To: Holly

Very busy. Hey maybe you can appeal against it? Let's see it.

From: Holly
To: Trisha

What? It was verbal?

From: Trisha
To: Holly

Yeah but they give you something don't they? Something on paper?

Subject: Lying

From: Holly
To: Jason

I need help quickly. Tell me a 'verbal' is just that—a verbal warning and I don't get something on paper too?

Subject: From Mr Fraser your friendly upstairs neighbour

From: Frank
To: Holly

Saw another mouse today.

From: Holly
To: Frank

Did you, Frank?

From: Frank
To: Holly

He escaped through a hole in the skirting board. It's amazing how small they can make themselves.

From: Holly
To: Frank

I know.

From: Frank
To: Holly

My brother says it's because it's mainly fur on a very tiny skeleton.

Subject: Early Inheritance

From: Mum
To: Holly

Holly

I've sent you some an early inheritance gift. Let me know when you get it.

Love Mum xx

From: Holly
To: Mum

Sounds exciting! What is it, Mum?

From: Mum
To: Holly

You'll see when you get it.

Before I forget to ask, have you had any calls from Charlie this week? We do worry about him. Why is it everything he does involves sex?

From: Holly
To: Mum

I don't know, Mum. No I haven't heard from him.

From: Mum
To: Holly

Do you think something happened to him at school?

From: Holly
To: Mum

No, Mum, I don't think something happened to him at school. He's not that bad, stop worrying.

Is Granny back online yet?

From: Mum
To: Holly

I'm setting her up over the weekend. Please email her next week, you know how to make her happy.

Love Mum

Subject: Lying

From: Jason
To: Holly

You definitely would get something written down.

From: Holly
To: Jason

That's it, I'm just going to have to be brave…
X

Subject: Something I've been meaning to tell you.

From: Holly
To: Trisha

About that meeting I had.

From: Trisha
To: Holly

Yes?

From: Holly
To: Trisha

You won't believe what happened.

From: Trisha
To: Holly

Go on?

Subject: IMPORTANT

From: Richard
To: Holly

Dear Holly

Thank you for attending the meeting, we will be in touch in due course. In the meantime, I have to insist that you refrain from discussing this with the rest of the team.

Yours sincerely

Richard Mosley

Head of Facilities, DK Huerst, 50 Cabot Square, Canary Wharf, London

Subject: Something I've been meaning to tell you.

From: Holly
To: Trisha

When I came out of the room, I looked down, and I had something stuck to my foot.

From: Trisha
To: Holly

What was it?

From: Holly
To: Trisha

A label.

From: Trisha
To: Holly

Is that it?

From: Holly
To: Trisha

Yes.

From: Trisha
To: Holly

Your stories are getting worse.

From: Holly
To: Trisha

Thanks.

From: Trisha
To: Holly

My pleasure. I thought being with Toby you might have something worth telling me.

From: Holly
To: Trisha

Like?

From: Trisha
To: Holly

Like 'I was looking in the fridge when I heard Toby come through the door behind, and he had a tux on'.

From: Holly
To: Trisha

How could I see what he was wearing if my head was in the fridge?

From: Trisha
To: Holly

Cause I told you, because I'm there watchin.

From: Holly
To: Trisha

Trisha!!!!

From: Trisha
To: Holly

You're in my bl**dy house.

From: Holly
To: Trisha

Why are we in your house???

From: Trisha
To: Holly

I don't know! You shouldn't be there, my Les'll be home any moment. Get out, you mucky cow.

From: Holly
To: Trisha

You're making me laugh.

From: Trisha
To: Holly

You can go back to telling me about this label of yours now if you want. Just wait a minute while I slit me wrists. Before I do—did you tell Richard I'll train you up better or what?

From: Holly
To: Trisha

Yes.

From: Trisha
To: Holly

What did he say?

From: Holly
To: Trisha

That might help and I should just double check my work.

From: Trisha
To: Holly

I told you, I said double check the scheduler at the end of the day.
What did I say?

From: Holly
To: Trisha

I know you did.

From: Trisha
To: Holly

No reason looking upset, just check your work then you'll be OK.
When you've been doing it as long as I have, you learn to look
after yourself.

From: Holly
To: Trisha

Thanks X

Subject: Spilling my beans

From: Holly
To: Jasón; Aisha

Couldn't do it, couldn't tell Trisha. I'm such a coward. Tomorrow,
I'm telling Trisha first thing tomorrow.

From: Jason
To: Holly; Aisha

Good—before she hears it from someone else.

From: Aisha
To: Holly; Jason

Hey last Friday, why did we meet in that pub again? I remember you both telling me, but I'll be honest I wasn't listening at all.

From: Jason
To: Aisha; Holly

That's something I've been meaning to ask you. What happens when we're all out together and you finish talking and someone else starts?

From: Aisha
To: Holly; Jason

Nothing, I carry on in my head? Only a bit louder so I can hear myself.

From: Holly
To: Aisha; Jason

Nice.

From: Aisha
To: Holly; Jason

Sorry, love you both though, kiss kiss. Oh and sometimes I'm thinking about who I can phone next? If that makes you feel better?

From: Holly
To: Aisha; Jason

Fabulously, we were in the Garrick again, because it's where Jason does his stalking.

From: Jason
To: Aisha; Holly

I'm not stalking, I just like his voice. He sounds nice and I want to know what he looks like in person, I'm just curious.

From: Holly
To: Aisha; Jason .

But he isn't, Jason, he's totally uncurious, he's married, with children.

From: Aisha
To: Holly; Jason

Who?

From: Holly
To: Aisha; Jason

Chris Brooks, he's a DJ.

From: Aisha
To: Holly; Jason

Who?

From: Holly
To: Aisha; Jason

Chris Brooks.

From: Aisha
To: Holly; Jason

Who?

From: Holly
To: Aisha; Jason

Stop it, Ayshie. He's a radio DJ.

From: Aisha
To: Holly; Jason

He'll be ugly then, that's for sure.

From: Jason
To: Aisha; Holly

He's not.

From: Aisha
To: Holly; Jason

He'll have a face like my granddad's gerbil.

From: Holly
To: Aisha; Jason

I'm hoping that's an animal you're talking about?

From: Jason
To: Aisha; Holly

miss-know-it-all, check out his picture on the link. http://www.facebook.com/people/Brooksie_Brooks/675250609

From: Aisha
To: Holly; Jason

Made up photo, this is really how he really looks. http://www.bonenet.net/bonenetMedia/mole-rat.jpg

From: Holly
To: Aisha; Jason

That's horrible. What is it?

From: Aisha
To: Holly; Jason

It's a mole-rat, someone sent it to me. Thought I might buy one as a pet, scare off unwanted exes?

From: Jason
To: Aisha; Holly

Anyway, so he's meant to drink in there, but if it's too much effort for everyone to meet there then we can meet somewhere else. See if I care.

From: Aisha
To: Holly; Jason

Ooooooh, Jason's getting stroppy.

From: Holly
To: Aisha; Jason

I'm happy meeting there honey, we can stalk him together. Ooooh home time, I'm off.

xxxxx

tuesday

Subject: Inheritance Gift

From: Mum
To: Holly

Holly
Can you please get in touch? I want to know if you've received your parcel safely. You should have got it this morning?
Mum

Subject: My inheritance???

From: Holly
To: Alice

Why has our mother sent me what looks like a toupee in a package?

Subject: Morning

From: Aisha
To: Holly

How are you? Do you need a friend to talk to??

From: Holly
To: Aisha

Why?

From: Aisha
To: Holly

Because I'm guessing Trisha isn't your friend anymore?

From: Holly
To: Aisha

Haven't told her yet.

From: Aisha
To: Holly

Are you going to?

From: Holly
To: Aisha

In a moment, anyway she might not care that much.

From: Aisha
To: Holly

If I was her I'd pour orange juice over your head and quit, that's what she'll probably do.

From: Holly
To: Aisha

Well you're not and she won't. We don't have any orange anyway.

From: Aisha
To: Holly

Ribena then.

From: Holly
To: Aisha

We don't have any Ribena either.

From: Aisha
To: Holly

I'd go buy some, and I'd slap you, hard, then quit, probably spread some gossip about you first on the company website, maybe throw your shoes down the toilet too.

From: Holly
To: Aisha

Goodbye Aisha, it's been nice chatting.

Subject: DK Bank

From: Marie on the Switchboard
To: Holly; Trisha; Claire

Does anyone know when I'll be moving to your building?

Marie

Switchboard, DK Huerst, 50 Cabot Square, Canary Wharf, London

Subject: News

From: Holly
To: Trisha

You haven't heard anything about Marie have you?

From: Trisha
To: Holly

Not a squeak. What's she like? You've seen her. Sounds foreign.

From: Holly
To: Trisha

Mexican, sweet, quite glam, a bundle of fun.

From: Trisha
To: Holly

Don't like the sound of her.

From: Holly
To: Trisha

Give her a chance. Also I was thinking, you know we're always shuffling everyone around on this scheduler from room to room, and each time there's a change, we have to let the PAs know?

From: Trisha
To: Holly

Yes.

From: Holly
To: Trisha

Why don't just not tell them anything.

From: Trisha
To: Holly

Because it'll cause a few rows darling. If we don't let them know what room their bosses are in, they won't be able to call them in an emergency, will they?

From: Holly
To: Trisha

No, but we can. They can call us if they have a message and we'll pass on messages, kind of like a concierge service. I was telling Tanya from Catering about it at that party. She said she would help with letting the butlers pass on messages if it became busy.

From: Trisha
To: Holly

Could work, might save time.

Subject: Moving on

From: Holly
To: Marie

No, Marie, sorry, I don't know when you're moving in here.

Regards
Holly

From: Marie
To: Holly

Oh Holly, I'm so worried, it doesn't feel right, sitting over here answering calls. Surely I should be in the new building with you three by now. What do you think has happened, do you think there's a problem? Maybe they aren't going to keep me, what do you think?

From: Holly
To: Marie

You'll be over here soon, Marie, I'm sure, I haven't heard anything different so don't worry.

From: Marie
To: Holly

What are the toilets like there?

From: Holly
To: Marie

Nice, clean.

From: Marie
To: Holly

Do they have hand driers or towels?

From: Holly
To: Marie

Paper towels.

From: Marie
To: Holly

Oh good, I think those hand driers spread infection. What do you think?

From: Holly
To: Marie

I think they do too.

X

Got to go check one of the rooms.

Subject: Toupee in a package

From: Alice
To: Holly

Oh I expect it's because you're getting close to 30.

From: Holly
To: Alice

I'm 29.

From: Alice
To: Holly

Oh well, she's thinking ahead I expect.

xxx

From: Holly
To: Alice

No not xxx!! That doesn't explain anything. What is she thinking ahead to—me being bald? Or is this some Spanish tradition I'm not aware of—your daughter hits 30, it must be toupee in a package time?

From: Alice
To: Holly

She must have mentioned it before. I've got one, Charlie's had one, now it's your turn... remember—Denham Family Hair-tree?

From: Holly
To: Alice

I don't remember. This sounds revolting, it's not my hair is it?

From: Alice
To: Holly

Oh no, it's much better than that. This is three generations of Denham hair. I think it includes some of your great great grandparents' hair too.

From: Holly
To: Alice

You are joking.

From: Alice
To: Holly

Each generation had cut some off and added it to the package. She's split it between us. We're meant to add to it and give it to our children. Sweet, isn't it?

From: Holly
To: Alice

It's the most disgusting thing I've ever heard of.

From: Alice
To: Holly

I agree, problem is, you can't throw it away. You'll try, but knowing all these people have bothered to keep it for you for over a century ... kind of makes it hard. Mine is sitting in a box under the bed. Every year I want to throw it out, but I can't. Sometimes at night, I'm sure I feel it watching me.

Good luck

Alice

Subject: My inheritance

From: Holly
To: Mum

Yes, I got the package, thank you.

From: Mum
To: Holly

Remember to add some to it when you have children.

From: Holly
To: Mum

I'll remember.

From: Mum
To: Holly

You should tell Toby.

From: Holly
To: Mum

Thanks Mum.

Subject: PRIVATE AND CONFIDENTIAL SECRET MESSAGE

From: Holly
To: Elizabeth on Tour

Agent Fox, Agent Fox, when you get online, please get in touch, there's an important message from London… and it's coming through now… DON'T RUN AWAY GRANNY I LOVE YOU!!!!!!!!!!!! AT LEAST TAKE ME WITH YOU????
xx hope you're OK, love Holly.

Subject: Gossip

From: Jason
To: Holly; Aisha

She's banned him!

From: Holly
To: Jason; Aisha

I know, for six months.

From: Jason
To: Holly; Aisha

How did you know who I was talking about?

From: Holly
To: Jason; Aisha

Read it this morning, I wondered when you'd notice.

From: Jason
To: Holly; Aisha

So what do you think then?

From: Holly
To: Jason; Aisha

He's lucky, he's got another chance.

From: Aisha
To: Holly; Jason

That's them finished.

From: Holly
To: Jason; Aisha

No, not necessarily.

From: Aisha
To: Holly; Jason

Come on, if he couldn't keep it tucked away before, what chance is there now?

From: Jason
To: Holly; Aisha

Oh I say, he'll be like a raging bull, it won't be safe to go out any more.

From: Holly
To: Jason; Aisha

I don't think you have to worry, honey.

From: Jason
To: Holly; Aisha

Hey do you think they'll be like two teams, like Jen and Angie?

From: Aisha
To: Holly; Jason

If there are, his will have about 11 in it, and one miserable manager.

wednesday

Subject: Cats

From: Toby on Blackberry
To: Holly

Got your message, feeding them now.

From: Holly
To: Toby on Blackberry

Just Monkey—Gretel's already eaten, so don't give her any.

From: Toby on Blackberry
To: Holly

I haven't but she's still sitting next to him chewing, why?

From: Holly
To: Toby on Blackberry

She's pretending to eat because she doesn't want him thinking he's got something she hasn't.

From: Toby on Blackberry
To: Holly

She has problems.

From: Holly
To: Toby on Blackberry

It's a female thing.

From: Toby on Blackberry
To: Holly

You want to meet up for lunch today?

From: Holly
To: Toby on Blackberry

You taking me out somewhere???

From: Toby on Blackberry
To: Holly

Won't have time to leave the bank, but what about half hour in the staff restaurant?

From: Holly
To: Toby on Blackberry

Really a half hour, for me, are you sure??????? Why thank you Mr Williams!!

Subject: Late Catch up

From: Jason
To: Holly; Aisha

How was everyone's weekend?

From: Holly
To: Jason; Aisha

Hangover on Sunday, feel fine now. How was everyone else's?

From: Jason
To: Holly; Aisha

So you did go to Ticky's dinner party in the end?

From: Holly
To: Jason; Aisha

No, we never got there, we had a few drinks while we got ready to go. I couldn't find an outfit that made me look glamorous—like I imagined all her friends would look. But one of them must have been alright, because we ended up having sex instead.

From: Jason
To: Holly; Aisha

Good sex?

From: Holly
To: Jason; Aisha

Amazing sex.

From: Aisha
To: Jason; Holly

For you two.

From: Holly
To: Jason; Aisha

I'll ignore that comment, Aisha. Some people can enjoy it without all the paraphernalia.

From: Aisha
To: Jason; Holly

What paraphernalia?

From: Holly
To: Jason; Aisha

Like a bag of bondage equipment, drugs and, knowing you, a few people standing by in case someone needs oxygen or something.

From: Aisha
To: Jason; Holly

Actually sex on laughing gas is amazing.

From: Holly
To: Jason; Aisha

?

From: Aisha
To: Jason; Holly

It is, I dated this guy once who always kept a canister by the bed.

From: Holly
To: Jason; Aisha

Where do you meet these men?

From: Jason
To: Holly; Aisha

More importantly, I want to know how he broached the subject with you, Aish—I'd like to have sex, but first of course you'll need to slip on this gas mask?

From: Holly
To: Jason; Aisha

Anyway, afterwards we decided to miss the party and go to bed. So what's this I hear about Marco?

From: Jason
To: Holly; Aisha

I'm definitely splitting up with him and this time I mean it. It's going to be the hardest thing I've ever done. I care about him so much, Holly, I still love him.

From: Holly
To: Jason; Aisha

I know you do. Xx

From: Jason
To: Holly; Aisha

I've thought about it all weekend, I've just got to do it this time, but I want to stay close friends.

From: Holly
To: Jason; Aisha

Honey, how are you going to do that?

From: Aisha
To: Holly; Jason

I told him he's just got to go do it, fast as possible, get it over with, not to worry, like ripping off a plaster.

From: Jason
To: Holly; Aisha

That would be impossible, I could never do that. I can't hurt him, I couldn't see him cry, it would kill me, so he's got to be happy about it. I just don't know how that's possible.

From: Holly
To: Jason; Aisha

It'll be very difficult.

From: Jason
To: Holly; Aisha

There must be a way though, I just need to come up with a plan.

From: Holly
To: Jason; Aisha

OK, well I'll try racking my brains for something too.

From: Jason
To: Holly; Aisha

Thanks.

From: Holly
To: Jason; Aisha

Whatever you do, I don't think he'll be happy, but he'll live.

From: Aisha
To: Jason; Holly

Unless he dies in some horrible sick suicide thing, you come back to the flat and find his corpse in the bath, with a note or something.

From: Jason
To: Holly; Aisha

Excuse me a minute, Holly, I've just got to do something.

Subject: That was really childish, Jason!

From: Aisha
To: Jason; Holly

I could have been electrocuted! Right, for that I'm taking an extra long break to reapply my makeup.

Subject: A chance of a lifetime

From: Holly
To: Toby

For one lucky person, you have the chance to win our star prize today. All you have to do is guess which of these destinations you could be whisked away to…

A: A weekend in Washington

B: A fortnight in France

C: A summer in Sicily

Or

D: A half hour in the food hall at DK Huerst!!!!

Yes, you've won D, but you get to sit next to Holly, our hostess of the week!

Meet you in five minutes, lovely man, you!

From: Toby
To: Holly

xxx That's so funny, brilliant, but also can we push it back to 2pm?
I've still got things to kind of finish before I break?

From: Holly
To: Toby

Can't, I've booked my lunch shift.

From: Toby
To: Holly

Sorry, sugar, don't hate me, it's not my fault. I'm trying to make us
money…

From: Holly
To: Toby

Whatever.

From: Toby
To: Holly

And with money comes a future, and happiness and all things
nice??

From: Holly
To: Toby

Nice, or nice and shiny??

From: Toby
To: Holly

All things bright and beautiful, sorry, back to work xxx love you.
PS we could go to the gym together? I'm going to start doing a half
hour each day—fancy?

From: Holly
To: Toby

No?

Subject: Natasha Springer

From: Trisha
To: Holly

You want to know who she is then?

From: Holly
To: Trisha

She doesn't own the bank does she?

From: Trisha
To: Holly

Not yet.

From: Holly
To: Trisha

Oh go on then.

From: Trisha
To: Holly

Natasha Springer has made more for the company in the first two months of this year, than the rest of them did in her department… for the whole of last year.

From: Holly
To: Trisha

So you're saying what?

From: Trisha
To: Holly

I'm saying she could pretty much take a dump on your desk and get away with it.

From: Holly
To: Trisha

How lovely.

From: Trisha
To: Holly

Oh and the PAs have a name for her.

From: Holly
To: Trisha

Let me guess, Fluffins?

From: Trisha
To: Holly

No.

From: Holly
To: Trisha

Cuddles?

From: Trisha
To: Holly

Not quite.

From: Holly
To: Trisha

Fluffy cuddly kitten face?

From: Trisha
To: Holly

The Wicked Witch of the Wharf…

From: Holly
To: Trisha

Dan dan DAHHHHH! Damn that's a good name, I should have thought of it.

thursday

Subject: Hello

From: Claire
To: Holly; Trisha

I'm going running tonight, do you two want to come?
Love Claire

From: Trisha
To: Claire; Holly

Not really.

From: Holly
To: Claire; Trisha

I can't tonight, but thank you, where are you going, honey?

From: Claire
To: Holly; Trisha

Just up and down, you know.

Subject: Attention

From: Trisha
To: Holly

You think that girl's alright?

From: Holly
To: Trisha

Yes, she's lovely.

From: Trisha
To: Holly

I think the height up there's making her dizzy.

Subject: Also

From: Claire
To: Holly; Trisha

I'm meeting my boyfriend after my run, we're having bagels.

From: Trisha
To: Claire; Holly

Good. Enjoy it you, lucky thing.

From: Claire
To: Trisha; Holly

I will

:)

Subject: Serious Attention

From: Trisha
To: Holly

She's nuts I'm telling ya.

From: Holly
To: Trisha

Don't be unkind, Trisha, take some more sunny pills.

From: Trisha
To: Holly

Also I don't trust her, she's up to something, believe me.

From: Holly
To: Trisha

Claire? Up to something?

From: Trisha
To: Holly

Closes something on her screen every time she sees me come out of the lifts towards her.

From: Holly
To: Trisha

You're making that up, how would you know?

From: Trisha
To: Holly

Don't you know when someone's trying to hide something on their screen?

From: Holly
To: Trisha

They turn it around?

From: Trisha
To: Holly

No, I can't believe you don't know. I know straight away if someone writing about me, it's bl**dy obvious.

From: Holly
To: Trisha

How?

From: Trisha
To: Holly

Like I always know when you do it.

From: Holly
To: Trisha

When I do what?

From: Trisha
To: Holly

When you write something about me.

From: Holly
To: Trisha

When do I do that??

From: Trisha
To: Holly

You used to do it a lot when you first got here, when you thought I was a right moody cow.

From: Holly
To: Trisha

You are, but I love you.

From: Trisha
To: Holly

I'd pinch you if you were closer, you could fit three receptionists on this desk. I hope they're not thinking of putting another one down here, I won't have it.

From: Holly
To: Trisha

Happy thoughts, happy thoughts. You were saying?

From: Trisha
To: Holly

You would type something with your left hand only, cause you'd have the right one holding the mouse in case I came over, so you could close it down quickly.

From: Holly
To: Trisha

Did I?

From: Trisha
To: Holly

Also, if you think someone's writing about you, watch their eyes, cause Claire always looks at the top right corner and then she clicks her mouse. Means she's shutting something off. She's either always writing something about me when I go up and I know I'm interesting, but not that interesting, or she's up to something.

From: Holly
To: Trisha

I never thought about it.

Subject: What a lovely email

From: Elizabeth on Tour
To: Holly

Dear Holly

I'm back amongst the living and it was so nice to open up my emails and find one sitting there waiting for me. What a lovely surprise. I'm sitting at my desk now, so if you have time I can have a bit of a chin wag.

Lots of Love from your granny.

From: Holly
To: Elizabeth on Tour

Granny!!

I'm so glad you're feeling better, I was really worried about you. Mum told me you'd removed all your addresses from your things?

Holly

From: Elizabeth on Tour
To: Holly

Holly

I most certainly did remove them, I don't like being labeled. I'm not a parcel and I have told your mother many times I'm not Paddington Bear either. I was fine and dandy and didn't need 'rescuing'. I was having a nice chat with a gentleman from Gibraltar who invited me fishing on his boat. I am not sure whether fishing is really my cup of tea, but he was ever so polite and a very handsome chap too. I'm back with your mother now, for my sins. At least I'm rid of that wretched place with all those old dears. How I was ever meant to be happy in such a miserable place, I'll never know; every time I made a friend they died.

Love Granny.

PS when are you coming to see me? Are you still with your man?

From: Holly
To: Elizabeth on Tour

Soon, Granny, there are lots of changes going on here, but I'll book a trip to see you soon. I'm still with Toby, yes, and very happy.

xxx

From: Elizabeth on Tour
To: Holly

Don't listen to your mother. You look after him, he sounds just perfect for you.

Subject: Just thought of another

From: Trisha
To: Holly

Another one, if someone types something then stabs the return key after, followed with a sideways glance at you, they're pissed off and they're emailing a mate about you. Trust me.

From: Holly
To: Trisha

You're so crafty, Trisha.

From: Trisha
To: Holly

You got to be, so don't you forget it.

Subject: Party in the Park

From: Tickie
To: Holly

I've got a spare ticket to see Fatboy Slim play in Hyde Park on Saturday July 5th. Would love you to come!! Please say you will sweetie.

xxx Ticks

From: Holly
To: Tickie

Wow! Of course I'd love to, thank you!!!

Holly

From: Tickie
To: Holly

Great, it's £50, just add it to the other money when you send that cheque.

xxx

Subject: Oi wake up you moron!

From: Holly
To: Trisha

YOU STUPID BL**DY IDIOT! REMEMBER to ask if things are FREE before accepting them!!

From: Trisha
To: Holly

What?

From: Holly
To: Trisha

Ooops, sorry that was meant as a reminder to me.

Subject: UPDATE

From: Richard Mosley
To: Holly

Holly

I have just come out of a meeting with the CEO. He's looking at a number of different options and ways of running our client services. If we do employ a manager you will also have some outside competition for the role, but it is an achievement in itself to have even been considered. ·

Kind regards

Richard

Subject: Gossip

From: Jason
To: Holly

How's it going with Toby?

From: Holly
To: Jason

Fine.

From: Jason
To: Holly

You mentioned this promotion thing yet?

From: Holly
To: Jason

No, hope I get it, sometimes he looks at me like, you know when he's all stressed and I'm trying to tell him something. Sometimes I get the feeling he thinks I'm a bit childish.

From: Jason
To: Holly

No?

From: Holly
To: Jason

Really, I think he does.

From: Jason
To: Holly

Childish, you!!!???
Did you sulk?

From: Holly
To: Jason

I will in a minute.

From: Jason
To: Holly

So do I hear the sound of wedding bells yet?

From: Holly
To: Jason

If you do, they'll probably be Aisha's. She's bound to get married again before me.

From: Jason
To: Holly

Stop feeling sorry for yourself. Come on now, what about the patter of tiny feet?

From: Holly
To: Jason

What about the patter of large feet, mine running towards you with an axe???

From: Jason
To: Holly

You won't get anywhere with that attitude. Mentioned babies??

From: Holly
To: Jason

No, actually yes, I said I wasn't really a child kind of person.

From: Jason
To: Holly

Good, long-term future?

From: Holly
To: Jason

Never.

From: Jason
To: Holly

Buying a place together?

From: Holly
To: Jason

No.

From: Jason
To: Holly

Holidays?

From: Holly
To: Jason

Once.

From: Jason
To: Holly

Fancying male celebrities?

From: Holly
To: Jason

Of course, but it didn't make him jealous, he didn't even know who David Schwimmer was. Did you see him in *Hello*?

From: Jason
To: Holly

Concentrate, Holly, concentrate!

From: Holly
To: Jason

Oops important email just come through.

Subject: Important Email

From: Toby
To: Holly

Actually not that important, just me. You called me, do you need me?

From: Holly
To: Toby

Not any more, busy busy busy.

xxx

Subject: Back again

From: Holly
To: Jason

It was just him.

From: Jason
To: Holly

OK, what about eating habits?

From: Holly
To: Jason

He's still using a knife and fork, if that's what you mean?

From: Jason
To: Holly

No, although I guess that's reassuring, the adorable Neanderthal that he is. I actually meant your eating habits?

From: Holly
To: Jason

I'm not spilling as much and I'm sticking to things without smell or taste.

From: Jason
To: Holly

Good girl, toilet doors?

From: Holly
To: Jason

Remain locked by both parties.

From: Jason
To: Holly

As they should, mentioned meeting his family?

From: Holly
To: Jason

Never, which is really annoying actually, I want to meet them. I think they'd like me.

From: Jason
To: Holly

What about your belly button?

From: Holly
To: Jason

I doubt they'd like that.

From: Jason
To: Holly

I doubt it too, unless you've given it a scrub recently.

From: Holly
To: Jason

Can we get off the subject please, they give me the creeps.

From: Jason
To: Holly

Yours gives everyone the creeps, wash it!

From: Holly
To: Jason

OK, fine. It's time I left for the day, can we carry on with my grilling tomorrow?
X

From: Jason
To: Holly

You can count on it.
x

Subject: Thought of another

From: Trisha
To: Holly

When you've got two people next to you, and one writes something, stabs the return key, then does nothing, then her friend clicks the mouse with a pause while she's reading, laughs, then taps away, stabs return, then pretends to do something with the mouse. Glances at her friend waiting for her to laugh. They think you don't know, but you do, you know what they're doing, they are being nasty little backstabbing toe-rag bitches, that's what they're doing.

From: Holly
To: Trisha

Thanks Trisha. What does it mean when someone sends you this?
[See attached pic of kissing lips]

From: Trisha
To: Holly

That you've got too much time on your hands. You're daft, and I love ya.

friday

Subject: Your vermin problem

From: Alice
To: Holly

I've had an idea :)
xxx

From: Holly
To: Alice

No, I'm not doing it.

Subject: Quickly

From: Toby
To: Holly

I have to go back to France again, they want me in the DK Paris office on Monday, so I thought I may as well go tonight and help Dad with the boat over the weekend.

Will you be OK? Back Tuesday?

From: Holly
To: Toby

Why can't someone else go to the Paris office?

From: Toby
To: Holly

Because I have more to prove.

From: Holly
To: Toby

No you don't.

From: Toby
To: Holly

I do. When I quit this job last year, it took a lot of time, interviews and effort to get them to take me back, it's like being the new boy again. When they say go the Paris office, I go.

From: Holly
To: Toby

You shouldn't have quit then.

From: Toby
To: Holly

If you'd told me you liked me before I quit I wouldn't have!

From: Holly
To: Toby

Fine, on my own again.

From: Toby
To: Holly

Will you be OK?

From: Holly
To: Toby

Of course, I'm not a child, I can look after myself. Remember to put in lots of good words for me with your dad. You seeing your sister too?

From: Toby
To: Holly

Not sure if she's around. I'll call you later.

x

Subject: FRANCE!!!

From: Holly
To: Jason

FFFFFFRANCE NASTY HORRIBLE FRANCE

From: Jason
To: Holly

What's happened?

From: Holly
To: Jason

Something's going on!!!?

From: Jason
To: Holly

Holly, calm down and tell me.

From: Holly
To: Jason

Toby! That's what's happened, nasty low down lying channel hopping, bed hopping, yes that's what he's doing, sleeping with some French thing, some nasty Prada-wearing thing. Is Prada French?

From: Jason
To: Holly

No, Italian.

From: Holly
To: Jason

Whatever, the lying son of a man with a boat is going to France again, didn't even ask if I wanted to go. Why???????

From: Jason
To: Holly

You didn't ask to go with him, did you?

Subject: STOP STEWING

From: Jason
To: Holly

Stop sitting there muttering to yourself and poking your tongue out at your screen. People will think you're mad.

From: Holly
To: Jason

I might not be doing that. You think you know me.

Subject: I have an idea

From: Alice
To: Holly

About the mice problem and it's not as bad as before.
Pretty please :)

From: Holly
To: Alice

No!

From: Alice
To: Holly

Pretty please?

From: Holly
To: Alice

No. Anyway we don't have a mice problem, just a mad neighbour problem.

From: Alice
To: Holly

OK, forget the mice, I've heard one of my friends has got his hands on some good rats though. Frozen, just like last time.

From: Holly
To: Alice

Sorry, Alice, the last lot defrosted in my case when our plane was diverted. I could have been searched by customs officials. What would I have said if they'd found them???

From: Alice
To: Holly

That your sister breeds snakes??

From: Holly
To: Alice

They'd have locked me up for being a lunatic. Sorry, I'm not meeting anyone called Ferret, Badger or Stoat, I am not storing them in my freezer, I don't want to be your rat smuggler anymore, I want out.

xxx but I love you.

Subject: Are you still huffing?

From: Jason
To: Holly

Are you still huffing?

From: Holly
To: Jason

Yes, but about a number of things now.

From: Jason
To: Holly

You didn't ask him if you could go along too, did you?

From: Holly
To: Jason

No, I didn't ask him if I could go. But I should have asked him, because if he loved ME I WOULD BE GOING TOO I HATE HIM DIE DIE DIE.

From: Jason
To: Holly

Feel better?

From: Holly
To: Jason

No.

From: Jason
To: Holly

But when the cat's away, the mice can play…

From: Holly
To: Jason

Bad choice of words. You take me out somewhere?

From: Jason
To: Holly

Your carriage awaits, actually Arabs await, a big group of them, got to go. Xxx don't worry about Toby, do you really think he'd do that to you?

From: Holly
To: Jason

No.

Subject: Friday night

From: William Duncan
To: Holly

I'm thinking pasta, good wine, maybe some dancing, could be on the river...

From: Holly
To: William Duncan

Is this a quiz???? Are you in Italy?????

From: William Duncan
To: Holly

Holly,
I find this refusal for you to at least acknowledge you are deeply attracted to me foolish.

From: Holly
To: William Duncan

You are so mistaken.

From: William Duncan
To: Holly

But the teasing thing you do, I love.

From: Holly
To: William Duncan

It really isn't teasing.

From: William Duncan
To: Holly

So I'm just wasting my time here, am I?

From: Holly
To: William Duncan

Yes.

From: William Duncan
To: Holly

Fine, I'll go.

From: Holly
To: William Duncan

OK.

Subject: So don't worry about me

From: William Duncan
To: Holly

I'm gone.

From: Holly
To: William Duncan

OK.

From: William Duncan
To: Holly

I'll not bother you again.

From: Holly
To: William Duncan

Good.

From: William Duncan
To: Holly

You won't see good old Will around here anymore. There'll be no more fun emails landing in your inbox, no more compliments, no more 'oh Holly you look so hot,' no more 'meet me tonight at Corney and Barrow's—8pm.' You don't want to, do you?

From: Holly
To: William Duncan

What?

From: William Duncan
To: Holly

Meet me?

From: Holly
To: William Duncan

NO!

From: William Duncan
To: Holly

FINE! But don't feel bad if you see me crying in the lift. They'll call me Cry Baby Will, I'll be an outcast.

From: Holly
To: William Duncan

I'm sorry, I really am in love with Toby and happy etc.
Got to go now.

From: William Duncan
To: Holly

Hey you know Claire? Does she have a boyfriend?

From: Holly
To: William Duncan

Go away, Will.

From: William Duncan
To: Holly

That's all you had to say. You girls have just got to stop being so ambiguous.

Subject: Leaving

From: Toby
To: Holly

I'm off at 5. You will be OK, won't you? Have you got any plans yet?

From: Holly
To: Toby

Yes, I'm out with Jason tonight.

From: Toby
To: Holly

Are you going to eat something before you go?

From: Holly
To: Toby

Might do.

From: Toby
To: Holly

Please, I'll worry about you if I'm not there to look after you, promise me please.

From: Holly
To: Toby

Well, you should be here to look after me shouldn't you? Maybe I won't eat a thing for three days or you might even come back to find I've moved in with my friendly upstairs neighbour. What d'you think of that?

From: Toby
To: Holly

I wouldn't. I think he's two pints short of a milk float. You know I'm sure there's someone famous called Frank Fraser. Anyway, see you Monday.

xx

Subject: Tonight

From: Holly
To: Jason

Is Aisha coming out tonight too?

From: Jason
To: Holly

Your guess is as good as mine. We have to hope she remembers us once she's pulled.

What time are we meeting up with her?

From: Holly
To: Jason

11pm.

From: Jason
To: Holly

By then, she'll have pulled, said she's not that type of girl, gone home with him anyway, fallen in love, changed her mind, lost her phone and at 11pm we should get a call from a phone box.

Got to go again. x

Subject: Tonight

From: Holly
To: Trisha

Are you sure you can't make it?

From: Trisha
To: Holly

I have bingo darling, with me mum, otherwise I would go with you.

Subject: Tonight

From: Holly
To: Tickie

Hi sweetie, darling lovely knickers, can you come out tonight to play, we're going clubbing?

xxx

Subject: Tonight

> **From:** Holly
> **To:** Tanya

Hi Tanya

We're going out tonight, should be a good night if you want???

Holly

Subject: Tonight

> **From:** Holly
> **To:** David Chislehurst

Are you out tonight, a few of us are going clubbing?

Regards

Holly

> **From:** David Chisliworth
> **To:** Holly

Who is this?

> **From:** Holly
> **To:** David Chisliworth

Oh sorry, must have the wrong email.

Subject: Meeting

> **From:** Human Resources Administrator
> **To:** Holly

Holly Denham

You are requested for a further meeting at 2pm on Monday Room 27 on the 30th Floor. Richard has arranged for a www. FrontRecruitment.com temp to cover you as we're not sure how long the meeting will last.

Kindest regards

Human Resources

DK Huerst,50 Cabot Square, Canary Wharf, London

Subject: You won't believe it...

From: Holly
To: Trisha

I've got to go for another meeting on Monday at 2pm

From: Trisha
To: Holly

What you done this time?

From: Holly
To: Trisha

I don't know.

From: Trisha
To: Holly

Sh*t, you must know. You double booked anyone or been rude to anyone?

From: Holly
To: Trisha

Not that I know of.

From: Trisha
To: Holly

Something's not right, you got to watch me more.

From: Holly
To: Trisha

Sorry.

From: Trisha
To: Holly

I'll drop Richard a quick email and ask him if I can spend some time with ya, doing some more training or something, get it into that thick skull of yours.

week 3
monday

Subject: Something I noticed.

From: Mum
To: Holly

I'm looking through the local paper here and there seem to be quite a few jobs for English-speaking workers. I can see Joe's bar in the port is looking for a couple of new bar girls, interviews next week. Plus there's a lifeguard vacancy. There's a supermarket in Torremolinos, looking for young lively staff, not sure how young, it doesn't say. Maybe we should leave that one, it's a bit far anyway. I'll keep looking.

Love Mum

Subject: Morning

From: Holly
To: Trisha

What's your mum like, Trisha?

From: Trisha
To: Holly

Lovely, how's yours?

From: Holly
To: Trisha

Unhelpful, how was your weekend?

From: Trisha
To: Holly

Didn't go out. You?

From: Holly
To: Trisha

I went for a quiet drink in my local on Saturday. It started quietly—I even took a book to read—but I met some people and it got a bit messy, ended up inviting them all back to mine.

From: Trisha
To: Holly

Not randoms, again?

From: Holly
To: Trisha

I know, don't have a go at me, I wasn't on my own though, I knew the barmaid and she's nice. I actually had fun until someone broke Toby's CD player. No idea what's wrong with it, have to get it looked at before he notices. Still haven't cleared up yet.

From: Trisha
To: Holly

You want to hope he doesn't come back early.

From: Holly
To: Trisha

Don't care, it's my flat.

From: Trisha
To: Holly

Bet you do care.

From: Holly
To: Trisha

Well it's his fault anyway, leaving me on my own. Having said that even when he is at home it's like being alone, he's always thinking about work.

From: Trisha
To: Holly

My Les does that, head's in the clouds.

From: Holly
To: Trisha

But what can you do?

From: Trisha
To: Holly

Punch him?

From: Holly
To: Trisha

I probably wouldn't do that.

From: Trisha
To: Holly

Or grab his inside thigh, there's a bit of soft skin there, don't half hurt if you get it right. I like to wait till Les is watching a thriller so he's all wrapped up in it. I'll creep up behind him, really quiet like so he doesn't know I'm around, then I'll clout him hard around the side of the head. That does it.

From: Holly
To: Trisha

Does what?

From: Trisha
To: Holly

Gets him.

From: Holly
To: Trisha

Thanks, I'll remember that.

Subject: Sports Relief

From: TCartwright@DKHuerst
To: WHOLE ADDRESS BOOK

Sports Relief is here again. Already £20,747,375 has been raised and with our own late company event this Bank Holiday Monday, which I expect everyone to attend, I'm hoping we can show some great support for this fantastic charity. Sports Relief helps people living incredibly tough lives both at home in the UK and across the world's poorest countries.

Prizes on the day will be handed out to the winners of the various heats, including the sack races, wheelbarrow races, three legged races, egg & spoon races and many more.

I look forward to seeing you all at the DK Huerst Olympics 2008 on Monday 24th March from 10am.

Yours sincerely

Timothy Cartwright

CEO, DK Huerst, 50 Cabot Square, Canary Wharf, London

Subject: Olympics

From: Trisha
To: Holly

Shame I can't go, I'll be up north still.

From: Holly
To: Trisha

I wish you were coming. Toby's going.

From: Trisha
To: Holly

Bet it's a right laugh, hey, I hope they don't make you wear shorts and trainers.

From: Holly
To: Trisha

They wouldn't, surely???

From: Trisha
To: Holly

Just refuse, say you've got some nasty disfigurement or something.

From: Holly
To: Trisha

Thanks.

Subject: Your email

From: Tanya
To: Holly

Holly

I just picked up your email today, it's so busy here it got a little lost. I don't think I'm going to make a particularly good friend to you, I have so little time to see my oldest and best friends that any new ones always end up losing out. Please don't take this the wrong way, I don't mean to sound rude, I am just very busy managing the catering team and don't have much spare time.

Tanya Mason
Catering Manager, DK Huerst, 50 Cabot Square, Canary Wharf, London

Subject: Tanya Mason

From: Holly
To: Jason

Read the below email:

Holly

I just picked up your email today, it's so busy here it got a little lost. I don't think I'm going to make a particularly good friend to you, I have so little time to see my oldest and best friends that any new ones always end up losing out. Please don't take this the wrong way, I don't mean to sound rude, I am just very busy managing the catering team and don't have much spare time.

Tanya Mason

Catering Manager, DK Huerst, 50 Cabot Square, Canary Wharf, London

From: Jason
To: Holly

Oh, I'm dying for you.

From: Holly
To: Jason

I actually feel quite sick.

From: Jason
To: Holly

Silly cow, ignore her.

From: Holly
To: Jason

I can't, I have to talk to her all the time about lunches and stuff.

From: Jason
To: Holly

Oh how embarrassing, I wouldn't be able to look at her. I'm embarrassed just knowing you; go and hide in a hole somewhere.

From: Holly
To: Jason

Thanks.

From: Jason
To: Holly

It's so cheeky of her, does she even know who you are??? You're the famous Holly, she should be so lucky to know you. Did you say 'do you know who I am??!'

From: Holly
To: Jason

She knows who I am—I'm the one hiding in a hole.

From: Jason
To: Holly

Forget her, any news on the job?

From: Holly
To: Jason

About to go in. This time they said it's not just a chat—it's a formal interview with competency-based questions, whatever they are??
Three of them grilling me, my poor stomach is doing somersaults.

From: Jason
To: Holly

Bit of trapped wind?

From: Holly
To: Jason

Nerves. I think I want it too much, I won't be able to talk

From: Jason
To: Holly

You'll be fine. Just don't mess anything up this week, keep happy and busy.

From: Holly
To: Jason

What kind of questions do you think they'll ask?

From: Jason
To: Holly

Nothing you can't answer. Be confident. Whatever you do if they ask you for your strengths, don't say you're 'a people person.' It's a stupid annoying answer and it makes me want to kill people that

say it. And don't give them a weakness. Say being 'a perfectionist'—
it does the same thing.

From: Holly
To: Jason

OK.

From: Jason
To: Holly

Also they'll probably ask for you to give an example of where you've
overcome a difficult situation.

From: Holly
To: Jason

Once a director wasn't happy because he'd told all his clients he was
away on a business trip in Dubai but I put a call through to him by
mistake, which he answered.

From: Jason
To: Holly

How did you deal with that?

From: Holly
To: Jason

I hid and blamed the temp.

From: Jason
To: Holly

Good. You'll have no problems.

From: Holly
To: Jason

Here I go.

From: Jason
To: Holly

xxx

tuesday

Subject: Help

From: Granny
To: Holly

Dear Holly

I think your mother is trying to kill me, she's pouring cement on everything I eat.

All my love

Granny

Subject: Toby

From: Aisha
To: Holly; Jason

What did he get up to in France then?

From: Holly
To: Jason; Aisha

He saw his dad, that's about it.

From: Aisha
To: Holly; Jason

Really.

From: Holly
To: Jason; Aisha

Yes really, and I know you think I'm stupid Aisha, but I trust him, he's a nice guy.

From: Aisha
To: Holly; Jason

That's what they said about Jack the Ripper.

From: Jason
To: Holly; Aisha

No they never.

From: Aisha
To: Holly; Jason

Bet they said it about some murderer somewhere.

From: Jason
To: Aisha; Holly

They said it about Kevin Federline.

From: Aisha
To: Holly; Jason

No they didn't.

From: Jason
To: Aisha; Holly

They said it about Ychudi Menuhin.

From: Aisha
To: Holly; Jason

Who's he?

From: Jason
To: Aisha; Holly

A composer.

From: Holly
To: Aisha; Jason

Of what?

From: Aisha
To: Holly; Jason

Maybe that's why he nips over to France???

From: Jason
To: Aisha; Holly

He's a composer of music—it's amazing what you learn when buying a violin.

From: Holly
To: Jason; Aisha

Why were you buying a violin?

From: Aisha
To: Holly; Jason

I said—MAYBE THAT'S WHY HE NIPS OVER TO FRANCE!

From: Holly
To: Jason; Aisha

Sorry Jason, got to deal with the chirping cherub in the background. What are you nattering about Ayshie?

From: Aisha
To: Holly; Jason

Toby goes there because he's a serial killer—he kills a few French people, buries the bodies, comes back, no one knows. Makes sense, doesn't it??

From: Holly
To: Jason; Aisha

Why are you buying a violin, Jason?

From: Jason
To: Aisha; Holly

Not sure, tell you tomorrow.

From: Aisha
To: Jason; Holly

Are you two ignoring me?

Subject: Dinner tonight

From: Holly
To: Toby

What you fancy?

From: Toby
To: Holly

I'll cook you something special. Did you miss me?

From: Holly
To: Toby

Of course, tell me all about France then?

From: Toby
To: Holly

I've told you most of it, very dull.

From: Holly
To: Toby

What did you do Saturday night?

From: Toby
To: Holly

Went to a casino with Steve and the guys.

From: Holly
To: Toby

Didn't think you liked to gamble?

From: Toby
To: Holly

They were going, so I went, but I like the occasional flutter.

From: Holly
To: Toby

You haven't mentioned the French girls?

From: Toby
To: Holly

What French girls??

From: Holly
To: Toby

Ze ffffrench girls who dress all sex-eee for Tobee?

From: Toby
To: Holly

Oh those ones, not interested.

From: Holly
To: Toby

Not even when zai pout zair lips and flick zair hair for nortee tobee?

From: Toby
To: Holly

No, but I am now.

From: Holly
To: Toby

Tobee, you naughty English boy, get on your naughty English knees and kiss my French stocking-top.

From: Toby
To: Holly

I'm doing it, what next?

From: Holly
To: Toby

Next you tell me where my present is hidden for being gone the whole weekend?

From: Toby
To: Holly

At home, tonight, what happened to the stocking top????

From: Holly
To: Toby

You took off the stockings off with your teeth and discover knobbly knees, hairy legs, varicose veins and sweaty feet.

From: Toby
To: Holly

Lovely stuff, rough and ready, keep going.

From: Holly
To: Toby

On that note, I hear the phone ringing.

Subject: Forgot to tell you

From: Holly
To: Jason GrangerRM

By the way, Tickie gave me a signed Take That CD.

From: Jason GrangerRM
To: Holly

Give it!

From: Holly
To: Jason GrangerRM

No.

From: Jason GrangerRM
To: Holly

I'll swap it for a bottle of Ashley's aftershave. It's called 'unforgivable'???

From: Holly
To: Jason GrangerRM

Funny but even if it existed, call me Mrs Unadventurous, but I don't want to smell like a sweaty footballer.

From: Jason GrangerRM
To: Holly

It does exist, I think it's Puff the Magic Daddy's one.

What about a sweaty football player like this one attached?

[Attachment: Christiano3]

From: Holly
To: Jason GrangerRM

Pretty—when he's not shouting, who is he?

From: Jason GrangerRM
To: Holly

My future husband, now David's got another tattoo.

wednesday

Subject: Today

From: Richard
To: Holly

Dear Holly

It's unfortunate that the interview process has taken so long, however it has to be the right decision for everyone concerned. You will definitely hear an answer by the end of today.

Regards

Richard

Subject: Tell me then

From: Holly
To: Jason

Why the violin?

From: Jason
To: Holly

It's part of my plan with Marco, it's going to take ten weeks.

From: Holly
To: Jason

Oh, do tell?

From: Jason
To: Holly

I'm not happy about doing it, but I can't see any other way.

From: Holly
To: Jason

If it did work, couples would be asking your advice all the time.

From: Jason
To: Holly

They would, wouldn't they.

From: Holly
To: Jason

You might become famous?

From: Jason
To: Holly

I would have to serialise it in OK! magazine first and foremost.

From: Holly
To: Jason

Of course.

From: Jason
To: Holly

I'd get on *Big Brother*, marry a celebrity and get voted Rear of the Year.

From: Holly
To: Jason

I thought you were?

From: Jason
To: Holly

Only in your eyes. Then I'd bring out a perfume, release a crap record, write a book, have a few children and get voted best celebgay-Dad of the Year.

From: Holly
To: Jason

It's just beautiful.

From: Jason
To: Holly

I'd need to retake my marriage vows (for an OK! exclusive), reveal why I had a secret nose job (to the world in OK!), clear up any confusion about my tit job by denying it, write another book, retake my marriage vows again, admit to bigger tits and finally I will retire to an island which I've turned into a retreat for sexually over-active males.

From: Holly
To: Jason

What are you going to do then?

From: Jason
To: Holly

Shag them.

From: Holly
To: Jason

So back to the point????

From: Jason
To: Holly

Can't, I'll call you tonight and tell you all about it, just got a call from general manager.

Xx

Subject: Holly Denham

From: Natasha Springer
To: Holly

How's your day going?

Natasha Springer

Head of Commodities Trading, DK Huerst, 50 Cabot Square, Canary Wharf, London

Subject: Strange

From: Holly
To: Trisha

Natasha's asking me how my day's going???

From: Trisha
To: Holly

Don't answer her.

From: Holly
To: Trisha

Maybe she's going to apologise for being so rude last week?

From: Trisha
To: Holly

Doubt it.

From: Holly
To: Trisha

I haven't done wrong that I know of, maybe she is being nice??
She's even calling me by my name instead of 'receptionist'?

From: Trisha
To: Holly

She's a witch and she eats human flesh, that's what they said. Now
she's got your name too.

From: Holly
To: Trisha

Oh stop trying to scare me.

Subject: HELP

From: Holly
To: Claire

Anything gone wrong today that you know of?

From: Claire
To: Holly

I think the Central line was down this morning.

From: Holly
To: Claire

Within the bank…?

From: Claire
To: Holly

No, under the City…?

From: Holly
To: Claire

I mean has anything gone wrong here in the bank with reception
today?

From: Claire
To: Holly

Why? Has someone complained about me again?

From: Holly
To: Claire

Don't worry. x

Subject: Morning

From: Holly
To: Natasha

Natasha
Yes thank you, so far so good.
How are you?
Holly

Subject: Problems Problems

From: Claire
To: Holly

Thinking about it, yesterday a woman called up who wasn't very happy at all, can't remember which room, but something about the food not turning up. They were being very rude, so I switched off and after a while, then they weren't there anymore.
Xxx hope this helps :)

Subject: Glad you're so happy

From: Natasha
To: Holly

So you're unaware of the cock up yesterday?

From: Holly
To: Natasha

I can see from the system you ordered one English Breakfast for your meeting. Did you not receive it?

From: Natasha
To: Holly

Yes, we did, thanks for that. I actually ordered a finger buffet though. Four Japanese clients, one full English, there you go lads, get stuck in, fancy some brown sauce with that, no? What—you don't share forks in Japan?

I will now be informing HR.

Yours sincerely

Natasha

Subject: Interesting

From: Mum
To: Holly

Holly

I'm sending you an article I cut out of The Times about life in the police force.

Love

Mum

Subject: SCHEDULE OF PAYMENTS

From: SouthernDebtManagementLtd
To: Holly

Reference No: 730809

We now intend to take further action against you in order to recover the outstanding balance; this action could include an agent visiting your address at a date to be advised.

This outstanding balance is not going to go away and trying to avoid your responsibilities will only make the situation worse.

Unless we hear from you within 5 working days from the date of this email, we will instruct our agents Red Debt Collections & Removables to take the appropriate action.

Recovery Dept

Subject: Job offer

> **From:** Alice
> **To:** Holly

Have you heard anything yet about your promotion yet?

> **From:** Holly
> **To:** Alice

Yes I thought I had it, but I think I lost it already.

> **From:** Alice
> **To:** Holly

London is so very fast isn't it, it's a lot slower here, maybe you'll get another promotion tomorrow, fingers crossed.

:)

Alice x

Subject: Promotion

> **From:** Holly
> **To:** Jason

Hi

Just saw Richard walk past and he ignored me, so I guess that's it then.

In big places like this, when they've found someone from outside, they can't just give them the job. They first have to interview someone from within the company, so it looks like they've at least tried promoting first.

xxx

I'm off home now, if you're there have a lovely night.

Subject: Your interview

From: Nigel Thorn, HR Director
To: Holly

Dear Holly Denham

Thank you for coming in for all our meetings.

On careful consideration of your application, we believe you obviously have the organizational skills that would work well within a supervisory role. You have a good understanding of project management procedures—shown by your recent success in organizing our Annual Results 2007. With the merger of the two companies there will be many structural changes occurring within DK Huerst, where all these skills would definitely come in useful.

A recent memo from Natasha Springer delayed our decision until now. You also lack people management experience, which is absolutely essential to this position; unfortunately you wouldn't be able to lead a team of staff without it.

Therefore we will be sending you on an intensive staff management training course, then you will begin a contract as our interim DK Huerst Front of House Manager. The offer will include a management benefits package.

We have two contracts waiting for you to read and sign. Please come up as soon as you're in and we'll go through them with you.

Can we remind you of the necessity for haste. You will need to employ another receptionist and you will have Marie from what was previously known as DK Bank coming over to join your team in a week's time.

Congratulations on the new post. I believe you'll make an excellent manager.

Kindest regards

Nigel Thorn

Director of Human Resources, DK Huerst, 50 Cabot Square, Canary Wharf, London

thursday

Subject: I spoke to Mum

From: Holly
To: Granny

She told me it's definitely not cement, but some kind of protein powder and it helps your cholesterol. She says it can go a bit hard if you leave it for too long.

xxx

From: Granny
To: Holly

Holly

Your mother talks such rot, it is cement, but I want you to see what you think.

Lots of love

Granny

Subject: The Newspaper

From: Mum
To: Holly

Holly

I just wanted to check to make sure you received my email about the police force? You've certainly got the height and I believe they give a very good pension?

What do you think?

Mum

From: Holly
To: Mum

What about?

From: Mum
To: Holly

Joining the police?

From: Holly
To: Mum

Not given it any thought yet, Mum, but now you mention it, no thanks.

x

From: Mum
To: Holly

I just know you're so much more capable of doing more than what you're doing now.

You had a fabulous education, that we paid for, and you don't want to be looking back at the wrong end of 40 wondering what you're going to do next.

We're allowed to worry about you Holly, it's what parents do.

Love Mum

From: Holly
To: Mum

Thanks, Mum. But I'm happy doing this, so don't worry.

Holly

From: Mum
To: Holly

I'm not saying you don't like it, and being a receptionist is nothing to be ashamed of. One of your great grandparents worked in the sewers, and he liked it, as far as I know. I'm just thinking about your career. Life can be so uncertain.

From: Holly
To: Mum

One email from you and pushing staples through my eyelids doesn't seem to hurt anymore.

But you needn't stress, I've just been given a promotion, I'm the new FOH manager. I think it comes with a good pension too, so you can rest easy at night.

Love you.

Holly

Subject: You won't believe it

From: Holly
To: Jason

Had a strange email from HR waiting for me this morning…

From: Jason
To: Holly

Don't tell me you got it?

From: Holly
To: Jason

I did—YAYAYAYAYAYAYAY! YIPPEEEEE for meeeee, I'm the new FOH manager for DK Huerst. Yipeeee and now I think I'm going to dance and it goes a little something like this… err huh err huh.

From: Jason
To: Holly

BRILLIAAAAAAAAAAAAAAAAAAAAANT!!!!
YOU'RE SO CLEVER!!!!!! CLEVER CLEVER
OH no she's going to dance, somebody stop her.

From: Holly
To: Jason

Yes I am clever, aren't I !!!!

Thank you, Jason.

I actually want to go outside and scream, but I'm thinking I should sign the contracts first.

Went to the lifts and did a little secret dance, nearly twisted my ankle.

xxx

Subject: Did I miss something?

From: Trisha
To: Holly

You OK there? Why you limping?

From: Holly
To: Trisha

I got my heel stuck in the edge of the lift.

From: Trisha
To: Holly

Why you all flushed and out of breath?

From: Holly
To: Trisha

It was really stuck. I might go up to Facilities and tell them about it in a minute. It was dreadful.

Subject: The Metropolitan Police

From: FraudInvestigationUnit@Yahoo.co.uk
To: Holly

Dear Holly Denham

Crime Reference Number 20080303

We have reason to believe that a crime has recently been committed within the Maida Vale area and your help would be much appreciated.

A CD—signed by a well known pop band, made up of four fabulously talented and perfectly formed boys was stolen from a bar.

If you know anything about this, or come into contact with this CD, it is IMPERATIVE that you quickly contact one of our undercover operatives, staying at a secret London location. It's probably just best if you leave it on the front desk of the lovely five star LHS Hotel in Mayfair for him to pick up.

Cheers

Mr Plod

From: Holly
To: FraudInvestigationUnit@Yahoo.co.uk

Dear Mr Plod

That sounds like theft not fraud?

Somewhat confused??

Holly Denham

From: FraudInvestigationUnit@Yahoo.co.uk
To: Holly

Listen Denham. Don't get shirty with us or we'll be using your peachy white booty as target practice in the new darts wing of Plod House.

Hand over the CD now!

From: Holly
To: FraudInvestigationUnit@Yahoo.co.uk

No.

Subject: Management position

From: Holly
To: Richard

Dear Richard

Having had a brief moment to go through everything, I've noticed it says the position is just a month's contract. I thought this was a permanent position with a month's probation period?

Kindest regards

Holly

From: Richard
To: Holly

Dear Holly

I did explain they have been considering outsourcing the whole reception area to a specialist reception management company and will be studying tenders already submitted over the coming weeks.

This position offered to you is initially on a contractual basis for a month. However, if you prove you can successfully manage the team during this period, the CEO will be more than happy to cancel the other proposals and offer you a straight permanent position as our FOH manager.

Your future is your own hands. You have been with the company for little over a year and so to progress within that time to FOH manager will be a fantastic achievement. I understand however if you chose not to accept this offer.

Yours sincerely

Richard Mosley

From: Holly
To: Richard

Richard

Thanks and please don't think I'm being ungrateful, just considering this seriously. Can you hang on till next week for me to send the contracts back? Also if it's decided at the end of a month that outsourcing would be the best option what would happen to me?

Holly

From: Richard
To: Holly

Dear Holly

I don't think you're being ungrateful at all and I perfectly understand your caution. If unsuccessful you would revert to being a standard receptionist at DK Huerst.

Have a great Easter. If I don't see you at the Olympics we'll speak Tuesday

Kind regards

Richard

sunday

From: Jason
To: Holly

I'm at work, on Easter Sunday, wish you were too.

week 4
tuesday

Subject: My Olympics Bank Holiday Weekend

From: Holly
To: Jason

Are you ready then?

From: Jason
To: Holly

I have shut myself in my office, I have a 'do not disturb sign' on the door, I am ready.

From: Holly
To: Jason

So the company Olympics Event didn't sound like the perfect romantic date, but I thought—at least I'm going to spend a whole day with Toby. The bank had reserved a corner of the park and it was a beautiful day. There was a fair, games, rides, stalls and a bar. Toby was wearing jeans, t-shirt and suit jacket, my favourite look on him, smart/messy sexy.

From: Jason
To: Holly

Hair?

From: Holly
To: Jason

Usual, wavy, bit of stubble etc. He was on good form, upbeat, making me laugh all morning. We walked arm in arm in the sun around the stalls. He went on the rifle range and won me nothing, but he kept going back all morning, which was sweet. He did end up winning me a bear on this kicking game though. I didn't realise how good he was at football. I think that's why he hates it now although he won't admit it (I think he's bitter because he was meant to be trying out for a club, but his parents wouldn't let him before taking him to France.)

Anyway, the day was just perfect, then Tanya Mason appeared.

From: Jason
To: Holly

Don't like the sound of this.

From: Holly
To: Jason

She was all perfect and pretty and full of giggles and pouts. He went to introduce me but she told him she knew me already and said 'me and Holly are already friends' and flashed me a big warm smile before grabbing his arm and the three of us were heading towards the athletics races. Which were about to begin.

From: Jason
To: Holly

I want to punch her already.

From: Holly
To: Jason

I had no idea what she was up to. I started thinking maybe she's nice again. She kept chatting to both of us, we all seemed to get along.

From: Jason
To: Holly

I still want to hit her.

From: Holly
To: Jason

I didn't like the way she had her arm around Toby's, then a call went out for volunteers for the three-legged race and Tanya had put her hand up for all of us to enter. I didn't want to do it but I wasn't about to say it and be the only one against the idea. So they start giving us arm bands with numbers on and she's still chatting away to him and making him laugh and I'm still trying to work out whether I should like her or not, when someone begins strapping THEIR legs together.

From: Jason
To: Holly

Bastards.

From: Holly
To: Jason

I want to say they'd got it wrong, he was MY boyfriend, not hers. If any legs were getting strapped together they would be Holly's and Toby's—NOT Tanya's and Toby's. Why did he presume they were a couple, Jason?

From: Jason
To: Holly

Probably didn't even look up, saw two legs, strapped them together. He's a strapper, they're not paid to think, just strap. Please tell me you didn't shout out?

From: Holly
To: Jason

I wanted to.

From: Jason
To: Holly

But you didn't?

From: Holly
To: Jason

No, I didn't, Toby tried to say something and was looking around for me, but then she had her nasty arm around his waist and they were being led off.

From: Jason
To: Holly

What did you do????

From: Holly
To: Jason

I did what any self respecting woman would do when she's jealous—I grabbed the nearest man who looked half decent and pull him to the front with me.

From: Jason
To: Holly

Perfect.

From: Holly
To: Jason

Nasty Tanya and Two Timing Toby were ahead of us and about to set off arm in arm on their romantic stroll. They were against six other couples. I couldn't decide if I wanted them to win or lose?

From: Jason
To: Holly

Lose surely?

From: Holly
To: Jason

But what if it meant they fell over? They'd be rolling around on the grass all tied up, yuck, sick. Win and they might hug and then their eyes would meet—and there'd be this hidden meaning. Oh I feel sick again.

From: Jason
To: Holly

Stop it, so what did you decide?

From: Holly
To: Jason

That it didn't matter, because the gun went off and they raced away and won the race.

From: Jason
To: Holly

Bitch. I hate Toby too.

From: Holly
To: Jason

Wasn't his fault, he was looking for me as soon as he got to the end.

From: Jason
To: Holly

Did you win with your guy?

From: Holly
To: Jason

There was so much noise, everyone was cheering and shouting. I was grabbed and pushed to the front, but our legs hadn't been strapped together, so I was getting worried. My big rugby player type asked who I was, I shouted back, but I later found out that he misheard me (never got his name either).

From: Jason
To: Holly

Tell me more about him, describe his legs.

From: Holly
To: Jason

No! I couldn't get anyone to hear me and then we were lining up and I could see Tanya and Toby at the end watching. The man on the microphone said something about wheelbarrow races and I turned around to protest, but the rugby guy twizzles me back around, the gun goes off, he pushes my head to the ground, yanks my legs up behind and yells 'Move it, Mary!!'

From: Jason
To: Holly

Oh mother of mercy.

From: Holly
To: Jason

Legs held up behind me, I struggle up on my arms and he's away, pushing me hard and I'm scrabbling with my hands as fast as I can, trying to save my life while he's shouting 'come on come on MOVE IT WOMAN, get those arms moving!' My arms suddenly give up on me, and I land on the ground, but he doesn't stop! Now he's just pushing me along on my face, my skirt over my backside and I'm trying to get up on my hands but he won't wait and now I'm being slid along on my front.

From: Jason
To: Holly

No, please stop, I don't want to hear any more.

From: Holly
To: Jason

I get my hands up in the end and struggle on, face covered in mud, arms pumping, miles behind everyone, him bellowing 'Move it, Mary!' every now and then. The crowd are cheering 'Maaa-ry Maaaa-ry'. I'm scampering off in the wrong direction. We are the very last to finish.

From: Jason
To: Holly

Oh Holly.

From: Holly
To: Jason

I couldn't look at Tanya's face directly but I'm sure I saw her smirking, then lots of fake sympathy. I just rushed off to the toilets to get fixed up.

From: Jason
To: Holly

Lordy lordy, I don't know what to say, you poor poor thing. I'm so glad I wasn't with you. What happened the rest of the day?

From: Holly
To: Jason

We all met up again, and had some lunch together. Got rid of her in the end.

From: Jason
To: Holly

She knows you two are going out then?

From: Holly
To: Jason

I made it crystal clear. I even mentioned living together and looking for a house together.

From: Jason
To: Holly

But you're not.

From: Holly
To: Jason

Don't care, it was war. And now I can't even lift a cup, my arms are still hurting so much.

From: Jason
To: Holly

I bet it keeps you fit, OH MY GOD!

From: Holly
To: Jason

What??

From: Jason
To: Holly

An idea. What are the two most meaningful, glorious words in the English language? Exercise & Video!!!! It will instantly catapult you to D list heaven!!! You in your dress again, me wheeling you down the street to Kylie's 'locomotion'??? I'd look fabulous, you'd look mad, but we'd make a fortune! What do you think??

From: Holly
To: Jason

I'm going now.

From: Jason
To: Holly

We could start a craze. Instead of passing joggers in the mornings, Maida Vale would be littered with burly men pushing their sweaty wives up and down the high street?????

From: Holly
To: Jason

Goodbye.

From: Jason
To: Holly

Wait, before you go, have you signed the contracts yet?

From: Holly
To: Jason

No.

From: Jason
To: Holly

Go do it now!

From: Holly
To: Jason

Still not sure about it. I'm thinking.

x

Subject: Keeping secrets from me!

From: Trisha
To: Holly

So when did you think you was going to tell me?

From: Holly
To: Trisha

What?

From: Trisha
To: Holly

You know what!!!! Why am I the last to know, I thought we were friends, I thought I was your Aunty Trisha??

From: Holly
To: Trisha

You are?

From: Trisha
To: Holly

Then why don't you tell me why people keep calling you Mary?

From: Holly
To: Trisha

Oh, I have no idea, didn't know they were.

From: Trisha
To: Holly

Liar, that last PA did.

From: Holly
To: Trisha

OK, fine, it wasn't nice, I'll tell you later.

x

From: Trisha
To: Holly

Wait a minute, also I want to know who that guy was before?

From: Holly
To: Trisha

Which one?

From: Trisha
To: Holly

You know the one, dashingly handsome, my Mum would say, a right sort.

From: Holly
To: Trisha

No idea.

From: Trisha
To: Holly

Look at me!

From: Holly
To: Trisha

OK, I think his name's William something, but he's a friend of Toby's.

From: Trisha
To: Holly

He's lovely he is, you got to introduce me next time.

Subject: Finished

From: Toby
To: Holly

I'm finishing early, you ready? We can go home together.

From: Holly
To: Toby

Yay! Come pick me up big boy. Just got to get my coat from the 30th and then I'll be back on the ground floor desk waiting. You want to have dinner somewhere—have one or two drinks on the way back? :)

From: Toby
To: Holly

We could do, but I'd prefer to just spend a nice night at home, just the two of us. I don't want to share you at all! And I promise I won't just crash out early.

xxxx

From: Holly
To: Toby

Perfect!
xx

Subject: The Break Up

From: Jason
To: Holly

Forgot to say—I've bought the violin, a Bible, a bottle of petunia oil, some French bangers and I've borrowed a heap of S&M equipment (off Aisha). Just keeping you informed.

I'm off home, speak later.

X

wednesday

Subject: He's back

From: Holly
To: Trisha

And I'm glad he didn't forget to pack his eyebrows, I would have missed them.

From: Trisha
To: Holly

I wouldn't. He's watching you again, underneath them.

From: Holly
To: Trisha

That's scary, one bush goes up, and you see an evil glaring eye.

From: Trisha
To: Holly

Evil or stupid. You seen the diary? We got meetings all day long.

From: Holly
To: Trisha

I know, it's back to back.

From: Trisha
To: Holly

Richard must be looking for another receptionist. Look at this one coming now. Thinks she's so great but she looks like she's been tie dyed by a drunk from Stepney Green.

From: Holly
To: Trisha

Trisha!! How can you say that and then be so nice to her! Shame on you!

From: Trisha
To: Holly

I'm paid to be nice. I like her hair though, might get mine done like that. Good legs an all, although it's a shame she forgot to dye the back of her knees. Hope he doesn't get us a Muppet who can't find her arse from her elbow.

From: Holly
To: Trisha

Deep breaths, Trisha, deep breaths.

From: Trisha
To: Holly

Wonder how our space farmer is doing up there.

Subject: Morning

From: Trisha
To: Claire; Holly

You alright, Claire?

From: Claire
To: Trisha; Holly

Fandabidozi Trisha, what's it like down there?

From: Trisha
To: Claire; Holly

Building up, so get yourself ready for the rush. They'll be heading up to you soon, girl.

From: Claire
To: Holly; Trisha

OK, it's going to be a bit difficult doing everything while I'm folding these envelopes though.

From: Holly
To: Claire; Trisha

What envelopes are those, sweetie?

From: Claire
To: Holly; Trisha

Don't know, I've got to fill them with these cards.

From: Holly
To: Claire; Trisha

What cards?

From: Claire
To: Holly; Trisha

Invitations to a party at a house in Pimlico. There was a mysterious pile of them waiting for me on my chair when I came back from the toilet.

From: Holly
To: Claire; Trisha

Was there a note or message attached?

From: Claire
To: Holly; Trisha

Yes, it said I had to get them done "ASAP" and after I should run them down to the post room.

From: Holly
To: Claire; Trisha

That's not right. Who's signed it off?

From: Claire
To: Holly; Trisha

T. Mason.

From: Trisha
To: Holly; Claire

That's Tanya, she's a cheeky bitch, you'll get in trouble.

From: Holly
To: Claire; Trisha

Don't be caught filling envelopes. If someone sees you doing that in front of clients, they'll have a fit.

From: Trisha
To: Claire; Holly

Too right darlin and Tanya knows it too, she's taking the piss, don't get yourself in trouble for her.

From: Claire
To: Holly; Trisha

I've got myself into a real pickle haven't I? What to do, what to do, no idea. What do you think I should do?

From: Holly
To: Claire; Trisha

You can blame it on me if you want. When she comes back just say I told you not to do it.

Subject: Splitting up

From: Holly
To: Jason

How's it going with Marco?

From: Jason
To: Holly

Difficult.

From: Holly
To: Jason

I noticed your new laugh.

From: Jason
To: Holly

Like it?

From: Holly
To: Jason

Not at all.

From: Jason
To: Holly

Good.

From: Holly
To: Jason

Don't use it when we're out.

From: Jason
To: Holly

I've got to keep it up.

From: Holly
To: Jason

What's next on the list?

From: Jason
To: Holly

Working out, at home.

From: Holly
To: Jason

Let me know what nights I need to avoid.

xxxx

Subject: Monday

From: Tanya Mason
To: Holly

Dear Holly

It was nice meeting you and Toby the other day, thank you for letting me join you both. You certainly make a wonderfully interesting couple.

Regards

Tanya

Catering Manager

From: Holly
To: Tanya Mason

Dear Tanya

Thank you, it was great seeing you too, I had so much fun.

Have a fab day

Holly

From: Tanya Mason
To: Holly

Holly

On a separate note, this morning I gave Claire on the hospitality floor some event invitations to put together for me, but she said she'd been told by you to stop doing them?

I presume the poor thing must have got confused about it all, anyway she's off doing them again now.

We must catch up again soon.

Kind regards

Tanya.

From: Holly
To: Tanya Mason

Hi Tanya

Yes, sorry, I did actually tell her to stop, because I thought she might get in trouble if she's caught filling envelopes there. Earlier in the year I was doing something similar for a PA and got in trouble.

We aren't even allowed to keep a mug of tea on the desks, just a plain glass of water. The desks have to be clear and spotless, definitely not with a pile of envelopes.

Regards

Holly

From: Tanya Mason
To: Holly

Holly

I don't want to argue with you, but a few envelopes will not be noticed. If this is about me being too busy to be able to come out with you and your friends, then don't you think that's a little childish??

Tanya

Subject: Quick question

From: Mum
To: Holly

I was thinking about getting your granny electronically tagged, like we did that dog of Alice's. What do you think?

From: Holly
To: Mum

No Mum, you can't do that.

From: Mum
To: Holly

OK, didn't mean to disturb you when you're busy managing things. All our love, Mum

Subject: Cards

From: Holly
To: Tanya Mason

Tanya

No of course it isn't about that. I totally understand you are very busy, and as I said it was great meeting you the other day. It's simply for the reasons I have stated.

We really do have strict guidelines on our professional conduct on reception.

Sorry

Holly

From: Tanya Mason
To: Holly

I know the guidelines. I am telling you I want these done. I have told her to carry on with them.

Tanya

From: Holly
To: Tanya Mason

I think your actions could cause a member of the reception team to get into trouble. I really think it's unfair of you to ask her to do this.

Holly

From: Tanya Mason
To: Holly

It is kind of you to watch out for her, but this would have gone completely unnoticed if you hadn't made a big deal out of it. Claire is doing a small task for me and unfortunately, Holly, that is the end of it, unless you would like to assist her? Let me know if this is the case and I will forward some down to you?

If not then I'll presume the conversation is now closed.

Tanya Mason

Subject: Management position

From: Holly
To: Richard

Having considered it, I would be very happy to take the challenge of this position and will be signing the contracts now and sending them back. As FOH manager I presume I am at the same level as Tanya Mason and therefore have priority over duties given to the reception team?

Regards

Holly

From: Richard
To: Holly

Dear Holly

That's great news. Yes your team is your area of authority. You will be answering to me and you have a month to get things improved. Unfortunately, as we're short staffed, your training will have to fit around your hours. Tomorrow and Friday I'm getting a temp in to cover you. I want you working up on the hospitality floor with Claire sitting down with Trisha. I've booked out room 22 for us all day and during any quiet periods we'll meet up and go through a few bits and pieces. I will be forwarding the current stats to you shortly. These will detail the areas needing most attention. I will be informing the whole Facilities/FOH team on Friday. This will give you tomorrow to let them all know you've been promoted first.

I think you will be a successful manager and look forward to being able to give you further news of a full-time placement.

Regards

Richard

Subject: Sorry, Tanya

From: Holly
To: Tanya Mason

Sorry but we are unable to package your personal 'event' invitations. Please remove them from Claire's desk before 5pm.

Thanking you in advance.

Holly

thursday

Subject: Repairs

From: HIFI CityDU
To: Holly

Dear Holly

Yes we could look at your CD player. However, there is a call out fee of £50. It is likely we may also have to send it away for repairs. Let us know what you would like to do.

REPAIRS

Subject: Accounts

From: Holly
To: Jason

I had a quick look through my outgoings for the first time in months and I've discovered something important.

From: Jason
To: Holly

You're about to be taken to court?

From: Holly
To: Jason

No, apart from that, my monthly debts now equal my monthly salary.

From: Jason
To: Holly

That's nicely balanced.

From: Holly
To: Jason

It is.

From: Jason
To: Holly

At least you know where you stand?

From: Holly
To: Jason

I do and I'm not great at accounts, but I have realised something important—get this—I've realised more money needs to come in than goes out each month.

From: Jason
To: Holly

Clever.

From: Holly
To: Jason

In one month I'll have more money coming in than going out, from being given the full-time management job—if I keep it—so I just need to hide from everyone for a month and survive, then I'll call them all up with the good news.

From: Jason
To: Holly

If you're not in prison by then?

From: Holly
To: Jason

And those kind of comments aren't helpful or needed.

From: Jason
To: Holly

Sorry. I think you've got it all worked out perfectly. You want to go out tonight and celebrate?

From: Holly
To: Jason

You're a bad influence, Jason.

x

Subject: From Granny

From: Granny
To: Holly

Dear Holly

I'm looking out at the garden this morning and I'm wondering whether it might be a glorious day to go out into the sun. I might do some pottering around. What do you think?

From: Holly
To: Granny

I think you should potter away. Thought you hated the sun?

From: Granny
To: Holly

I don't hate anything, Holly, I just miss the rain and fog and mist. Every day it's sun sun sun here. Someone said to me the other day, 'You are so lucky living where you are, you can ski in the morning and sunbathe on the beach in the afternoon.' What a damn silly thing to say to an old woman. I said to him, where I came from it could snow in the morning, give us hot sunshine in the afternoon and in between if we were lucky we could get some thunder, some lightning, rain and even a drop of hail. Try and beat that!

From: Holly
To: Granny

What did he say?

From: Granny
To: Holly

Well what could he say, I think I scared the poor man. Right, sunshine it is. Are you going anywhere nice this weekend?

From: Holly
To: Granny

Are you pottering locally?

From: Granny
To: Holly

My dear girl, are you asking me whether I intend to bolt from my rabbit hutch? Never fear, my days of running are over. Celia comes over from across the road and there we sit on the Internet talking on chat sites. They are so much fun, and I took the liberty of registering your name on a few to see what you thought.

Xxx Love Granny

Subject: Here we go...

From: Holly
To: Jason

I'm on the 30th hospitality floor today, Claire's downstairs with Trisha, so I'm going to do it now.

X

From: Jason
To: Holly

Could you get any further away???

From: Holly
To: Jason

Yes—the 41st floor, but then I don't have anywhere to run to.

From: Jason
To: Holly

Coward.

From: Holly
To: Jason

I know!

Subject: Things

From: Holly
To: Trisha

Hi Trisha, how's it going today?

From: Trisha
To: Holly

Not good. I'm not happy about sitting with Claire for two days. She's never quiet and I told her we're not meant to talk. I said imagine a library, email me as much as you want but don't sit nattering to me about your boyfriend troubles with clients sitting in front of you. You know me, I was even rude, but did she care? No, on she goes whispering. It's like sitting next to Les's mum in church, I'm telling you.

From: Holly
To: Trisha

Be patient with her. Please, she's sweet.

From: Trisha
To: Holly

I'll try, I'll really try.

From: Holly
To: Trisha

Trisha, you know I told you I'd been given a verbal warning.

From: Trisha
To: Holly

Yes.

From: Holly
To: Trisha

I hadn't, it wasn't about being told off, it was all just such a shock I didn't really know what to say, and you were so worried for me, I couldn't just come out with it.

From: Trisha
To: Holly

So what's it all about then?

From: Holly
To: Trisha

They started talking to me about a promotion, but I felt so bad that I'd been so wet about it all, thinking I was getting in trouble, that I couldn't bring myself to tell you straight away.

From: Trisha
To: Holly

Promotion? What promotion?

From: Holly
To: Trisha

For a management role.

From: Trisha
To: Holly

Where?

From: Holly
To: Trisha

Here, managing the reception team, the whole team, amazing isn't it?

From: Trisha
To: Holly

Management role??? YOU?? That's nice, nice of them to think of me!!!! Bet you don't get it though, they're just interviewing you to show they've done someone internally, like a token Huerst person. Wouldn't raise your hopes, darlin.

From: Holly
To: Trisha

I got it.

From: Trisha
To: Holly

RIGHT< Wheres myf**ing meeting, an my fuisning porotion, that's just typical f or the se b*&(LKJF , right, I'm going up there right now t ohave it out with t hem all F***ing ****ds!!!!KJKLJLK(*&^*&%* and you 're coming with me, see you in a minute DARLIN

From: Holly
To: Trisha

Trisha?

Subject: TRISHA??

From: Holly
To: Claire

Is Trisha there still?

From: Claire
To: Holly

No, what happened? She just got up, threw the switchboard across the room and marched into the lift. :(

friday

Subject: Are you lonely/sad/depressed?

From: Registration@CPNT.UK.com
To: Holly

Do you sometimes feel out of place amongst other people?

Do you fear that no one is talking to you? Are you occasionally left in the corner, shunned, alone, at lunch time?

Are you finding it difficult to make friends at work?

Do you spend your nights by yourself??????!

If so, then maybe you need

CHATLINE !!

For £5/min you could have a friend!!!!!??

Don't feel SAD feel CHAT-ASTICK!!!

No more being the lonely Joe in the corner.

Calls charged at £5 standard rate, although rates may vary

Subject: Need to talk

From: Holly
To: Trisha

Email me when you get in please.

Holly

Subject: Changes

From: Richard
To: Holly

Dear Holly

Marie will be joining us in this building in a couple of weeks to continue her role as the overflow switchboard operator. The hospitality floor is getting busier by the day so we'll need to take on another full-time receptionist to sit with Claire. Between myself and

HR we've already interviewed a lot of candidates for this reception role and have whittled them down to just nine; all of whom you are booked in to interview on Tuesday.

I'd like you to pick the best two you could see fitting into your team. HR will have the final say in which one joins the company.

Richard

PS Have you told the team yet about your appointment?

From: Holly
To: Richard

Richard

Thank you, and yes, I told the team last night.

Holly

From: Richard
To: Holly

Good, I can't imagine it was easy. Well done.

Richard

Subject: Newsletter

From: Charlie@SubmissionEnterprises
To: Holly; Alice; Mum

Dear Family

Just to let you know, the band has split up and now I'm heading off to Brazil.

Regards

Charlie

From: Mum
To: Charlie; Holly; Alice

Dear Charlie

I'm glad you're sending us these newsletters, but a call once in a while would be nice too.

Such a shame the band split up, it must be very disappointing for you, after all that hard work you put into it. What happened?

Love Mum

From: Charlie
To: Holly; Alice; Mum

Therese caught herpes, Tina has the flu, Tatiana ran off with a roadie, then caught herpes and the monkey got a call from Sir Andrew Lloyd Webber, because he's written a new stage production of Cats, but this time with monkeys.

Terrible news for everyone.

Charlie

From: Alice
To: Charlie; Holly; Mum

Sorry Charlie—the monkey got a call?

From: Charlie
To: Alice; Holly; Mum

Obviously monkeys can't speak, Alice, but he has an agent.

I'm going to Brazil now, my flight's leaving soon, got to run.

Charlie

Subject: Stop it!

From: Holly
To: Rubber Ron

Just stop writing rubbish?

From: Rubber Ron
To: Holly

Holly, I'm keeping in touch with his business clients so no one knows he's not around and he's given me instructions of what to write to your family.

Ron

From: Holly
To: Rubber Ron

OK, when you speak to him next, can you get something which involves fewer sexual diseases and monkeys. Something which makes him out to be less of a pervert and more of a nice guy?
Holly

Subject: Someone is lying

From: Alice
To: Holly

Come on, where is Charlie really?

From: Holly
To: Alice

I know as much as you do.
xx

Subject: Morning, Mr Williams

From: Holly
To: Toby

I thought of something to bring a little sunshine into your morning. Have you got a few spare minutes? xxxx

From: Toby
To: Holly

Yes, sunshine is much needed, things aren't going well today. Tell me.

x

From: Holly
To: Toby

I've got some exciting news that I've been dying to tell you, but... as you're a gambling man and you like the occasional flutter... I'm going to give a list of floor numbers: either 20, 25, 30, 35 or 40.

They'll be a prize waiting for you on the other side of one of those special steel doors, but you only have five minutes from the moment you get this email to guess the correct floor.

If you don't get to the right floor in time, then the prize will be removed and you lose the game.

Do you understand the rules?

From: Toby
To: Holly

Yes, that's so funny.

Subject: What happened?

From: Holly
To: Toby

Did you look?

From: Toby
To: Holly

No.

From: Holly
To: Toby

WHY????

From: Toby
To: Holly

I thought you were joking?

From: Holly
To: Toby

I was waiting like an idiot on floor 25 for ten minutes?????

From: Toby
To: Holly

Oh, sorry, I really thought you were joking. Do it again, I'll look this time, I promise. What was the news?

From: Holly
To: Toby

Forget it, I can't go again now, I'm manning the desk.

From: Toby
To: Holly

I'm really sorry baby. x

Subject: Rabbits

From: Holly
To: Jason

Want to come rabbit shopping this weekend?

From: Jason
To: Holly

Yes yes yes! I've seen a really cute one that looks like it's been put in a tumble dryer. Its hair is all sticky up and fluffy. I thought Toby wasn't keen though?

From: Holly
To: Jason

He's not, but I'm not going to tell him.

From: Jason
To: Holly

You're such a rebel!

Subject: TRISHA!!!

From: Holly
To: Trisha

Are you there yet??

From: Trisha
To: Holly

Yes???

From: Holly
To: Trisha

Why did you turn your phone off last night?

From: Trisha
To: Holly

Personal probs, darlin. Sorry were you trying to get hold of me?

From: Holly
To: Trisha

Yes, strangely I was!!!???

From: Trisha
To: Holly

Why?

From: Holly
To: Trisha

Why do you think?!

From: Trisha
To: Holly

I can't imagine, I've done nothing wrong, unless you were just miffed because I didn't invite you to bingo with me mum?

From: Holly
To: Trisha

Yesterday I was up here for ages waiting for you!! Wondering when you were going to come out of the lift steaming, and when people were going to be carried off in ambulances, AND YOU'D GONE HOME!!

From: Trisha
To: Holly

I know, can't be late for Bingo, or I would be in trouble.

From: Holly
To: Trisha

Claire told me the truth!

From: Trisha
To: Holly

I'd taken a half day, darlin, anyway my fighting days are over.

From: Holly
To: Trisha

TRISHA!

From: Trisha
To: Holly

They told me all about it a while ago, I knew where you'd been all along. Verbal warning, you dopey lying cow. Call yourself a friend!!

From: Holly
To: Trisha

What???

From: Trisha
To: Holly

They asked me two weeks ago if I'd be upset if they talked to you about it. I told them I thought you'd be useless, but I certainly wouldn't mind. I'm a receptionist not a manager, wouldn't want the stress.

From: Holly
To: Trisha

TRISHA!

From: Trisha
To: Holly

So I couldn't let you just have an easy ride, had to get me enjoyment out of it somehow.

From: Holly
To: Trisha

TRISHA!!

From: Trisha
To: Holly

Some manager, can't even write a flipping sentence, I ask ya.

From: Holly
To: Trisha

You know it's just for a month to start with.

From: Trisha
To: Holly

I know you'll keep the job anyway, you're what this place needs. So you going to come down and give me a hug or what?

From: Holly
To: Trisha

I'll get someone to cover me and come down with my hug.

xxxx

Subject: Unknown

From: UnknownAngel101@yahoo.co.uk
To: Holly

And the Lord said "secrets are the undoing of the soul".

month 2

week 1

monday

Subject: PLAN FOR 2008

From: Holly
To: Holly

Count down to May 5th.

Five weeks to prove myself.

Then I'm going to:

Get permanent management job with increase in salary & bens

Get back in touch with the world and begin paying off my debts
again

Holly Denham

FOH Manager, DKHuerst, 50 Cabot Square, Canary Wharf, London

Subject: Missed call

From: William Duncan
To: Holly

Had a missed call on my mobile. I'm presuming it was you fluffins.
What was it?

From: Holly
To: William Duncan

It wasn't me! I don't even have your number?

From: William Duncan
To: Holly

Oh, do you want it?

From: Holly
To: William Duncan

No.

From: William Duncan
To: Holly

Why not?

From: Holly
To: William Duncan

Because I have no reason for it?

From: William Duncan
To: Holly

Oh come on, don't lie to me, I know about the photo.

From: Holly
To: William Duncan

What photo?

From: William Duncan
To: Holly

The one you have in the top drawer of your desk.

From: Holly
To: William Duncan

I don't have any photos in there.

From: William Duncan
To: Holly

Would you like some? Will on a bike, Will relaxing by the pool, Will on a surfboard in his lounge, Will holding up his school boxing medals? Will at home cooking. Do you like Lobtherhoop?

From: Holly
To: William Duncan

What is it?

From: William Duncan
To: Holly

Lobster Soup, sorry I was eating when I wrote that. I'm a great cook, so how about it sexy? Want to know what makes young Duncan really tick?

From: Holly
To: William Duncan

Not whatsoever.

Subject: An interesting discovery

From: Toby @ Blackberry
To: Holly

What do you think I found in my shoe this morning?
Toby

From: Holly
To: Toby

I don't know, maybe some magic beans???

Subject: Targets

From: Richard
To: Holly

Dear Holly

In answer to your question about how you can quantify your achievements, I have been provided with some clear targets, ones you must achieve to ensure the reception is not outsourced in a month's time. Currently Client Services has been given an overall score of 62 out of 100. This needs to be brought up to 80 by the 5th May; then you will become our permanent FOH manager.

Each area has been given a score out of twenty, they are:

Room reservations—10

Organization, presentation and assignment

Face to Face Contact—12

Meeting and greeting, taking clients to rooms, providing information, warmth, discretion, ability to cope with difficult clients

Telephone etiquette and techniques—12

Screening sales calls, accurately transferring calls, time taken to answer calls, warmth, professionalism, ability to cope with difficult clients

In-house relationships—13

Co-operating within the team, liaison with PAs, directors, catering team and overall team spirit

Beyond the call of duty—15

Going further to ensure client satisfaction, additional extras— providing a memorable service overall

I would suggest looking at each area and trying to think of some new systems or procedures to ensure these are improved.

Yours sincerely

Richard

Subject: Morning

From: Holly
To: Jason

I've been thinking all weekend about fun ways to improve what we're doing. I'm so excited about it all, I can't wait.

From: Jason
To: Holly

I think you'll make a fab manager, better than me—as I forgot this morning about the clocks going forward—I was an hour late again.

From: Holly
To: Jason

Oh dear, I was going to call you about it. Sorry.

From: Jason
To: Holly

Don't worry. Any gossip? How was your Sunday?

From: Holly
To: Jason

Spent it planning things here. How was yours?

From: Jason
To: Holly

Unusual.

From: Holly
To: Jason

Why?

From: Jason
To: Holly

Because on Sunday morning at about 7am, while Marco was still asleep, I found myself questioning the meaning of life.

From: Holly
To: Jason

Deep.

From: Jason
To: Holly

I know.

From: Holly
To: Jason

I sometimes do that—lie awake in the mornings next to Toby, thinking about everything.

From: Jason
To: Holly

I wasn't lying next to him, I was standing in the lounge in front of the TV in nothing but trainers and a very tight pair of shiny pink spandex shorts.

From: Holly
To: Jason

Oh.

From: Jason
To: Holly

I stood for a moment, wondering what it was all about, I remember even Jordan looked unusually thoughtful staring back at me from her metallic fuchsia hotpants.

From: Holly
To: Jason

That is unusual. Was she on the TV?

From: Jason
To: Holly

Of course?? You think I'd look that stupid if she was actually in my lounge?

All the same I whacked up the volume, and began my squat thrusts as Marco rushed out of his room and stared at me bleary eyed. Poor me. Poor Marco. Maybe we should just stay together before I lose him and the last of my dignity. What do you think?

From: Holly
To: Jason

Baby, are you really sad? You OK?

From: Jason
To: Holly

I'm OK. To cheer myself up I've got the staff picking on people with big noses, kind of team bonding.

From: Holly
To: Jason

How sweet.

Subject: Your weekend

From: Holly
To: Granny

Hi Granny

Hope you had fun with your neighbour at the weekend. How are things?

Love Holly

From: Granny
To: Holly

Dear Holly

Very kind of you to ask and yes I did enjoy my weekend. Celia really is so much fun.

Do you have a neighbour who is fun?

Granny

From: Holly
To: Granny

I have one who's mad? He's called Frankie Fraser and Toby thinks he used to be famous. I'm meeting him for lunch on Sunday to talk about problems in the building.

From: Granny
To: Holly

I think Toby could be right, I remember a singer called Frankie Fraser. You enjoy your lunch.

Love Granny x

From: Holly
To: Granny

Thanks

xxxx

Subject: Interviews

From: Richard
To: Holly

Holly

Your first candidate is waiting for you in room 8.

From: Holly
To: Richard

Thank you. Claire has just arrived to cover and I'm off now to interview her.

Regards

Holly

Subject: Interesting

From: Toby
To: Holly

Not magic beans. I found rabbit pooh in my shoe this morning.

From: Holly
To: Toby

How very strange.

From: Toby
To: Holly

I'd say.

From: Holly
To: Toby

I guess it's one of those great mysteries which will never really be solved.

xx

Subject: JASON YOU BAD MAN!

From: Holly
To: Jason

I'VE BEEN TRYING TO CALL YOU, ARE YOU HIDING????!

From: Jason
To: Holly

Me, hiding, why would I hide?

From: Holly
To: Jason

Then would you like to guess who was waiting for me in one of my interview rooms?

From: Jason
To: Holly

Not Brian Harvey from East 17??? Either way, can't talk, away from my desk for a bit. I'll email you when I'm back.

From: Holly
To: Jason

You're in trouble, Mr Granger!

Subject: I'm guessing

From: Toby
To: Holly

If we have a rabbit lurking somewhere, that pretty much solves it.

From: Holly
To: Toby

Not sure, I'll check when I get home.

Love you xx

From: Toby
To: Holly

Continuing on the surreal note, you had some post which included a torn envelope with what looks like cement in it???

From: Holly
To: Toby

That'll be from my granny.

From: Toby
To: Holly

Thoughtful.

From: Holly
To: Toby

I know.

From: Toby
To: Holly

Your granny really spoils you sometimes.

Subject: Jason!

From: Holly
To: Jason

Are you back yet?

From: Jason
To: Holly

No.

From: Holly
To: Jason

Right, waiting for me in that meeting room was your favourite receptionist...

From: Jason
To: Holly

Astrid! And she should be in the middle of a hysterectomy. That must have been messy?

From: Holly
To: Jason

Aisha!

From: Jason
To: Holly

WHAT???? That naughty squirrel!! How? Why?

From: Holly
To: Jason

You're such a liar!!! You knew all about it!!!!!!

From: Jason
To: Holly

I didn't, I promise.

From: Holly
To: Jason

LIAR.

From: Jason
To: Holly

She is late for work though. Gosh, I'll have to bring her up on it.

From: Holly
To: Jason

LIAR.

From: Jason
To: Holly

Anyway, how do I know you weren't trying to headhunt her from me?? Maybe you are trying to steal her from under my very nose? Hmmm???

From: Holly
To: Jason

What?

From: Jason
To: Holly

I thought as much, some friend you are, oh well, you win some you lose some. I forgive you. When's she starting then?

From: Holly
To: Jason

I'm still in a state of shock, seeing that much flesh on view first thing.

From: Jason
To: Holly

Oh bless her. Listen I'm gay and I had to put up with it for a year. So what are you going to do then, must be difficult?

From: Holly
To: Jason

I don't know, anyway she can't do it, because she'd have to start on Wednesday next week, the latest—we need immediately available candidates.

From: Jason
To: Holly

No problem at all, she never signed a contract with us anyway, she can start when she wants.
Xx

From: Holly
To: Jason

I can't believe you find this so funny, it's an awkward situation and you're being a sick, unhelpful man. Got to interview another one now.
Bye.

Subject: Your neighbour

From: Granny
To: Holly

Holly

I just remembered Frankie Valley was the singer. The man you have living above you sounds like Mad Frankie Fraser the gangster.

What a very exciting life you lead!

Love Granny

INTERVIEWING ALL AFTERNOON
tuesday

Subject: Morning

From: Holly
To: Toby

Why don't men make lists?

From: Toby
To: Holly

What do you mean?

From: Holly
To: Toby

Women make lists, men don't, it said in the paper this morning. What does that mean?

From: Toby
To: Holly

You aren't reading a broadsheet?

From: Holly
To: Toby

You should make a list, lists help you organise your mind better. You could make one of all the things you like about me????

From: Toby
To: Holly

I don't need one, you are perfect.

From: Holly
To: Toby

OK, I am now sitting here with a big grin.
X
PS so are you.

Subject: REMINDER

From: Holly
To: Holly

Holly!
Make a list of all the compliments he's given you then re-read them every time you have doubts. It'll be like reliving them again.
Also you can use them to cheer you up when you've had a row with someone. Seeing as Trisha is determined you will be having them with people soon.

Subject: Also

From: Toby
To: Holly

Someone said they keep seeing you go in to meeting rooms with people, is everything OK?

From: Holly
To: Toby

Fine, I'm interviewing them.

From: Toby
To: Holly

As long as you're OK. I'll see you later.

xx

Subject: Morning

From: Holly
To: Jason

I've got five weeks, so I've decided I'm going to tackle one area a week; introduce new procedures then move on. Otherwise it's too many changes at once. What do you think?

From: Jason
To: Holly

Perfect, what are the areas again?

From: Holly
To: Jason

Face to Face Contact—12

Room reservations—10

Telephone etiquette and techniques—12

In-house relationships—13

Beyond the call of duty—15

So I need to get them all up to around 16 to get to 80. I'll tackle Face to Face this week and Room Reservations next week and so on.

From: Jason
To: Holly

What's the last one about?

From: Holly
To: Jason

Going further than your standard job description—to ensure clients' happiness.

From: Jason
To: Holly

Aisha's done that many times.

From: Holly
To: Jason

I don't think they mean quite that far. Anyway I didn't think she had done that for a while?

From: Jason
To: Holly

She hasn't. I was being serious, I mean she's really good at her job, not joking.

From: Holly
To: Jason

Promise?

From: Jason
To: Holly

I promise, I just like taking the Michael, she's good, really.

Subject: Front Entrance

From: Holly
To: Richard

Dear Richard

When you come into the building through the main entrance, it's all a little cold and unwelcoming. Because the reception desk is so high you don't get any eye contact from us until you're nearly leaning over the desk. Any chance of a lower desk? It was much lower in the last building and that way we can see clients approaching and

by the time they're standing at the desk we may have even worked
out who they are and can greet them accordingly.
Holly

From: Richard
To: Holly

Dear Holly
Sounds feasible, I'll look into it.
Also the CEO just told me he wants to introduce some changes
which Tanya Mason has put forward from Catering. Apparently
she had a chat with him on Monday with some great proposals.
Kind regards
Richard

From: Holly
To: Richard

Dear Richard
Sounds good, do you know what they are?
Regards
Holly

Subject: My love for you

From: Aisha
To: Holly

Holly
The journey through life can be a perilous one, not knowing what could
be waiting for you around every corner. Luckily for me, I've had such
a good friend, to help guide me through difficult times. Our friendship
is more valuable than anything else in the world. More valuable than
a job, so if you feel that working with me could compromise our
friendship... then, although feeling deeply disappointed, I understand
the pressure you must be under at this time.
Love Aisha

From: Holly
To: Aisha

Thanks, Aisha. That's such a relief, I didn't really fancy putting you through anyway, glad you understand.

xxxx

From: Aisha
To: Holly

WHAT??? YOU BITCH!!!!!
You are kidding me, aren't you????

Subject: My news

From: Mum
To: Holly

Holly
We've sent out our Spring Newsletter to family and friends which lets them all know about your promotion to bank manager.
Lots of love
Mum

From: Holly
To: Mum

Reception manager.

From: Mum
To: Holly

Same thing.

Subject: New ideas

From: Richard
To: Holly

Holly
In answer to your question, the CEO said Tanya Mason's idea involves the PAs not being told the day before what room their

bosses will be in. Instead the reception staff should liaise a little more with the butlers, providing more of a concierge-type service. Sounds like it has possibilities to me.

Regards

Richard

Subject: Tanya MASON!

From: Holly
To: Trisha

That woman is a revolting, disgusting shitbag thief and a liar!

From: Trisha
To: Holly

What's she done?

From: Holly
To: Trisha

Stole an idea I had—which would save us all time. Told the CEO herself directly.

From: Trisha
To: Holly

I told you to keep your cards closer to your chest.

From: Holly
To: Trisha

I know.

From: Trisha
To: Holly

This is what I told you about, it's not going to be a bed of roses every day. You're going to have to fight sometimes, sort out squabbles day in day out, win people over and if that don't work stick the odd knife in. I don't want to see my Holls getting hurt all the time.

From: Holly
To: Trisha

I'll be OK.

From: Trisha
To: Holly

You sure you're up for it all?

From: Holly
To: Trisha

Yes.

From: Trisha
To: Holly

Then you'll have to learn quick.

From: Holly
To: Trisha

I will.

wednesday

From: Charlie
To: Mum; Alice; Holly

Hi

Having arrived in Brazil I quickly headed to the nearest bar, you know me. And there I heard a story which, although you may find this difficult to believe, actually made me cry. I feel different, you could say refreshed, and maybe this is a turning point where I become more of the 'nice guy' I always thought I was capable of becoming.

There is a jungle tribe close to extinction, they lack the basic knowledge needed to keep their water supply fresh and free from bugs and things. I've been on the web for the last couple of days learning about sanitation and along with some others I intend to seek out this village full of backward thick people and help them improve their impoverished depleted existence.

From: Ron
To: Holly

What do you think!!!!???

From: Holly
To: Ron

I give up.

Subject: Motivating the team

From: Richard
To: Holly

Holly

I've set a budget for your day out with your staff. I suggest that once you've recruited the new receptionist you take everyone somewhere fun. It would help team spirit—bonding etc.

Richard

Subject: Thinking

From: Jason
To: Holly

I was wondering, are you going to tell Toby that Tanya's such a cow?

From: Holly
To: Jason

I've thought about it all. I started saying it but I stopped when I realised how it would come out. He'll think I'm saying it because I'm jealous of her, I couldn't have that. I'd look a lot worse.

From: Jason
To: Holly

I suppose so.

Subject: Take That

From: MarkOwenFromTakeThat@Hotmail.com
To: Holly

Alright our kid, I heard you got me CD like. I'm pleased for you, but don't it make more sense if you give it to your friend Jason? He's so funny and sexy and he knows all the words to me music and even sings them in the bath.

Love Marky

Subject: Tonight

From: Holly
To: Toby

Can we go out tonight or Thursday somewhere?

From: Toby
To: Holly

It's unlikely. I did have an idea though. If you joined the DK gym, we could grab a half hour together around 6pm? We could work out together?

From: Holly
To: Toby

I'm not going to the company gym????

From: Toby
To: Holly

We could join another gym nearby then?

From: Holly
To: Toby

Why do you want me to go to any gym?

From: Toby
To: Holly

I don't—that's not the point, I just thought we could spend my gym time together, or we could go running somewhere across the Wharf?

From: Holly
To: Toby

I don't want my night out with you to involve a chase sequence, sorry.

From: Toby
To: Holly

Fair enough.

From: Holly
To: Toby

A nice meal, a bar or maybe the theatre. Call it a confidence thing— but when I'm talking to you, I don't want you running away from me. Got to go.

x

Subject: Break up

From: Holly
To: Jason

How's it going with Marco?

From: Jason
To: Holly

OK. I know I joke about it, but I'm not feeling very good about myself, which is a first. Do you think I'm doing the right thing?

From: Holly
To: Jason

Honey, I've only met him once. He seems like a nice guy, but you said that he doesn't like the same things you do, he doesn't go out, and you're always arguing which can't be good. You're just both very different.

> **From:** Jason
> **To:** Holly

Sounds like you and Toby, but you're not splitting up.

> **From:** Holly
> **To:** Jason

We don't really argue much. He still shows me lots of affection and although the thoughtful little cards and flowers have dried up, I think that's down to his work.

You've got to give it lots of thought. If you think you are very unhappy at home though, no I don't think you should carry on just because it's the easy option. It's not fair on either of you.

x

> **From:** Jason
> **To:** Holly

I think I'll carry on with my plan, so how is the dark wanderer?

> **From:** Holly
> **To:** Jason

He's frustrating me. I knew it would be difficult while he was living in France and me just seeing him at weekends, but this last month since he started back with the company and we've been living together, things should have got better, but they haven't.

> **From:** Jason
> **To:** Holly

You think he's changed since school?

> **From:** Holly
> **To:** Jason

I think the ten years I haven't seen him are there, somewhere and unaccounted for.

I used to like it all. Found it very sexy, the unanswered questions, now I'm like 'can you just answer the f-ing question please!'

From: Jason
To: Holly

I think I could live with the mystery. He reminds me of Woody Harrelson in *Will and Grace*—but with longer hair obviously.

From: Holly
To: Jason

You're just thinking bad thoughts now, aren't you?

From: Jason
To: Holly

I am, I can't lie, Aisha's been talking about sex all day and it's finally getting to me, I'm a broken man. Please give her a job, I beg you.

From: Holly
To: Jason

Hmmm. Meet you at the Garrick later.

Subject: Our brother

From: Alice
To: Holly

How come we never get any pictures from him?

thursday

Subject: Excuse me

From: Holly
To: Toby

Also you still haven't answered my question.

From: Toby
To: Holly

I did.

From: Richard Mosley
To: Holly

Holly

I am sorry to have to heap the pressure on you. In an ideal world we would have much longer, but unfortunately time is running out.

We need to know which two candidates you feel are best by midday so we can have someone in place for next Wednesday the latest.

Richard

Subject: Not good

From: Jason
To: Holly

How are you feeling?

From: Holly
To: Jason

OK, been worse.

From: Jason
To: Holly

I'm rough as hell, we didn't eat again, and apparently I smell of garlic.

From: Holly
To: Jason

I think you wandered off to get Chinese around ten.

From: Jason
To: Holly

I remember.

Subject: From your friend?

From: Aisha
To: Holly

I've had no call from your company yet.

No one loves poor Aisha, not even her best friend.

:(

Cry, sniff, sob sob.

Subject: New Receptionist

From: Holly
To: Richard

Dear Richard

Any chance of having someone cover me so I can go into a quiet meeting room to sift through the candidates?

From: Richard
To: Holly

Too late to get a temp in and I just checked and unfortunately we are short staffed in facilities today ourselves. Did you not have a chance to go over them last night?

From: Holly
To: Richard

I did, just doing a final check. No problem, I can do it while I'm on the desk.

Subject: Hello

From: Trisha
To: Holly

You awake?

From: Holly
To: Trisha

Yes, just thinking.

From: Trisha
To: Holly

Lend us a hand with this lot, I can't do them on me own.

From: Holly
To: Trisha

Sorry, Trisha.

Subject: What's up?

From: Trisha
To: Holly

I can see steam coming out of your ears.

From: Holly
To: Trisha

I have to work out which two candidates would be good for our team and I'm running out of time.

From: Trisha
To: Holly

Thought they only wanted one?

From: Holly
To: Trisha

They do, but they want me to offer them two possibilities. Should have emailed Richard at 12pm.

From: Trisha
To: Holly

You're late.

From: Holly
To: Trisha

I know.

From: Trisha
To: Holly

You should have said something.

From: Holly
To: Trisha

I know.

From: Trisha
To: Holly

Why midday? Why not tell them they'll get it tomorrow by 5pm?

From: Holly
To: Trisha

I can't, I just need a moment and I'll have it.

From: Trisha
To: Holly

You want to take a breather.

From: Holly
To: Trisha

Good idea, thanks Trish.

From: Trisha
To: Holly

Deep breaths, feel any better?

From: Holly
To: Trisha

No.

Subject: Urgent

From: Richard
To: Holly

I need that list.

From: Holly
To: Richard

I'll have it in five mins.

Subject: Actually

From: Toby
To: Holly

Yes I did.

From: Holly
To: Toby

No you didn't.

Subject: Candidates

From: Trisha
To: Holly

I'm a good judge of character. Come on, we'll do it together, I don't want you putting me next to another Claire or Marie.

From: Holly
To: Trisha

They're both lovely, I don't know why you don't like them.

From: Trisha
To: Holly

They do my head in. Now, any men on the list?

From: Holly
To: Trisha

No.

From: Trisha
To: Holly

Shame.

From: Holly
To: Trisha

I know, Richard saw a couple but they weren't good enough.

From: Trisha
To: Holly

So, apart from Aisha, who else you got?

From: Holly
To: Trisha

Next one I saw was Jodie. I thought she was sweet, answered all the questions well, told me she loved customer service and wanted to improve over time.

From: Trisha
To: Holly

She's a lying tart who'll steal your man the first chance she gets. Don't like her.

From: Holly
To: Trisha

You didn't even see her?

From: Trisha
To: Holly

Hello, I'm Jodie and I'm from Australia and I'm so pretty, I've got the perfect body and I like surfing and pole dancing. I won't like her and if you give her a job I'll leave.
Next?

From: Holly
To: Trisha

OK, as long as we're giving everyone a fair chance. The next one was confident, assured, has a background of 2 years' reception, from an insurance firm. She's married, lists her hobbies as long walks in the country, cooking, and childcare.

From: Trisha
To: Holly

What's her name?

From: Holly
To: Trisha

Donna Powers.

From: Trisha
To: Holly

Whore bag bitch who steps on people on her way up. Next?

From: Holly
To: Trisha

Why is she?

From: Trisha
To: Holly

Just is, next?

From: Holly
To: Trisha

Hold on.

Subject: Hello

From: Holly
To: Toby

OK, remind me what the answer was. Where were you—for 8 hours that night in December?

From: Toby
To: Holly

8 hours in December???? Maybe I should just keep a record of every second of every minute of every day from now on? Would that make you happier?????

From: Holly
To: Toby

Yes.

Subject: Next one

From: Trisha
To: Holly

See, we're racing through them now.

From: Holly
To: Trisha

Fourth one had six years at an outsourced reception. She described herself as highly customer focused.

From: Trisha
To: Holly

What's her name?

From: Holly
To: Trisha

Susan Flanagan.

From: Trisha
To: Holly

She's OK, put her to one side.

From: Holly
To: Trisha

You're just going on their names.

From: Trisha
To: Holly

So you should tell me their names first, it'd be quicker.

From: Holly
To: Trisha

Joanna Foster.

From: Trisha
To: Holly

You can trust her, bit horsey though.

From: Holly
To: Trisha

Angela Wong.

From: Trisha
To: Holly

Nice, she'd be OK.

From: Holly
To: Trisha

Amber Regan.

From: Trisha
To: Holly

Stripper.

From: Holly
To: Trisha

She actually had a lovely smile.

From: Trisha
To: Holly

Stripper.

From: Holly
To: Trisha

Maureen Fraser.

From: Trisha
To: Holly

Possible, but moans a lot.

From: Holly
To: Trisha

Tiffany Hamilton-Jones.

From: Trisha
To: Holly

You what?

From: Holly
To: Trisha

Tiffany Hamilton-Jones.

From: Trisha
To: Holly

?

From: Holly
To: Trisha

That's her name.

From: Trisha
To: Holly

???!!!

From: Holly
To: Trisha

I'm serious, you're making me laugh—stop looking at me like that, she's probably the best one.

From: Trisha
To: Holly

I couldn't even speak her language, darling. Is that it?

From: Holly
To: Trisha

That's the lot.

From: Trisha
To: Holly

Good, all sorted then.

From: Holly
To: Trisha

OK, so if I discount the whorebag bitch, we're left with two strippers, two OKs, one moaner and someone who's a bit horsey?

From: Trisha
To: Holly

Sounds about right.

From: Holly
To: Trisha

Good, thanks for your help.

From: Trisha
To: Holly

No problem, you get that off to HR, I'm going for a fag.

friday

Subject: Morning UPDATE—Important

From: Toby
To: Holly

I'm heading to the toilet.

From: Holly
To: Toby

Thanks for that.

From: Toby
To: Holly

Just keeping you up to date with my movements, I know you need to know minute by minute.

Subject: A job in your company???

From: Aisha
To: Holly

So what's the news? Did I get it?

From: Holly
To: Aisha

I have put you through.
X

From: Aisha
To: Holly

YES!!!!!!! I LOVE YOU I LOVE YOU I LOVE YOU
I'LL MAKE YOU SO PROUD! :)

From: Holly
To: Aisha

But it's not confirmed yet. The final decision is down to them and it's between you and someone else, but don't worry, you don't have to go back for another interview.

From: Aisha
To: Holly

Why put two through?

From: Holly
To: Aisha

I had to. Sorry baby.

From: Aisha
To: Holly

I'm sulking now.

From: Jason
To: Holly; Aisha

Please ignore the small child I work with. You should see her now, she's actually got her arms crossed and she's pouting, it's quite amusing bless her.

So is all well at the Holly home?

From: Holly
To: Jason; Aisha

All well, Toby's working late tonight.

From: Aisha
To: Holly; Jason

Really, does he have a secretary?

From: Holly
To: Jason; Aisha

Yes, a male one.

From: Aisha
To: Holly; Jason

Then he's probably bumming him.

From: Holly
To: Jason; Aisha

AISHA!!!!!!!!

From: Aisha
To: Holly; Jason

I'm sorry, but I wanted to work with you and I thought I was and now I'm upset. I love you lots and lots and Toby's probably not really.

From: Holly
To: Jason; Aisha

Thanks?

From: Aisha
To: Holly; Jason

But you should try following him to France next time, I would.

From: Holly
To: Jason; Aisha

You know he hasn't even noticed I'm managing the team.

From: Jason
To: Holly; Aisha

Why don't you tell him?

From: Holly
To: Jason; Aisha

I've dropped in so many hints. I've been so excited waiting for him to realise, I just keep waiting for him to ask me, but the longer it goes on the more I don't care anymore. :(

From: Aisha
To: Holly; Jason

One last thing, will I have to go back in and meet HR again then?

From: Holly
To: Jason; Aisha

No.

From: Unknown999@hotmail.com
To: Holly

Secrets will always be your downfall, Holly.

From: Holly
To: Unknown999@hotmail.com

Haven't they always been, Jason.

Subject: PLAN FOR 2008

From: Holly
To: Holly

Countdown to May 5th.

Four weeks to go

Then I'm going to:

Get permanent management job with increase in salary & bens

Get back in touch with the world and begin paying off my debts again

Get my legs, nails and hair done, roots badly showing.

Holly Denham

FOH Manager, DKHuerst, 50 Cabot Square, Canary Wharf, London

Subject: Night out

From: Richard
To: Holly

Holly

Thank you for your candidate submissions. Nigel Thorn in HR told me we'd have a decision on which one of the two they've selected by 5pm today. Have you decided where you're taking your team on Saturday afternoon yet?

Regards

Richard

Subject: Drinking

From: Holly
To: Jason

Worried about taking the team out for drinks. Remember what happened last time?

From: Jason
To: Holly

I'll never forget it. Avoid it at all possible cost, that's my advice. Don't mix alcohol with work, you don't want to lose your job before you've got it.

From: Holly
To: Jason

Thanks. I have an idea.

Subject: I saw you

From: Trisha
To: Holly

Don't think I don't know what you're up to.

From: Holly
To: Trisha

What?

From: Trisha
To: Holly

Putting that other candidate through with Aisha. I know which one you ended up choosing last week.

From: Holly
To: Trisha

I don't understand.

From: Trisha
To: Holly

She was awful and you know it.

From: Holly
To: Trisha

I thought she had qualities.

From: Trisha
To: Holly

Bad ones, very bad ones. If they chose her and I have to work with her, I'll be well pissed off.

From: Holly
To: Trisha

Surely they wouldn't?

From: Trisha
To: Holly

Stranger things have happened. I know why you did it, I probably would have done the same.

Subject: Illegal Activity

From: IT Services
To: Holly

Dear Holly

One of your staff is using their computer terminal for illegal activity.

Jeff Hedges

IT Support, DK Huerst, 50 Cabot Square, Canary Wharf, London

From: Holly
To: IT Services

Hi Jeff

Can you be more specific? Can I ask what kind of illegal activities and which member of my staff?

Regards

Holly

Subject: Just got a message from IT

From: Holly
To: Jason

One of my staff has been caught doing something illegal with their computer? ? ? ?

From: Jason
To: Holly

God, you don't think it's Trisha, do you? What do you think she's been doing?

From: Holly
To: Jason

God knows, it can't be, I'm sure it won't be.

From: Jason
To: Holly

But what if it is?

From: Holly
To: Jason

I'm not giving her a disciplinary, no way, Richard will have to do it.

Subject: Illegal Activity

From: IT Services
To: Holly

This is a disciplinary matter, and as such I have submitted my report to HR.

Yours sincerely

Jeff

From: Holly
To: IT Services

Can you at least tell me which member of staff?

From: IT Services
To: Holly

Dear Holly

Unfortunately I can't tell you, it is an HR issue, I just need to formally inform you and pass on my report. All procedure, sorry. But don't worry, they'll probably be in touch in the next day or two. Jeff.

Subject: New recruit

From: Nigel Thorn
To: Richard; Holly

Dear Richard and Holly

After some deliberation we've decided Aisha Peters would be the most suitable candidate for this role. She is currently at a good hotel and we feel her previous experience working as a member of the Cabin crew will bring something new to the table. She stated during her interview that she would be able to start immediately so if all goes well we should have her in place on Wednesday.

Yours sincerely

Nigel Thorn

tuesday

Subject: Outstanding Account

From: Red Debt Collections & Removables
To: Holly

Reference No: 730809

In spite of our previous letter the above account remains outstanding.

Your details may now be passed to our Litigation Department with instructions to take the appropriate action for pursuit through the Court. We would advise that all recoverable costs involved in such Litigation will be added to your debt and will have to be paid by you.

It is essential that you deal with this matter by contacting the undersigned immediately.

All cheques and Postal orders should be made payable to 'Controlaccount Clients Account' quoting reference number 730809

Yours faithfully,

P C Cutter

Collections Department

Subject: Aisha

From: Holly
To: Trisha

They gave her the job.

From: Trisha
To: Holly

Good, I didn't like the sound of that other one. When's she start?

From: Holly
To: Trisha

Tomorrow, fingers crossed.

From: Trisha
To: Holly

She'll keep you busy, do they know she's a friend of yours?

From: Holly
To: Trisha

No, I didn't think it was necessary to tell them.

From: Trisha
To: Holly

I bet you didn't. Just make sure she keeps it to herself.

From: Holly
To: Trisha

I will x

Subject: Aisha

From: Holly
To: Jason; Aisha

I had some news about your job.

From: Aisha
To: Jason; Holly

Tell me????

From: Holly
To: Jason; Aisha

I'm sorry, baby.

From: Aisha
To: Jason; Holly

What? I didn't get it?

From: Holly
To: Jason; Aisha

It's not my fault, I did all I could.

From: Aisha
To: Jason; Holly

Those bastards, I don't want it anyway, you wait, I'll show them. I'll start my own bank and outsell them or whatever. They're all losers, they missed out on me.

From: Holly
To: Jason; Aisha

I did all I could to change their minds, but they still wanted you. So I guess that's it, they want you to start on Wednesday, can you start Wednesday?

Is that OK Jason?

From: Aisha
To: Jason; Holly

YOU ARE JOKING????????

From: Holly
To: Jason; Aisha

NO, I'M NOT.

xxx

From: Jason
To: Holly; Aisha

Oh thank God. Oh you're a life saver, the whirlwind which is Aisha—is going. I keep my job, the hotel is left standing, if looking slightly bewildered. Everyone wins.

From: Holly
To: Jason; Aisha

Don't wind me up, Jason.

From: Aisha
To: Jason; Holly

I've just realised, I've got one day to get everything ready!!! Oh so little time, so much to do!!! Jason, can I have this afternoon off?

From: Jason
To: Holly; Aisha

Let me get this straight, you want me to let you leave—with just a day's notice—and half of that day you want to take off???

From: Aisha
To: Jason; Holly

Yes.

From: Holly
To: Jason; Aisha

Aisha, what is it that you have to do? Surely you just turn up tomorrow in a suit. You do have a suit, don't you?

From: Aisha
To: Jason; Holly

I have a 'now you see me, now you don't' suit, but not a banking suit. I used my hotel uniform to interview before, I guess I could steal it?

From: Jason
To: Holly; Aisha

No, I guess you couldn't.

From: Holly
To: Jason; Aisha

I don't like the sound of that 'now you see me' thing. You need a black corporate suit.

From: Aisha
To: Jason; Holly

Jason?????

From: Jason
To: Holly; Aisha

Yes yes, fine, just go.

From: Jason
To: Holly; Aisha

NOT NOW! At 1pm! Sit back down!

From: Aisha
To: Jason; Holly

Sulk.

Subject: URGENT PROBLEM

From: Richard
To: Holly

We're having complaints about the length of time it takes for people to answer the calls. Is it extremely busy today? I just tried and it wasn't picked up until the 20th ring????! Can you find out what is going on—is Marie sick or something?

Richard

From: Holly
To: Marie

Marie, are you there????

From: Marie
To: Holly

Yes dear.

From: Holly
To: Marie

Have you been away anywhere?

From: Marie
To: Holly

No dear, I'm here in the switchboard room.

From: Holly
To: Marie

What's it like there?

From: Marie
To: Holly

It's nice, I'm going to bring some pictures in tomorrow, cheer it up a bit you know.

Don't worry about me, Holly, I've been using a switchboards my whole life. When will I get a break? Is it the same as before, or will we get a bell or something?

From: Holly
To: Marie

No, it's just the same as before.

Subject: Switchboard problems

From: Holly
To: Richard

Marie is definitely there.

Subject: Hi

From: Toby
To: Holly

Tried playing my CD player this morning. It was broken. Do you know anything about it?

From: Holly
To: Toby

No, sorry.

Subject: Hello

From: Friends@UKMeetingPlaces.com
To: Holly

Some of your friends just took the 'I'm feeling fruity' test. You could compare your results with theirs, are you feeling fruity??

From: Holly
To: Friends@UKMeetingPlaces.com

No, not really no.

Subject: From Frank Fraser your friendly upstairs neighbour

From: Frank Fraser
To: Holly

I bought a new freezer this morning.

From: Holly
To: Frank Fraser

That's nice, Frankie.

From: Frank Fraser
To: Holly

It's got twelve compartments, you can separate your fish from your bread and vice versa. The old one was falling apart and there was a very strange smell coming from the back, so I bought a new one.

From: Holly
To: Frank Fraser

Good.

From: Frank Fraser
To: Holly

Would you like the old one?

From: Holly
To: Frank Fraser

No thank you, but thank you for asking, Mr Fraser, very kind of you.

Subject: Missing brother

From: Alice
To: Holly

Why did Charlie go to Brazil? I don't get it, and why don't we ever get any pictures through?

From: Holly
To: Alice

He doesn't have a camera?

Subject: Important

From: Holly
To: Jason

Mad Frankie Fraser, my friendly upstairs neighbour, has bought a new freezer.

From: Jason
To: Holly

That's nice.

From: Holly
To: Jason

Just bringing you the news as I get it.

From: Jason
To: Holly

Thanks.

Subject: Marie

From: Richard
To: Holly

What's she doing there, because she's not answering calls?

From: Holly
To: Marie

Marie, you are answering the calls there, aren't you?

From: Marie
To: Holly

No.

From: Holly
To: Marie

Why not?

From: Marie
To: Holly

I don't have a switchboard, Holly?

From: Holly
To: Marie

You do Marie, you're on it.

From: Marie
To: Holly

This is a computer, Holly. A switchboard looks very different. How long have you been a receptionist dear?

From: Holly
To: Marie

It is a switchboard and a computer, Marie, it does both. I'll be down to show you in a minute, I didn't realise you had not used a computerized one before. I'm really sorry Marie for not showing you, but you'll like it I promise.
Holly

From: Marie
To: Holly

Why didn't they just bring my old one across? I don't think I'm going to like this one. What do you think? Do you think I'll like this one?

From: Holly
To: Marie

You'll love it, just wait there.

Subject: One thing

From: Jason
To: Holly

One plus about employing Aisha—at least you know when your whole team turns against you, there'll be one friend on your side.

From: Holly
To: Jason

Why would they turn against me?

From: Jason
To: Holly

They just do.

wednesday

Subject: I am wondering

From: Holly
To: Toby

When I get to meet your dad?

From: Toby
To: Holly

Soon, I promise.

From: Holly
To: Toby

You keep promising. What about meeting your sister then?

From: Toby
To: Holly

Her too, they'll be over soon, if not we'll go over together. I've got to arrange something, I know, but it's been just so difficult recently with work the way it is. By the way, you want to meet up at lunch time for a few minutes?

From: Holly
To: Toby

I can't, I'm using the time to put together everyone's rotas for next week.

From: Toby
To: Holly

Rotas for what?

From: Holly
To: Toby

For the team, for their hours.

From: Toby
To: Holly

Oh, cool, what are you doing this weekend?

From: Holly
To: Toby

Depends whether I've got the pleasure of your company?

From: Toby
To: Holly

Friday night I'll be working till about nine, so I'll be shattered when I get back, but I'm up for a dvd or something if you want, have an early night? Saturday night I'm yours.

From: Holly
To: Toby

Sounds like the perfect weekend to me! Saturday I'm bonding with the team in the day, but I'm yours from 6pm.

Subject: Introduction

From: Holly
To: Aisha; Trisha; Claire; Marie

Hi

I would like to welcome Aisha to the team. It would be nice for us all to get together for a chat, but as we're all on different shifts and can't leave our posts it's going to be too complicated, unless we do it at the weekend—which I'm sure no one wants. On Saturday afternoon, as I hope you'll all remember, we are meeting up to do something fun, to get to know each other better. As a small summary of Aisha's relevant experience, she has been both a hotel receptionist and member of the cabin crew.

From: Trisha
To: Holly; Aisha; Claire; Marie

So nothing relevant unless someone wants to spend the night? Or we need to puke in a bag?

From: Holly
To: Aisha; Trisha; Claire; Marie

What she means is welcome to the company.

Now this Saturday I was thinking of booking an afternoon of 'paint-balling mayhem' at the Canary Wharf indoor paint-balling centre?

From: Aisha
To: Holly; Claire; Trisha; Marie

Have fun, you lucky thing.

From: Holly
To: Aisha; Marie; Claire; Trisha

For all of us, Aisha, not me on my own. For the team day out you're all meant to be coming to?

From: Marie
To: Holly; Aisha; Claire; Trisha

What is paintballing?

From: Holly
To: Aisha; Marie; Claire; Trisha

Shooting people with paint in guns.

From: Marie
To: Holly; Aisha; Claire; Trisha

I don't think so, Holly. Why don't we have a nice drink somewhere?

From: Claire
To: Holly; Marie; Trisha; Aisha

My boyfriend once worked in a place like that, he used to fill the guns with paint.

From: Trisha
To: Claire; Marie; Holly; Aisha

Good.

From: Claire
To: Holly; Marie; Trisha; Aisha

I never went there though.

From: Trisha
To: Claire; Marie; Holly; Aisha

No?

From: Claire
To: Holly; Marie; Trisha; Aisha

He used to say 'stay out, this is a man's place.'

From: Trisha
To: Claire; Marie; Holly; Aisha

Thanks for letting us know that, Claire, so do we have to go?

From: Holly
To: Aisha; Trisha; Claire; Marie

No, I just thought it would be nice to do something fun together that we'll want to remember.

From: Trisha
To: Claire; Marie; Holly; Aisha

What about something drunk that we'll want to forget?

From: Holly
To: Aisha; Trisha; Claire; Marie

I thought it sounded fun? What does everyone think?

From: Trisha
To: Claire; Marie; Holly; Aisha

OK, what about if me and Marie go to a boozer and you all come and meet us after?

From: Marie
To: Holly; Aisha; Claire; Trisha

Yes, that sounds good, Trisha.

From: Aisha
To: Holly; Claire; Trisha; Marie

I'm with them.

From: Claire
To: Holly; Marie; Trisha; Aisha

Holly, can I also go to the bar with the others and also meet you later?

From: Holly
To: Aisha; Trisha; Claire; Marie

Claire, if none of you are going I won't be going paintballing either. I'm not running around on my own shouting yahoo and firing my gun in the air?
So we'll all go for a drink then, fine.
Holly

Subject: Just had an idea

From: Holly
To: Jason

I'm going to hide in a cupboard!!! Yes I am!

From: Jason
To: Holly

My guess is—you've just heard that it IS Trisha who's doing illegal gubins on her computer and instead of confronting her in a professional manner, you've decided to jump into a cupboard instead. Correct?

From: Holly
To: Jason

No, you're wrong.
I meant I'm going to hide in a cupboard at home (they still haven't come back to me on the illegal computer thing). Now don't shoot me down till I've explained it all from my side. I'm not saying Toby's up to something and I completely trust him, but I just feel for my own sanity I need to hide in a cupboard.

From: Jason
To: Holly

How will it help things?

From: Holly
To: Jason

My choices are: follow him (that's too creepy and I can't do it) or get someone else to follow him (but imagine if the person gets caught, Toby would leave me and rightly so) or hide in a cupboard and listen in and see who he calls and what he does.

From: Jason
To: Holly

Why don't you just set up some surveillance equipment?

From: Holly
To: Jason

No money.

From: Jason
To: Holly

Then I think it's a great idea, it's just completely brilliant and exciting. Have you got a cupboard in mind?

From: Holly
To: Jason

The broom cupboard in the kitchen. It's big enough, I can sit down in it, he never goes there and I can hear everything, even if he's in the lounge.

From: Jason
To: Holly

As you're a friend I need to say something to you first—you do realise that you might hear something you won't like about yourself, even if he's just being honest?

From: Holly
To: Jason

Yes.

From: Jason
To: Holly

Right, got that out the way, now let's have some fun. Oh oh I want to sit in it with you!!!

From: Holly
To: Jason

You can't, it's too small, honey.

From: Jason
To: Holly

Damn. OK, we need a walky-talky, some chewing gum, a compass, a map, some Kendal mint cake, a watch that tells the time in various countries, an eye patch, an eye glass, a raincoat, a moustache, a trilby, some rubber waders (or leather chaps), two blonde wigs and man with a limp.

From: Holly
To: Jason

I'm just going to sit in the cupboard one night and text you what goes on.

From: Jason
To: Holly

OK, forget all that. While you're doing that I'll go deep deep undercover and mingle amongst the gay bars and clubs in the West End. See what filth I can shake down.

From: Holly
To: Jason

Good. Nice.

thursday

Subject: A show called Trading Places

From: Holly
To: Toby

I just heard Jason's bought us tickets to see this show on Friday night, it sounds quite camp, do you think you could finish work earlier?

From: Toby
To: Holly

I could try, I do want to see Jason again, he makes me laugh.

From: Holly
To: Toby

Great, you don't mind dressing up for it though?

From: Toby
To: Holly

What is it like *The Rocky Horror Show* type of thing?

From: Holly
To: Toby

Yes.

From: Toby
To: Holly

OK, I'll do it, if I can get the time off.

Subject: NOT WORKING

From: Holly
To: Jason

He wants to go to it!?

From: Jason
To: Holly

NO??

From: Holly
To: Jason

I told him it meant dressing up!?

From: Jason
To: Holly

Kinky! Well, who cares about the cupboards, I'm in. I'll be around at 7pm. I'm thinking suspenders, bra, stockings. I can get heels from Steve me queen. Oh just imagine that body in nothing but a thong?

From: Holly
To: Jason

NO, we're not ditching the plan just so you can see my boyfriend in a dress!

From: Jason
To: Holly

Why not?

From: Holly
To: Jason

Because we're not!

From: Jason
To: Holly

Spoilsport.

Subject: Friday night

From: Holly
To: Toby

That's all sorted then, I've just spoken to Jason and he's got a tranny friend of his to dress you up before we go, oh this is going to be so exciting!

From: Toby
To: Holly

I'm thinking it might be too much for me. Listen I'll go to another one of his shows, something with a little less audience participation?

From: Holly
To: Toby

Are you sure?

From: Toby
To: Holly

Yes, you go and have fun.
X

Subject: Help

From: Claire
To: Holly

Host of room 38 just came out and said they've been waiting for the next course for ten minutes.

From: Holly
To: Claire

I'll call up and find out what's going on.

Subject: Team work

From: Tanya
To: Holly

Dear Holly

I've already spoken to one of your receptionists about this, so there was no need for you to leave me a message.

Tanya Mason

Subject: Late meals

From: Holly
To: Claire

I wish you'd told me you'd already spoken with Tanya about this.

From: Claire
To: Holly

I had only just begun telling her the story and she'd gone, she does move very fast.

Sorry

Claire

Subject: Team work

From: Holly
To: Tanya

Better safe than sorry, that's what I say.

Regards

Holly

From: Tanya
To: Holly

Dear Holly

I am so sorry, you must think it rude of me, I almost forgot to congratulate you; well done for getting the temporary manager's contract! I'm so pleased for you.

Also I know you're doing your best there at such short notice and I'm sure your team are still trying to adapt to the unexpected pleasure of having you supervise them, but if you teach them to keep you in the loop it'll save you a lot of extra time. As I say I'm always here if you need any advice or handy hints.

Kind regards

Tanya

From: Holly
To: Tanya

Thank you, Tanya

Handy hints are welcome, from someone so full of them.

I read recently about your new concierge idea, astounding, brilliant, but more importantly so original! You must have a wealth of ideas just cooking away in that creative pot of yours, waiting to be shared.

I really am lucky you're there to help.

Regards

Holly

Subject: Reservations

From: Holly
To: Richard

Dear Richard

With the amount of rooms we've now got, the reservations system we use is unable to cope, also we are wasting space.

Regards

Holly

From: Richard
To: Holly

What do you mean re wasting space?

From: Holly
To: Richard

Rooms are being booked without any concern for the size of the meeting i.e. if there are just two guests arriving, often they end up in a meeting room which seats ten.

I've been checking some of the figures, but the amount of space we're wasting could be used for something else. You could probably run another bank in the amount of wasted space.

From: Richard
To: Holly

What do you suggest?

From: Holly
To: Richard

Buying meeting-room-booking software that can do searches on room occupancy and size etc. These programs seem to be quite expensive though.

From: Richard
To: Holly

If you think it will make that much of a difference, you find us some new software.

From: Holly
To: Richard

Really?

From: Richard
To: Holly

Yes, but if it's expensive, it better do what you say it will, or I'll get it in the neck.

Also I just had a forward from Tanya of your email complimenting her about her ideas and help she's been giving you, I am glad you're looking for other influences. A good manager takes on board as much advice as possible and then filters out the parts which won't work for them.

Well done

Regards

Richard

friday

Subject: In the closet

From: Jason
To: Holly

Have you prepared everything?

From: Holly
To: Jason

I'm putting a cushion in there tonight. He's coming back from work around 9pm he thinks, so I'll get myself all comfy a half hour before and just wait.

From: Jason
To: Holly

How do you feel?

From: Holly
To: Jason

Nervous, really really nervous.

From: Jason
To: Holly

So am I and I'm feeling for you. Can you see when you're in there?

From: Holly
To: Jason

No, I wanted to read a book, but it's going to be dark.

From: Jason
To: Holly

I want texts all night long. I'm in Old Compton Street, and I'm having a "hiding in the closet" party for you, so you need to keep us informed to make it exciting!!!

From: Holly
To: Jason

Thanks.

From: Jason
To: Holly

You can back out of it you know?

From: Holly
To: Jason

I know. So far, I'm not going to. I am beginning to get butterflies though. What happens if he says something like—he was really disappointed when he saw me again after so long but he thought he'd stick with me anyway and now he's regretting it????

From: Jason
To: Holly

He won't!!!

From: Holly
To: Jason

Or he could say something even worse??? Oh god.

From: Jason
To: Holly

He won't. He better not say anything bad, or I'll bring the whole party straight around and we'll jump on him or something.

From: Holly
To: Jason

Thanks. Please don't.

From: Jason
To: Holly

Shame, the offer's there though.

From: Holly
To: Jason

x

Subject: Confidential

From: Nigel Thorn
To: Holly

Holly

You have received notification from IT regarding one of your staff's illegal misuse of company equipment. This is an issue we take very seriously so you will need to issue them with a verbal warning. The employee in question is Claire Miller. She has spent some considerable time looking at pornographic sites over the past few weeks.

I suggest you take her into a meeting room on Monday and explain to her the strict laws we have for our employees etc. Please carefully follow the disciplinary procedures we went through in your training. This is a difficult but extremely important issue and needs to be dealt with sensitively.

Regards

Nigel

Subject: Claire's The Pervy Porn Queen !!! Just got your text!!

From: Jason
To: Holly

Naughty Claire, likes them bare. Me too, so find out what the sites are and send me back the link!

xxxx

From: Holly
To: Jason

PLEASE try and be more cryptic when you email about this. I left the message on your phone because I wanted to make sure you got the email. It's personal confidential stuff about an employee.

From: Jason
To: Holly

Understood, full security will be used during our email exchange about the dirty pervert.

From: Holly
To: Jason

Stop it! I only told you because you don't know her.

From: Jason
To: Holly

Sorry. But I wish I was a fly on the wall during that meeting. This is going to be fun, who can I tell???

From: Holly
To: Jason

NO ONE!!!

From: Jason
To: Holly

OK, I mean out of my friends???

From: Holly
To: Jason

NO ONE!

From: Jason
To: Holly

Hate you. What are you going to say to her???

From: Holly
To: Jason

No idea, I've gone red just thinking about it. I'm just glad it wasn't Trisha or Marie, I couldn't think of anything worse than telling someone older than you to stop looking at porn.

From: Jason
To: Holly

What are you going to say then?

From: Holly
To: Jason

Stop looking at porn?

Subject: Saturday night

From: Toby
To: Holly

I've been thinking about somewhere to go. You wanted to go to the theatre, what about it?

From: Holly
To: Toby

Love to, oh oh can we see Mamma Mia, please please, I've been wanting to go for ages?????

From: Toby
To: Holly

I really couldn't handle that much Abba.

From: Holly
To: Toby

Oh OK, well, whatever you fancy, I'm happy. What time?

From: Toby
To: Holly

We could do a matinee, think there's one at 3pm, then we could have an early dinner, go home early…

From: Holly
To: Toby

Can't, I've got a works thing in the afternoon.

From: Toby
To: Holly

Alright 7.30pm it is, anyway the matinees are packed with kids, you'd hate it.

From: Holly
To: Toby

Children, yuk,
So, good—you book it then for the night, any show, I'm easy.

Subject: Closet

From: Jason
To: Holly

How are you going to finish it? Get out when he's gone to bed??

From: Holly
To: Jason

Of course.

From: Jason
To: Holly

Don't fall asleep in there.

From: Holly
To: Jason

I won't. Once he's gone to bed for an hour or so I'll get out, down a mouthful of wine, slam the door and fall on the bed.

From: Jason
To: Holly

Maybe just fall on the floor, more realistic?

From: Holly
To: Jason

Yeah yeah.

Subject: Late shifts

From: Holly
To: Aisha; Claire; Marie; Trisha

Can we have a quick email meeting? Something Aisha brought up about the late shifts. Why don't you start, Aisha?

From: Aisha
To: Holly; Claire; Marie; Trisha

I'm meant to be doing the late shift next week. Does anyone want to do it more than me?
Aisha

From: Holly
To: Marie; Claire; Aisha; Trisha

The system at the moment is that everyone does one late shift a month. Does anyone like doing the late shifts more than others?

From: Aisha
To: Holly; Claire; Marie; Trisha

Sorry, there is a reason, I'm not just trying to be difficult.
I don't mean to cause a fuss on my first week, don't get me wrong I love the job, Holly, and think you're the best manager in the world. God, I just wish they were all like you, I've learnt so much. I love this job and the fact it's got its own gym—has everyone seen the hot men in the gym?

From: Holly
To: Marie; Claire; Aisha; Trisha

You were saying, Aisha?

From: Aisha
To: Holly; Claire; Marie; Trisha

Yes, I'll have to get the night bus and I'm not willing to die just to work here.

From: Claire
To: Aisha; Holly; Marie; Trisha

Last time I was on a night bus a man sat next to me and I'm sure he had a knife under his jacket.

From: Marie
To: Holly; Claire; Aisha; Trisha

When I was on the train, this man sat down near to me, and started chatting, and I thought how nice—a well dressed man and he had this suit on, and he had a bag with him from John Lewis so I thought he has been shopping, you know, on Oxford Street. Wait a moment I have to deal with these calls.

From: Holly
To: Marie; Claire; Aisha; Trisha

Was this a late night train, Marie?

From: Marie
To: Holly; Claire; Aisha; Trisha

No, Holly, it was in the daytime, who would have believed? Well, let me tell you girls, I thought how nice to have a chat on my way to work. Made me feel very special, but there was this smell and I promise you would not believe the smell.

So I'm looking around at the people you know and I'm thinking who smells like this, and then the man wants to show me what he's bought and he opens a John Lewis carrier bag and it is full of dog's dodos, you know, the whole bag was full of it. What kind of man carries a bag like that with him?

From: Trisha
To: Marie; Claire; Aisha; Trisha

Not a nice man that's for sure, Marie. You don't want to take him to meet your mum.

From: Aisha
To: Marie; Claire; Trisha; Holly

Unless he leaves his shopping behind.

From: Marie
To: Holly; Claire; Aisha; Trisha

London is a very strange place sometimes, you have to be careful who you talk to.

From: Trisha
To: Marie; Claire; Aisha; Holly

Don't talk to men with pooh in their bags, Marie, that's my advice.

From: Holly
To: Aisha; Claire; Trisha; Marie

So, are we agreed that no one likes doing extra late shifts here?

From: Marie
To: Holly; Claire; Aisha; Trisha

I don't want to, Holly, you have a nice man to drive you home at night. How did you meet him, Holly? Do tell us because I am looking for someone from here.

From: Claire
To: Holly; Aisha; Marie; Trisha

It's so romantic, he was her boyfriend at school, then his parents took him to France with them, then they didn't see each other for years and years, then he starts working here and then they're in love all over again.

From: Holly
To: Aisha; Claire; Trisha; Marie

He doesn't have a car Marie.
But Claire—why and how do you know about Toby?

From: Claire
To: Holly; Aisha; Marie; Trisha

Everyone knows, it's the first story I was told when I got here.

From: Aisha
To: Marie; Claire; Trisha; Holly

You meet men in the gym, Marie, I'll take you.

From: Marie
To: Holly; Claire; Aisha; Trisha

Oh, good, we can go after work on Monday?

From: Holly
To: Aisha; Claire; Trisha; Marie

So if no one likes late shifts I'll see what I can do about it all.

Catch up again soon.

Holly

Subject: Tonight

From: Toby
To: Holly

Have fun. If you're late back don't make too much noise please, I need a good night's sleep.

From: Holly
To: Toby

Of course I'll be quiet

xxx see you tomorrow.

PS You do love me don't you?

From: Toby
To: Holly

Yes, so much!!

From: Holly
To: Toby

Good. xxx

holly's mobile

TEXTING friday NIGHT

From: Holly
To: Jason

I'm in the cupboard.

From: Jason
To: Holly

Is he there yet?

From: Holly
To: Jason

No, but I can hear him coming down the stairs.

From: Holly
To: Jason

OMG!!!

From: Jason
To: Holly

What's he doing now?

From: Holly
To: Jason

Inside.

From: Jason
To: Holly

He's inside???

From: Holly
To: Jason

Y

From: Jason
To: Holly

What now? Everyone wants 2 know, we've turned the music down

From: Holly
To: Jason

He's groaning.

From: Jason
To: Holly

Everyone just cheered, we do like a man to groan.

From: Holly
To: Jason

Can't hear anything.

From: Jason
To: Holly

Have you got water, honey?

From: Holly
To: Jason

Y

From: Jason
To: Holly

I'm having a Piña Colada for you.

From: Holly
To: Jason

X

From: Jason
To: Holly

What's happening? Any news?

From: Holly
To: Jason

N

From: Jason
To: Holly

What about now?

From: Holly
To: Jason

N

From: Jason
To: Holly

What about now?

From: Holly
To: Jason

N

From: Jason
To: Holly

Come on, Holly, entertain the troops. Has he taken off any clothing that you know about?

From: Holly
To: Jason

He's had a shower.

From: Jason
To: Holly

A shower!! And we missed it!!! More details, Holly, come on.

From: Holly
To: Jason

He's coming back.

From: Jason
To: Holly

And?

From: Holly
To: Jason

Making a call.

From: Jason
To: Holly

House phone?

From: Holly
To: Jason

Mobile.

From: Jason
To: Holly

Oh, this is it. Everyone's gone quiet, are you OK??

From: Holly
To: Jason

Yes. He's murmuring.

From: Jason
To: Holly

What?

From: Holly
To: Jason

Just murmuring, the other side of the door.

From: Jason
To: Holly

Why?

From: Holly
To: Jason

That's what he does, he murmurs, when he's thinking.

From: Jason
To: Holly

Weirdo.

From: Holly
To: Jason

Oh no, please don't tell me.

From: Jason
To: Holly

What?

From: Jason
To: Holly

Please don't tell you what???

From: Jason
To: Holly

Where are you, Holly??

holly's
inbox

saturday

I think we could be friends.

week 3
monday

Subject: PLAN FOR 2008

From: Holly
To: Holly

Countdown to May 5th.

Three weeks to go.

Then I'm going to:

Get permanent management job with increase in salary & bens.

Get back in touch with the world and begin paying off my debts again.

Get my legs, nails and hair done, roots badly showing.

Buy two cheap suits for work.

Holly Denham, FOH Manager, DK Huerst, 50 Cabot Square, Canary Wharf, London

Subject: Targets

From: Richard
To: Holly

The team's performance has improved since you've taken over, but at this rate it won't be sufficient for me to take you on permanently.

Previously Since you took over

Room reservations 10 10

Face to Face Contact 12 14

Telephone etiquette and techniques 12 12

In house relationships 13 14

Beyond the call of duty 15 15

You haven't much time and I apologise for this.

Richard

Subject: Confidential

From: Nigel Thorn
To: Holly

Dear Holly

Have you spoken to Claire Miller yet?

Regards

HR

Subject: Hi

From: William Duncan
To: Holly

I understand your need for ground rules. I've got a few of my own too.

From: Holly
To: William Duncan

That seems fair, what are yours?

From: William Duncan
To: Holly

Firstly I know you mentioned your fear of taking things too fast. I'm fine with that, I'm equally cautious about new people.

From: Holly
To: William Duncan

Good.

From: William Duncan
To: Holly

Secondly, I think we should keep it a secret at work, so no signs of affection in open-plan offices.

From: Holly
To: William Duncan

OK.

From: William Duncan
To: Holly

Although empty lifts and meeting rooms are optional, but this place is just so full of gossips.

From: Holly
To: William Duncan

It is. Would you like my ground rules now?

From: William Duncan
To: Holly

Absolutely, fire away.

From: Holly
To: William Duncan

I need you to explain what the hell you're talking about??

From: William Duncan
To: Holly

Oh, I just thought I'd bluff it and see if you went for it.

From: Holly
To: William Duncan

I think I'd remember if we'd started a relationship?

From: William Duncan
To: Holly

You're keen, I was just thinking of something very casual?

From: Holly
To: William Duncan

Goodbye, Will.

From: William Duncan
To: Holly

Ta-rah.

Subject: Meeting

From: Holly
To: Claire

Hi Claire

Hope you had a good weekend.

When you get in can we have catch up?

Regards

Holly

From: Claire
To: Holly

Hi Holly

What's it about? It's not about those clients from Morocco, is it?

From: Holly
To: Claire

It's just a catch up, mainly. What clients from Morocco?

Subject: Morning

From: Aisha
To: Holly

Not happy with my suit.

From: Holly
To: Aisha

It's a fabulous suit, Aisha, very classy, exactly the way it is. Please do not change it in any way. That includes any kind of alteration to make it shorter, tighter or more Aisha.

Subject: Chat

From: Claire
To: Holly

So am I in trouble?

From: Holly
To: Claire

Don't worry, it's just a chat. I've booked a meeting room for us tomorrow.
Holly

From: Claire
To: Holly

I won't be able to last that long. Can't you tell me now? You're making me nervous.

From: Holly
To: Claire

Please don't be.

From: Claire
To: Holly

I feel sick.

From: Holly
To: Claire

Honestly, don't worry.

From: Claire
To: Holly

I really do feel sick. I think I might have to go home. Can I go home?

From: Holly
To: Claire

No.

Subject: Stats

From: Holly
To: Richard

Hi

I can see why improving our overall performance is good for me, good for the company etc, but from my team's point of view it won't be so clear.

Regards

Holly

From: Richard
To: Holly

They get personal satisfaction of knowing they've improved?

From: Holly
To: Richard

I don't think that's going to drive my team on so much. I'd be the same. I think they'd be interested in either career progression or benefits, or simply money. Sorry to sound so mercenary, but a bonus would be good.

From: Richard
To: Holly

So, go on, you've obviously already thought it through. Hit me with it.

From: Holly
To: Richard

We introduce a performance bonus.

If the team achieves good things, then the team gets a performance bonus. I'm not asking for anything that most of the other people in the company don't already get. I know we're not fee earners, but if a private client is deciding between ourselves and another very similar company and the only difference is how warmly they were greeted here and how special and important we made them feel when they arrived—then we've contributed to securing their business. If I get the manager's job full time, that will be my incentive, but I think the team needs something too.

From: Richard
To: Holly

I'll come back to you on it.

Subject: Tonight

From: Toby
To: Holly

I'm back a bit later tonight. If you're trying to decide whether or not to hide from me again, I think not. I'll be edgy and stressed and to have you leap out from behind a curtain or something will probably send me to early grave. Sorry for being a misery.

From: Holly
To: Toby

I didn't leap out at you.

From: Toby
To: Holly

I know, but you would have done if I hadn't found you.

From: Holly
To: Toby

Wouldn't it have been funny!

From: Toby
To: Holly

I'm sure it would.

From: Holly
To: Toby

OK, no surprises, and I'll get something nice from the shops on the way back. Might try my luck at pie-making.

xxx

Subject: Not nice

From: Holly
To: Jason

I went shopping yesterday for something better to wear to work. I'm working in a team of gorgeous women who always look fantastic, and I'm their manager and I look the scruffiest. How does that work?

From: Jason
To: Holly

Why doesn't Toby buy you some clothes?

From: Holly
To: Jason

I haven't asked him and anyway why should he? He's got no money either, he's trying to keep the rent paid on two empty flats in France. So I've got my roots showing, bad nails, I'm running out of makeup and I wear the same suit every other day.

From: Jason
To: Holly

You can't go shopping, you haven't got the money for it.

From: Holly
To: Jason

I know, but this is important, this is very very important, this is our relationship. I wanted to wear one of those pencil skirts that Aisha wears and you know I'm a twelve don't you?

From: Jason
To: Holly

I know you are, sweetie.

From: Holly
To: Jason

THANK YOU! The rest of the high street doesn't seem to know it. I've spent all year trying to get myself back into a size twelve and

I'm there I've done it, I'm a twelve. I go out with my proud twelve body and guess what?

From: Jason
To: Holly

What?

From: Holly
To: Jason

The stupid shops have put it down again. So you pick up an item that says twelve and it's really a ten. They do this each year and it's really getting me down.

From: Jason
To: Holly

I don't think they do that.

From: Holly
To: Jason

JASON.

From: Jason
To: Holly

Bastards, they're shop-keeping size-manipulating bastards. Give us back our inches before we take you to court.

From: Holly
To: Jason

Thank you. My waist gets in, but my hips and bum get stuck. Thing is, I keep trying to squeeze in until I hear a ripping sound and an assistant telling me to stop. Do you know how many shops I can go back to now in Oxford Street?

From: Jason
To: Holly

One?

From: Holly
To: Jason

Two, Jason, two shops, and neither of them sell pencil skirts. In fact one's a delicatessen and he's not too happy with me either.

From: Jason
To: Holly

You have the shapely body women would die for, sweetie—hour glass figure. Do you want to be Marilyn Monroe or Kate Moss?

From: Holly
To: Jason

Marilyn.

From: Jason
To: Holly

Do you want to have a body men want or the one women want?

From: Holly
To: Jason

Men.

From: Jason
To: Holly

Good, are we going out tonight?

From: Holly
To: Jason

No, not feeling too good still.

Subject: Important!

From: Richard
To: Holly

That was fast, I think you've either rattled someone with your team bonus request, or one of your staff has really upset someone somewhere. I've just had a call from the CEO—he wants to meet you himself, 11.30am Monday. Whatever you do, make sure you're on time and fresh as a daisy.

Good luck

Richard

tuesday

Subject: Team Spirit

From: Richard
To: Holly; Aisha; Claire; Trisha; Marie

To the team

I wanted to just say how glad I am you all got on so well on Saturday. These team-building exercises are so useful to help develop stronger understandings within the group. This all encourages a more cooperative and efficient working environment. I hope you all had fun, but more importantly took the opportunity to learn more about one another.

Well done.

Regards

Richard

Subject: Team Spirit

From: Trisha
To: Holly

Yeah I learnt you're still trouble when you've had a drink.

From: Holly
To: Trisha

I forgot to ask yesterday, do you remember what happened to that pink bra?

From: Trisha
To: Holly

I have a photo of where it ended up.

[SEE ATTACHED]

From: Holly
To: Trisha

Oh God, why didn't you stop me?

From: Trisha
To: Holly

I tried, darling, you weren't having it.

From: Holly
To: Trisha

I hope I wasn't caught on CCTV. Do you think there's any chance I was?

From: Trisha
To: Holly

My Les says they've got about 2000 cameras on the wharf.

From: Holly
To: Trisha

Just gets better and better.

From: Trisha
To: Holly

Bet you never met Toby after. You were off to the theatre, weren't you?

From: Holly
To: Trisha

I did meet him but apparently I was 'In no fit state to be anywhere apart from bed.' I don't think he was too pleased, I'm still feeling sick.

Subject: Our little chat

From: Claire
To: Holly

Morning, Holly

If it is about those Moroccans, I can explain everything, then we don't have to have our chat?

Claire

From: Holly
To: Claire

Hi Claire

What happened with the Moroccans then?

Regards

Holly

From: Claire
To: Holly

Well, remember telling us that when we're taking clients to another floor in the lift and we're on our own with them—we should entertain them with idle chat?

From: Holly
To: Claire

I do remember, but I'm not sure why I said it now.

From: Claire
To: Holly

They told me they were from Morocco, so to keep them entertained I said I heard they sell really good rugs there. The thing is, I think they thought I said 'really good drugs' because that's what it sounded like to me too. They looked a bit shocked.

From: Holly
To: Claire

I bet they were. Don't worry, it's not about that, but maybe don't talk so much to the clients on the way up on the lift. Hum or something, or whistle. Now let's have our meeting, and don't worry!
Holly

Subject: Are you there?

From: Holly
To: Jason

I've just finished.

From: Jason
To: Holly

Tell me everything. What happened??

From: Holly
To: Jason

This has got to stay secret. Don't even ever ever tell Aisha or I'll never talk to you again, OK?

From: Jason
To: Holly

Of course, just tell me!

From: Holly
To: Jason

I met her in a meeting room. She looked so scared, completely pale, poor thing. I just wanted to give her a hug, but you can't do that kind of thing here. I told her she's broken a company rule about banned websites—she's been looking at sites she knew she shouldn't be.

From: Jason
To: Holly

So you managed to get around it without too much embarrassment??

From: Holly
To: Jason

She asked specifically which sites I was talking about.

From: Jason
To: Holly

Nice.

From: Holly
To: Jason

I told her these were specifically pornographic websites and of course I went bright red and so did she then. She insisted there was a legitimate reason for it all. I told her it really wasn't necessary to explain, just not to look at them again and I wanted to leave it at that. But she wanted to explain.

From: Jason
To: Holly

Had she clicked on them by mistake hundreds of times?

From: Holly
To: Jason

No, she said she wanted a chance to tell her side of it, and needed a computer to—show me.

From: Jason
To: Holly

Oh no.

From: Holly
To: Jason

OH yes.

From: Jason
To: Holly

Did she show you?

From: Holly
To: Jason

We couldn't use a computer at one of the reception desks because Aisha or Trisha would have been there. So, we found the conference room free, which had a 52inch screen at the end.

From: Jason
To: Holly

Lovely.

From: Holly
To: Jason

She found the sites. They were contact sites, for meeting people. The problem she found is that when you clicked on someone, you didn't know until you opened their profile whether the picture would be clothed or not. Some of them were, but others weren't so clothed... then we found this image which leapt up on the screen.

From: Jason
To: Holly

Fabulous, big boy was he?

From: Holly
To: Jason

NO, big girl actually. Claire's gay, so I got to see some five foot tall graphic images—of what you call lady-bits.

From: Jason
To: Holly

YUK!!!!

From: Holly
To: Jason

Close-up photos of lady bits.

From: Jason
To: Holly

Stop, please stop, I'll have nightmares.

From: Holly
To: Jason

Her boyfriend doesn't know, but she's decided she's gay.

From: Jason
To: Holly

Did you look at the pictures?

From: Holly
To: Jason

I couldn't miss them, they filled the room, Jason. She kept clicking on new ones. I really wanted her to stop.

From: Jason
To: Holly

But you were curious, were you?

From: Holly
To: Jason

No, Jason, I was not curious. I don't want to scare you - but I do have my own to look at if I want. I felt so bad for her though. I wish I could tell the IT lot they were wrong about her, but of course I can't.

Subject: ME

From: Holly
To: Toby

How's it going there, honey?

Subject: Red Fox to Golden Eagle

From: Holly
To: Granny

Dear Granny

Still planning to run away with you, so please don't leave without me!

Love you very much

Holly

xxxx

Subject: Yoga

From: Marie
To: Holly

Holly

Sorry to bother you, dear, but I've been looking at the rota and I can't see how I can still go to my yoga classes at lunchtime. I did tell you, Holly, I can't miss a class.

Marie

From: Holly
To: Marie

Marie,

Don't worry, I have it covered.

Regards

Holly

From: Marie
To: Holly

I knew there would be a problem with this when we merged. I'm sorry if it wasn't explained to you, Holly, but I really have to stand my ground on this one. I'm not happy, Holly. I am not missing a class, it just isn't fair. Why hasn't this been looked at before now? I really am upset, Holly. I feel like crying, I really do.

From: Holly
To: Marie

Please don't cry, Marie. I know all about your yoga classes and for those two days I will cover your lunches myself. It's not a problem, you will always be able to go—I give you my word.

Holly

From: Marie
To: Holly

You will cover me?

From: Holly
To: Marie

Yes. But if I can't do it, we'll rotate and someone else can cover you.

From: Marie
To: Holly

So you think I shouldn't worry then?

From: Holly
To: Marie

No, you shouldn't worry.

:)

Subject: Your Reservations System to go live

From: Richard
To: Holly

Holly

Datacraft's Hospitality Suite will go live on Friday. The company has taken a big risk following your suggestion here. If all the meetings get lost or get jumbled, it'll be havoc, and unfortunately down to you. I have arranged for a number of Frontrecruitment temps to spend the next two nights transferring all the old bookings onto the new system. Please read up on all training manuals so problems with the changeover are kept to a minimum. If the system goes into a meltdown or crashes there is no manual back up, so I'm putting a lot of faith in you.

This is your baby, make sure things go right.

Regards

Richard

wednesday

Subject: Mum

From: Trisha
To: Holly

Your mum's been calling, sounds upset.

From: Holly
To: Trisha

Thanks. Oh, I've just got an email from her.

Subject: Fire

From: Mum
To: Holly

Holly

I have been trying to call you all morning.

I found smoke pouring down the stairs from your granny's room earlier. I have been so worried about this kind of thing happening for such a long time now. I hadn't heard from her for a while so I went up to see what was going on. There was smoke everywhere and in the middle of the floor I found Mum in her nightie cooking bacon and eggs on a calor-gas camping gas stove perched on a stool. Can you have a word with her again? When I try and talk to her we only end up arguing, but she still listens to you. She's now made a friend with someone who lives over the road called Cynthia, and they sit upstairs all day on the computer. I have no idea what they're up to, but I'm very worried about them. Would you see if you can find out, Holly, please?

Love

Mum

From: Holly
To: Mum

Got your email, glad everything's OK. Try not to worry about her so much, she's a lot more capable than you think. But I'll ask her about being more careful.

X

From: Mum
To: Holly

Holly

I do worry about her, all the time.

Subject: Pssssst

From: Jason
To: Holly

I heard on the grape vine that you like nudie pics of lady-bits. Want to buy a large collection off a friend of mine??? All large format files, nothing too shabby, right up your alley????????

From: Holly
To: Jason

Go away

Subject: Me

From: Aisha
To: Holly

I've been looking at myself a hell of a lot recently and I think you're right—I do look great in this suit, so don't worry, I won't take it in.

xxx love you

From: Holly
To: Aisha

So pleased.

From: Aisha
To: Holly

By the way, some guy asked about you earlier.

From: Holly
To: Aisha

Really, who was that?

From: Aisha
To: Holly

Don't know, just asked if I knew you, nice, sweet, friendly, model looks, not my type at all, not rough enough.

From: Holly
To: Aisha

Really?

From: Aisha
To: Holly

Yes, he'd grab your shoulders and push you down, but I can't see him telling you what to do when you got there.

From: Holly
To: Aisha

Yes, I see.

From: Aisha
To: Holly

You'd be waiting, looking up all puppy eyed and he'd be like 'what do I say now, where do I go with this?'

From: Holly
To: Aisha

Please finish now, Aisha. Finish emailing me.

From: Aisha
To: Holly

Oh, OK.

xxx

Subject: Telephone techniques

From: Holly
To: Aisha; Marie; Trisha; Claire

We're all answering the phone in slightly different ways and as much as that doesn't sound like a problem, we should all be saying the same thing.

From: Trisha
To: Holly; Aisha; Marie; Claire

I've said the same thing for twenty years and had no complaints before?

From: Marie
To: Holly; Aisha; Trisha; Claire

I haven't either, Holly.

From: Holly
To: Aisha; Marie; Trisha; Claire

I'm not saying you have, but both your ways are different from each other.

From: Marie
To: Holly; Aisha; Trisha; Claire

So?

> **From:** Holly
> **To:** Aisha; Marie; Trisha; Claire

I agree there shouldn't be anything wrong with it. But you can't help what people take away from something so simple. If we're all answering it in different ways, it affects an overall picture of the company as a whole. We could look a little jumbled and disjointed.

I agree it's annoying and stupid, but it's people's perception.

> **From:** Trisha
> **To:** Holly; Marie; Claire; Aisha

Not having a go darling, but I'm not doing it, end of.

Subject: Team

> **From:** Holly
> **To:** Jason

How do you get people to do things they don't want to—but stay friends with them and not fall out with them?

> **From:** Jason
> **To:** Holly

Don't know, I have a team of twelve and I'm sure half of them hate me.

> **From:** Holly
> **To:** Jason

I thought they all loved you.

> **From:** Jason
> **To:** Holly

Don't think so. But you need to inspire them, give them a speech or something.

> **From:** Holly
> **To:** Jason

I'm not good with speeches.

From: Jason
To: Holly

Also make sure you put all the receptionists together who don't like each other.

From: Holly
To: Jason

Why?

From: Jason
To: Holly

If they're not talking to each other, they're not talking about you.

Imagine you're working with a bunch of pretty psychopaths who spend the day plotting your downfall and you won't be far wrong.

From: Holly
To: Jason

Wonderful.

Subject: Hi

From: Holly
To: Toby

Hello, lover, did you know you make goat noises when you sleep??

From: Toby
To: Holly

Probably the stress.

Subject: On another note

From: Holly
To: Jason

I think Toby barely knows I exist.

From: Jason
To: Holly

Rubbish.

From: Holly
To: Jason

Maybe I'm being a bit dramatic. He knows I exist and I think he loves me and everything, but I think I need to do something to get his attention.

From: Jason
To: Holly

Why don't you paint yourself gold?

From: Holly
To: Jason

Not sure about that.

From: Jason
To: Holly

And cover your back in lovely long feathers.

From: Holly
To: Jason

Why?

From: Jason
To: Holly

You'll look like a fabulous gold peacock, especially if you strut about the flat flapping your arms and squawking when he comes through the door!

From: Holly
To: Jason

He's only just found me hiding in a cupboard. Do you really think this would help?

From: Jason
To: Holly

No, not really.

Subject: Hello

From: Holly
To: Alice

How's things on the funny farm?

From: Alice
To: Holly

Not a bad name for it at the moment. We've had so many problems with our snakes. You remember we asked if we needed a license and the council said we did, and we got fined because we haven't got one?

From: Holly
To: Alice

Yes.

From: Alice
To: Holly

We were sent from government office to office in our attempt to find one and in the end they've admitted there isn't one. So they're making one (we're still fined for not having one though) and they're trying to work out what animals will be classed as dangerous, and interestingly enough they're doing it on weight. Don't even go there. So we're trying to slim our snakes down as fast as possible. Also bought some little lizards instead, so we've branched out a little.

From: Holly
To: Alice

I like lizards, they're not as scary as snakes. What do they eat? Bet it's something nicer than rats.

From: Alice
To: Holly

They eat flies and things.

From: Holly
To: Alice

Easy, I think you should stick with them.

From: Alice
To: Holly

Of course you have to breed the flies though and Matt thinks the ones out here aren't as big and juicy as the lovely ones you get in England (his words not mine) so he's trying to create a hybrid fly by feeding them on English meat.

From: Holly
To: Alice

Stop now.

From: Alice
To: Holly

OK, it was my turn to have the mothers around from Joseph's class at school today. Lots of coffee drinking and talk about baking cakes, but there was something buzzing around the living room and in the end it settled on an armchair and I'm looking at it and it's a nasty huge fly and I found myself thinking out loud, 'Oh dear, one of Matt's experiments has escaped again.' There was this silence and I've looked up and thought, great, I won't be hosting this meeting again. Do you think other mothers have the same problems?

From: Holly
To: Alice

No.

From: Alice
To: Holly

You're probably right.

> **From:** Holly
> **To:** Alice

Alice, I need to talk to you about something tonight. Are you in?

> **From:** Alice
> **To:** Holly

I'm always in, I don't live in party central here. Call me later.

x

thursday

Subject: Gossip

> **From:** Holly
> **To:** Jason; Aisha

So, any exciting news? What's the latest gossip? How's your love life, Aisha?

> **From:** Aisha
> **To:** Jason; Holly

I've got a date with a trader on Friday. He's not exactly good looking, but he's told me he's got a Lamborghini and I've never been in one.

> **From:** Holly
> **To:** Jason; Aisha

Good, so you're sorted for Friday. How's it going with Marco?

> **From:** Jason
> **To:** Aisha; Holly

I'm nearly there I think.

> **From:** Aisha
> **To:** Jason; Holly

What is this plan you're up to? You haven't told me? .

From: Jason
To: Aisha; Holly

It was going to take ten weeks, but I then decided to cram it all into five, as it's becoming too difficult to live with myself. It's me that's having the trouble. This was the original plan, a lot I haven't done yet, and some I just couldn't bring myself to:

WEEK 1
- Be smelly, the smellier the better. Make sure when he walks in that room that he wishes he had died—cheat if you have to, cat food is particularly repellent, keep an open sachet in your pocket
- Be physically repulsive, from rotting teeth to a new horrifying taste in clothes. Put fake sweat patches under the arms, let your hair grow long and out of shape, don't shave anywhere
- Develop a taste for the unusual. Leave whips, chains and strange looking sexual contraptions everywhere. Begin wearing a dog lead at home and sometimes bark during sex
- Take up the violin

WEEK 2
- Giggle nervously when he's around, stutter shake and dribble. Be waiting for him by the door, grinning. Keep tabs on him, ask where he is all the time, even when he's with you. Explain it's just because you love him so much
- Be horrible to live with, wait until he's in the bathroom before you run in there and use the toilet. Eat everything that doesn't agree with your digestive system, burp, fart, leave your pants on the floor
- Use the last of household products without replacing them
- Develop a hacking cough and put a spittoon by your bed
- Take up the clarinet

WEEK 3
- Play with matches a lot

- Buy an air horn and press it regularly, buy bangers and explode them in the garden every Sunday afternoon
- Find religion, begin quoting the Bible during arguments. When you win an argument, pummel the air and scream 10 points for the Grrrrrrangers (or your surname)
- Whenever he talks, slap your knees to an imaginary drum beat, wear your trousers up high to reveal odd socks, wear your pants on top of your trousers
- Always wear odd socks
- Exercise. Buy an exercise bike, work out at home, in spandex, in front of him, while he's on the phone, watch him closely
- Admire everyone else, tell him you wished you could only be as sexy as they are. Tell him every day you you're so lucky to be with him. Get caught sniffing his underwear

WEEK 4

- Say 'init' 'lovin it' and 'defo' in every sentence, throw in the obligatory 'am I bovered'
- Creep up on him and explode balloons behind his head regularly, then lie on the floor belly laughing afterward
- Accumulate a list of the oldest jokes ever, begin telling them when you're at dinner parties. Repeat one in particular all the time
- Leave black muck stains around the bath rim. Get caught sniffing his shoes
- Walk dirt through the house
- Puke in the bed at night and pee yourself in the morning
- Pick your teeth with your toe-nail clippings

WEEK 5

- Freshen your socks by stretching them over the cold drinks cans in the fridge
- Paint his portrait once a week, badly, and insist on hanging it in the gallery you've created in the hall, just of him

- Get caught putting pins into a doll, keep petrol in canisters under the bed. When someone comes on the TV you like, pinch your nipples and growl
- Rearrange everything in the cupboards in alphabetical order, and put labels on everything in the fridge which you've bought, with MINE written on them
- Spend the evening's polishing the doorknobs and scream in pain when he uses them without gloves. Sit around the house in rubber shorts

What do you think?

From: Holly
To: Jason; Aisha

That may do it.

From: Aisha
To: Jason; Holly

I can see it working, but after Marco's gone, the chances of you finding anyone at all interested in you whatsoever, ever again, are going to be slim.

From: Jason
To: Holly; Aisha

Thanks.

From: Aisha
To: Jason; Holly

Except maybe the police, the council and the odd docu-filmmaker covering freaks.

Subject: Confirmation

From: Admin@DKHuerstBeautyandtheBest
To: Holly

Appointment booked in from 1pm until 5pm on the ???? of ?????

Subject: The new reservations system

From: Holly
To: Marie; Trisha; Claire; Aisha

Hi everyone

My friend Jason made me read a book called *Who Moved My Cheese?* to help me acclimatize to change once. It's a story about mice in a maze and the point of the story is that good things can be just around the corner, but only if you look around the corner will you find them. I thought this might inspire you.

From: Trisha
To: Holly; Marie; Claire; Aisha

Did it inspire you?

From: Holly
To: Marie; Trisha; Claire; Aisha

No and it gave me a nightmare about being chased through a maze by a lump of cheese stuck to a horse ridden by Ted Danson.

From: Claire
To: Holly; Marie; Trisha; Aisha

A horse, not a huge mouse?

From: Holly
To: Marie; Trisha; Claire; Aisha

No, a horse. I suppose I should be grateful, a mouse would have been scarier.

From: Claire
To: Holly; Marie; Trisha; Aisha

Unless it was a tiny mouse, with a tiny Ted Danson.

From: Aisha
To: Holly; Marie; Trisha; Claire

Then you could just tread on them.

From: Marie
To: Aisha; Claire; Trisha; Holly

I'm lost, who is Ted Danson?

From: Trisha
To: Holly; Marie; Claire; Trisha

He was in *Three Men and a Baby*. I loved that film. My first came from it. I couldn't wait to get pregnant after I saw it, should have a health warning it should.

From: Aisha
To: Claire; Trisha; Holly; Marie

I hated it, put me off moustaches for a long time.

From: Holly
To: Marie; Trisha; Claire; Aisha

So anyway, the new reservations system will be up and running tomorrow. I'm hoping it will go perfectly and you'll love it, and it will make our lives easier and amongst a host of other advantages it will isolate who's made mistakes—good if it's not ours (so we can laugh and point the finger) and if it was ours we'll be able to adjust our routines etc. I kind of stuck my neck out on it all, so if you hate me, just spend the day making as many mistakes as possible and blaming everything on Holly's stupid booking system so next time I go up to see Cartwright he presses a red button and the bottom of the lift slides back and I disappear into his shark tank.

I hope it goes well.

Holly

From: Aisha
To: Claire; Trisha; Holly; Marie

Although I was straight back on moustaches when *Friends* came out. What was his name?

From: Holly
To: Marie; Trisha; Jason; Aisha

Tom Selleck?

From: Aisha
To: Claire; Trisha; Holly; Marie

No, his character?

From: Claire
To: Holly; Marie; Trisha; Aisha

His name was Richard. I should be a *Friends* guru. I have every episode, the board game, the album, everything.

From: Aisha
To: Claire; Trisha; Holly; Marie

Remind me never to go round to your place. Anyway I would have ridden Richard's moustache happily.

From: Holly
To: Marie; Trisha; Claire; Aisha

Aisha, put a pound in your bad-Aisha box for one count of nastiness and one count of just being revolting.

Subject: I forgot

From: William
To: Holly

Did I mention my boxing medals?

From: Holly
To: William

You did.

Subject: Birthday Boy

From: Holly
To: Toby

It's your birthday on Wednesday. What do you want to do for it?

From: Toby
To: Holly

A quiet, relaxing night in.

From: Holly
To: Toby

Sounds romantic…?

Subject: Advice

From: Mum
To: Holly

Dear Holly

I have been in the clinic all morning with your father's eye problem. He now has three different drops he uses. I think you should think about getting your eyes tested on a regular basis too.

Love Mum

Subject: Re Our conversation last night

From: Alice
To: Holly

Have to talked to him yet?

From: Holly
To: Alice

No, it's his birthday on Wednesday next week so I'm going to tell him then.

From: Alice
To: Holly

Sounds perfect. Have you told anyone else yet?

From: Holly
To: Alice

Only you.

From: Alice
To: Holly

I think that's best, it's so exciting.

xxx

Good luck, I'll send you some zaps.

friday

Subject: Youu

From: Holly
To: Jason

How you feeling, baby?

From: Jason
To: Holly

OK, not too pleased with myself, feeling a bit dirty actually.

From: Holly
To: Jason

That was unexpected, wasn't it?

From: Jason
To: Holly

Yes, out of the blue he said 'I'm off'. He was quite rude about it too actually. He's clearing out today. I didn't get to go through much of my plan, it's a lot harder than you think. It still means lying to someone you care about (well not lying, acting, but same difference). Probably keep up the violin for a bit, I think I'm getting quite good at.

From: Holly
To: Jason

You're not, it's awful. x

From: Jason
To: Holly

I know.

From: Holly
To: Jason

You want me to come around tonight??? We can watch a film?

From: Jason
To: Holly

Thanks, but I'm OK. I think it's because I'd got used to the idea for some time that this would happen. I'll hit the bars instead, might take my violin with me.

From: Holly
To: Jason

OK, whatever you do, do not go into the Garrick and PLEASE do NOT serenade that DJ. He will talk about you on the radio and it won't be nice.

From: Jason
To: Holly

But I'd be famous?????? Oh, Chrissy, come to mummy!!! OH you've cheered me up—Holly, I love you, oh oh oh I might even sing too!!!!

From: Holly
To: Jason

But, honey, you're REALLY awful at singing.

From: Jason
To: Holly

I KNOW!!! Isn't it just so perfect and meant to be?? It's like fate, I feel a shift in the planetary activity, something is saying, 'Jason, this is your time.'

From: Holly
To: Jason

Really—you think?

From: Jason
To: Holly

I'm going to be so bad, so fabulously awful he will just have to invite me to a live broadcast and I'll be up there with the greats. It worked for Peter Andre??!!! This could be the beginning of my showbiz life!!!!

From: Holly
To: Jason

It's meant to be, so you take your violin and you go stalk that DJ and play your heart out, princess, and play like you've never played before! Now fly, you musical marvel, fly!!!!

xxx

Subject: Mystery

From: Richard
To: Holly

Holly

Good luck today with your new bookings system.

Also, just to let you know, the way we work out our scoring on various topics is through the use of mystery shoppers, both calling in on the telephone and in person. These have been rating the reception team for the past month.

Hope this is useful

Regards

Richard

Subject: Today

From: Holly
To: Trisha; Aisha; Claire; Marie

Just so you're aware, for the last few weeks we've had mystery shoppers coming into the bank (only just found out).

From: Aisha
To: Holly; Claire; Trisha; Marie

That's out of order. I could have done with a new dress last Friday.

From: Holly
To: Trisha; Aisha; Claire; Marie

That's a personal shopper, Aisha. A mystery shopper is more like a spy.

From: Trisha
To: Aisha; Claire; Holly; Marie

I bet it was the nasty-looking one with the bushy eyebrow we saw a few weeks back, Holly.

From: Holly
To: Aisha; Marie; Claire; Trisha

That's what I was thinking. So just be aware that every client on the telephone or in person might be the mystery shopper. Also I need to know who wants to be involved in this charity do on the roof terrace next month? It goes towards someone really wonderful causes.

From: Aisha
To: Holly; Claire; Trisha; Marie

Is it staff only or can we bring someone?

From: Marie
To: Holly; Aisha; Claire; Trisha

Will you be bringing Toby or have you now split up, Holly dear?

From: Holly
To: Aisha; Marie; Claire; Trisha

What????

From: Aisha
To: Holly; Claire; Trisha; Aisha

You told everyone you thought he was probably having an affair (you were trashed).

From: Marie
To: Holly; Aisha; Claire; Trisha

And I'm always the last to know about these things. So do we know who he's having an affair with now?

From: Holly
To: Aisha; Marie; Claire; Trisha

Can everyone please stop saying he's having an affair?

From: Claire
To: Holly; Aisha; Marie; Trisha

I thought you knew he was?

From: Holly
To: Aisha; Marie; Claire; Trisha

No.

From: Marie
To: Holly; Aisha; Claire; Trisha

I can listen in on his calls if you want, Holly. It's very easy with this switchboard?

From: Holly
To: Aisha; Marie; Claire; Trisha

No, I do not want you listening in to his calls. Do not do that.

From: Aisha
To: Holly; Claire; Trisha; Aisha

Makes more sense than hiding in a cupboard?

From: Marie
To: Holly; Aisha; Claire; Trisha

Yes, why did you do that? I never understood that, Holly dear?

From: Holly
To: Aisha; Marie; Claire; Trisha

Can everyone just tell me if they're going to this bloody charity thing??

From: Marie
To: Holly; Aisha; Claire; Trisha

Yes.

From: Claire
To: Holly; Aisha; Marie; Trisha

Yes.

From: Trisha
To: Aisha; Claire; Holly; Marie

Yes.

From: Aisha
To: Holly; Claire; Trisha; Marie

Yes.

From: Holly
To: Aisha; Marie; Claire; Trisha

Thank you!

Subject: Missing

From: Natasha
To: Holly

Dear Holly Denham

I ask some questions below in the politest possible way I can, which is difficult because I am about to explode. Please give them some very careful thought before you venture an answer to them.

A: Where are my meetings? I can't see them on the system

B: Do you know what will happen to you if my 2 o'clock meeting is not in the board room?

C: One of my guests has special dietary requirements and it is now too late to order it in

D: Why have they made you manager?

Regards

Natasha

Head of Commodities

Subject: Important

From: Aisha
To: Holly

Holly

There are four clients up here waiting for a meeting that isn't on the system. I presume it's lost a booking. What should I do?

Aisha

Subject: Extras

From: Trisha
To: Holly

No room at the inn, we're over-run and too many extras for room 14

Sorry darling.

Trisha

Subject: Lost

From: Claire
To: Holly

I just dragged and dropped someone's event into thin air. It's all gone kaput. :(Sorry.

Subject: Interesting

From: Frankie Fraser
To: Holly

Did you know that our supermarket has a sale on? Fresh fish, four to the dozen, for under a fiver.

How's about that?

Subject: Lost meeting

From: Holly
To: Claire

I've brought it back for you. Don't worry, you can't lose things, there's a failsafe feature.

X

Subject: Extras

From: Holly
To: Trisha

We'll move the people from the room next door to another floor. It's only an internal meeting anyway, then we'll get the AV boys to remove the partition and make it into one big room.

From: Trisha
To: Holly

Sorted.

Subject: Clients waiting

From: Holly
To: Aisha

Just found out they're for Richard. He's going out to lunch with them, so they're going straight back down again. No room needed.

x

Subject: Fish

From: Holly
To: Frankie Fraser

Thank you, Frankie, but I've no idea what you mean I think you may have your figures wrong there though. Hope you're alright, must catch up soon.

Holly

From: Frankie Fraser
To: Holly

There's a suspicious-looking package in the hall way. Do you think I should open it?

Frank

From: Holly
To: Frankie Fraser

Who is it addressed to?

From: Frankie Fraser
To: Holly

You.

From: Holly
To: Frankie Fraser

Then no, Frank, but thank you very much for your concern. I think you should put it back.

Thank you again for keeping an eye out.

Holly

Subject: REMINDER

From: Holly
To: Holly

1: My friendly upstairs neighbour is Frank NOT Frankie.

Subject: Missing

From: Holly
To: Natasha

Dear Natasha

Thank you for your email. Having given your questions some careful consideration, please find answers below:

A: *Where are my meetings? I can't see them on the system*

They are there but you may be in the wrong screen. Just use the search facility and type in your ID number

B: *Do you know what will happen if my 2 o'clock meeting is not in the board room?*

You find it very difficult to forgive me, but in the end you do and we become best friends???

C: *One of my guests has special dietary requirements and it is now too late to order it in*

Yes I did know, and his unfortunate palate has been catered to

D: *Why have they made you manager?*

Because they thought I had nice shoes

I know you're busy and having to learn a new system was probably the last thing you needed, however I'm hoping it makes your life and ours here a lot easier, but feedback is appreciated.

Regards

Holly

Subject: Newsletter from Charlie

From: Charlie
To: Mum; Holly; Alice

It's a seven-mile walk to the nearest computer, but I thought this was important enough to let you know. This morning I caught Big Foot, one of the tribal people, thieving from the supply hut. The villagers wanted to cut his head off, soak it in vinegar, boil it in rotting cabbage and make it into a kind of soup, but I said NO, this is not how civilized people behave, take the pot off the fire now, you can keep the vinegar to pour on your chips, which you then wrap in newspaper. So they did and then we all sat around and smoked some grass.

From: Charlie
To: Mum; Holly; Alice

When I say grass, Mum, I meant the Brazilian herbal grass, which cures things.

From: Charlie
To: Mum; Holly; Alice

I don't mean something which makes you high.

From: Charlie
To: Mum; Holly; Alice

No one in my village gets high.

From: Charlie
To: Mum; Holly; Alice

Not even medicine man Sam, and you'd think it was his job to get high.

From: Charlie
To: Mum; Holly; Alice

But it isn't.

Subject: Hi

From: Alice
To: Holly

I don't believe any of this, why don't we see pictures of him if he's helping the starving? I've been thinking, why is it you think we don't get any pictures ever from Charlie. Surely he could send us something? Can you ask him if he ever calls you, and can you ask him to call me, I'd like to talk to him some time.

xxx

Subject: Police

From: Frankie Fraser
To: Holly

Your package is leaking now, I think it's a bomb, I'm going to call the police.
Frank

From: Holly
To: Frankie Fraser

Where is the package from? ? ? ?

From: Frankie Fraser
To: Holly

Spain, there's oil seeping out of it everywhere.

From: Holly
To: Frankie Fraser

Then it's from my granny, and it's a treacle tart.

From: Frankie Fraser
To: Holly

Why would it leak oil?

From: Holly
To: Frankie Fraser

That's how she makes them, she fries them. Now please don't call the police, put it back and forget my post.

Subject: Today

From: Trisha
To: Holly

You done all right with this thing. I was ready to moan, but I like it.
X

Subject: Hey you

From: Holly
To: Toby

I've had such a good day!!! I can't wait to tell you, two bits of news to tell you, both of which I've been holding back as a surprise. I could tell you tonight…
Holly

From: Toby
To: Holly

Hi
Great, looking forward to it, can't you tell me now?

From: Holly
To: Toby

Tonight.
xx

From: Toby
To: Holly

Very mysterious.

Subject: Congratulations

From: Richard
To: Holly

Well done today, really pleased for you. I think it was an out and out success.

Don't forget your meeting with the CEO on Monday. Be bright and bushy tailed.

Richard

Subject: Your appointment

From: Dr El Trazier
To: Holly

Dear Holly

Your appointment with the doctor is confirmed for Wednesday next week.

Regards

Jane

PA to Dr El Trazier

week 4

monday

Subject: PLAN FOR 2008

From: Holly
To: Holly

Countdown to May 5th.

Two weeks to go.

Then I'm going to:

Get permanent management job with increase in salary & bens

Get back in touch with the world and begin paying off my debts again

Get my legs, nails and hair done, roots badly showing.

Buy two cheap suits for work

Begin preparing things

Holly Denham

FOH Manager, DKHuerst, 50 Cabot Square, Canary Wharf, London

Subject: Our brother

From: Alice
To: Holly

Any more news/pictures yet from Charlie?

From: Holly
To: Alice

Yes, he called Saturday. He's well and happy, not much to report as I only spoke to him for about twenty seconds.

X

Subject: Charlie

From: Holly
To: Rubber Ron

You really need some photos if I'm going to be able to pass this off till he's out. Alice knows something's up.
Holly

From: Rubber Ron
To: Holly

Not long now, how was he on Saturday?

From: Holly
To: Rubber Ron

Good, he had me in stitches the whole time, he's a pain in the bum, but I love him.

From: Rubber Ron
To: Holly

He'll be out soon anyway, just a few more weeks.

From: Holly
To: Rubber Ron

Just as well. Speak later.
Holly

Subject: Your birthday

From: Holly
To: Toby

Honey, what do you fancy doing for your birthday?

From: Toby
To: Holly

Nothing too much, I'm happy just staying at home.

Subject: Worried

From: Holly
To: Jason

I re-organised Toby's wardrobe on Friday night.

From: Jason
To: Holly

What??

From: Holly
To: Jason

I know, I was so excited waiting for him to come home. I was going to tell him about me being promoted (seeing as he never picked up on it). I kept calling him and he kept saying he was on his way. I got bored and it started when I put one of his sweatshirts on.

From: Jason
To: Holly

You shouldn't do that.

From: Holly
To: Jason

Why? You must have worn someone's sweatshirt at some stage, don't say you haven't.

From: Jason
To: Holly

I have, but I wouldn't want you doing it.

From: Holly
To: Jason

Why?

From: Jason
To: Holly

Because I know why you like it.

From: Holly
To: Jason

It's comforting??

From: Jason
To: Holly

Yes.

From: Holly
To: Jason

So???

From: Jason
To: Holly

Until he gives you back as much in this relationship as you give him, I won't like it.

From: Holly
To: Jason

You don't think it's equal?

From: Jason
To: Holly

No.

From: Holly
To: Jason

If you don't think it's equal, tell me why it could be unequal. Sorry, Jason, but this is important.

From: Jason
To: Holly

I can't say one specific thing but I don't want you getting hurt. I don't like it. I wish I could put a force field around you to stop all the bad men getting to you.

From: Holly
To: Jason

That's sweet, but I really don't need a force field.

From: Jason
To: Holly

I'll only be happy when you're married, packaged off and stamped and sent to the land of love.

x

From: Holly
To: Jason

Thanks.

xx

From: Jason
To: Holly

You're welcome.

From: Holly
To: Jason

I really really wanted to tell him about my promotion and how good my day had been on Friday, how my idea had worked and things. Once again he was working late. Got bored of waiting and I did it, I ended up colour-coordinating his wardrobe. Put everything in a rainbow from yellow-orange-red-purple-blue-turquoise.

From: Jason
To: Holly

I know what a rainbow is.

From: Holly
To: Jason

It looked really good.

From: Jason
To: Holly

You need to watch more trash TV. You know *100 Greatest Housewives* was on?

From: Holly
To: Jason

?

From: Jason
To: Holly

The Greatest Ever TV Housewives.

From: Holly
To: Jason

?

From: Jason
To: Holly

Including soaps, series and films. The woman off the Fairy commercial won it.

From: Holly
To: Jason

So, I didn't watch that and I ended up putting his clothes in a rainbow.

From: Jason
To: Holly

You missed out. Does he really have that many coloured clothes?

From: Holly
To: Jason

No, I added a few of my own. Anyway I finished and shut his wardrobe and forgot all about it. Ended up going to bed and falling asleep with the light on. I heard him come in, and I knew he'd noticed it, there was this kind of sigh. Then he just took off his clothes and went to bed. I wish I hadn't done it now, I remember thinking I just wanted to do something nice for him, he works so hard. I know it was a terrible idea, and he'll think I'm even more stupid. But I just wanted him to laugh and come in and grab me, hold me and kiss me, like he did when we were first together.

From: Jason
To: Holly

Twelve years ago or when you got back together?

From: Holly
To: Jason

Either. I just wanted that passionate, tender—hell, I just wanted him to care about me!?? Not too much to ask I think, Jason. It's gone, you know that? The weekend was terrible, he's just so distant.

From: Jason
To: Holly

You need those gold feathers. Don't worry, we just need a plan.
X

Subject: Hate to disturb you, but

From: Trisha
To: Holly

Aren't you going to be late for the CEO ?

From: Holly
To: Trisha

Shit xx

Subject: CEO Meeting

From: Holly
To: Trisha

That was fun.

From: Trisha
To: Holly

What happened?

From: Holly
To: Trisha

You know the brand new boardroom at the top of the building?

From: Trisha
To: Holly

What's it like?

From: Holly
To: Trisha

They just finished it, looks great. You won't guess how much they've wasted on it though…

From: Trisha
To: Holly

10,000?

From: Holly
To: Trisha

500,000.

From: Trisha
To: Holly

That's stupid money.

From: Holly
To: Trisha

For a really stupid room. So we sat down opposite each other and I then noticed some fresh coffee on the side, so I said 'Oh good, fresh coffee,' and went to get up but I found my foot was stuck to the floor. So I didn't get up, and he looked at the coffee, then back at me and in the end he decided I was hinting that HE should get it.

From: Trisha
To: Holly

The CEO?

From: Holly
To: Trisha

I basically told the CEO to get me some coffee while I sat there like a princess. In the end I wrench my foot up and my knee hit the underside of the table, startling him as he was pouring. I think he thought I was a loon. I glance down to see chewing gum in long trails from a large flat lump on the new white zillion pound carpet—stuck to MY shoe. So I spend the rest of the meeting trying to quietly scrape it off on the antique table leg—so I'm not attached to the evidence. We finish the meeting and we're walking together back down the marble corridor to the lift but with each step I take there's this loud sticky squelchy sound echoing. He stops, I stop, the noise stops, and when we start off again, it starts.

From: Trisha
To: Holly

You poor thing.

From: Holly
To: Trisha

Awful, now I'm worried they'll discover it's me who's ruined their room and want to send me a bill.

From: Trisha
To: Holly

What was the meeting about?

From: Holly
To: Trisha

He told me some parable about bears hunting for fish—but only finding angry ducks then asked me if understood. I told him I understood completely. He went on to add that this was of the utmost importance and needed doing quickly because the reception area was essential to the look of the building.

From: Trisha
To: Holly

What was the important thing?

From: Holly
To: Trisha

I've have absolutely no idea—I was too busy gum-scraping, but I've learnt you shouldn't go fishing in duck ponds if you're a bear. At least I've picked up on that lovely nugget of know-how.

From: Trisha
To: Holly

Good on ya.

From: Holly
To: Trisha

Oh and he agreed a bonus scheme, so everyone will get a bonus if we achieve our targets.

From: Trisha
To: Holly

YOU DARLIN!!!!!!!!!

Subject: Newsletter from Charlie

From: Charlie
To: Holly, Mum, Alice

All going well. See attached pictures of me relaxing with Medicine Sam after a hard day in the Brazilian Forest excavating a new irrigation system.

Regards

Charlie

Should be home in two or three weeks.

[image attached]

Subject: Brazil

From: Alice
To: Charlie; Holly

In this Brazilian forest, are there many women with prams?

From: Charlie
To: Alice; Holly

No.

From: Alice
To: Charlie; Holly

So why is there one in the background of this photo?

From: Charlie
To: Alice; Holly

That's not a pram, that's an earth excavator.

From: Alice
To: Charlie; Holly

Why's she holding what looks like a mobile phone?

From: Charlie
To: Alice; Holly

Well it is 2008, even tribal excavators have phones, Alice. What did you expect?

From: Alice
To: Charlie; Holly

Frankly I expect the jungle to look less like communal gardens.

From: Charlie
To: Alice; Holly

You can't change the way the jungle looks.

From: Alice
To: Charlie; Holly

Hold on, it is a communal garden, at the bottom of Charlie's flat!

From: Charlie
To: Alice; Holly

No it isn't.

From: Alice
To: Charlie; Holly

Yes it is, and that's not Medicine Sam either.

From: Charlie
To: Alice; Holly

Yes it is.

From: Alice
To: Charlie; Holly

No it's Rubber Ron, and I don't think that's you, Charlie, that's your friend Pete, trying to look a bit like you. WHERE ARE YOU, CHARLIE????

Subject: Charlie

From: Holly
To: Rubber Ron

I'd say you've been rumbled.

From: Rubber Ron
To: Holly

Looks like it.

From: Holly
To: Rubber Ron

Do you want to explain it to her? I'll call her after your email and smooth things over?

Subject: Your brother

From: Rubber Ron
To: Alice; Holly

Hi Alice

You are right, Charlie is not in Brazil, he's in prison, but on the up side, he'll be out in the next few weeks. I've been emailing everyone pretending he's still around, because we didn't think it was good for his business really. Hope everything's going well out there.

How are the children?

Lots of love

Rubber Ron

From: Alice
To: Rubber Ron; Holly

WHAT?????

From: Rubber Ron
To: Alice; Holly

Charlie's inside, in the nick, gone down, away etc. Don't worry, he's fine, he still thinks it's very funny for some reason. He just got four months because the judge didn't have a sense of humour.

Ron

From: Alice
To: Rubber Ron; Holly

WHAT DID HE DO??

From: Rubber Ron
To: Alice; Holly

Oh, just convinced a load of big corporations to fork out lots of money for a language training course called the Harvard Training Matrix, then sent them a language dictionary with a set of blank labels and a note saying to look up the object in the dictionary, write the foreign word on the label and stick it on the object—that way you'll quickly pick up the language without noticing. The judge said it was a scam and it certainly wasn't written in Harvard and Charlie asked him if he really thought the Oxford Dictionary was written in Oxford (and smirked when the judge didn't know). So he got a bigger sentence for being a smart arse.

Ron

Subject: Our brother

From: Holly
To: Alice

I'll give you a call now, Alice. I'm really sorry, Charlie didn't want you worrying.

X

tuesday

Subject: Fun for Toby

From: Jason
To: Holly

When's his birthday?

From: Holly
To: Jason

Tomorrow.

From: Jason
To: Holly

OK, can you take tomorrow morning off?

From: Holly
To: Jason

Yes, why?

From: Jason
To: Holly

You need time to get yourself glitzy.

From: Holly
To: Jason

Can't :(

From: Jason
To: Holly

I know—no money, but what are fairy godmothers for???

From: Holly
To: Jason

You've got none either :(

From: Jason
To: Holly

Correct, but I have favours and gossip, and I've used both to wangle you some treatments here in the hotel.

From: Holly
To: Jason

NO!!!!

From: Jason
To: Holly

YES!!!

From: Holly
To: Jason

YIPEEEE. How many?

From: Jason
To: Holly

Everything.

From: Holly
To: Jason

What, a facial too?

From: Jason
To: Holly

EVERYTHING.

From: Holly
To: Jason

Everything on my head?

From: Jason
To: Holly

E.V.E.R.Y.T.H.I.N.G.

From: Holly
To: Jason

NO!!! Even the naughty bits?

From: Jason
To: Holly

Especially the naughty bits. I mean the top to bottom scrub, you will be as polished as they get.

From: Holly
To: Jason

NO WAAAAAAAAAAYYYYYYY.
I LOVE YOU I LOVE YOU I LOVE YOU I LOVE YOU I LOVE YOU!!!!!!

From: Jason
To: Holly

A team of permers, preeners, polishers and steamers will be waiting by their assorted torture devices to have you plucked, waxed and stamped. Personally I wouldn't do it, far too much pain at once, but in for a penny in for a pound, or as Mad Frank would say 'In for a dozen for under a fiver' or something equally bazaar, bless his cockney socks and his slightly mad scary heart. Be here 7am sharp!

From: Holly
To: Jason

I WILL!

xxx

Subject: Toby

From: Alice
To: Holly

What happened?

From: Holly
To: Alice

Haven't told him yet, just can't see an opportunity.

From: Alice
To: Holly

You have to do it today.

From: Holly
To: Alice

I'm going to tell him on Wednesday, it's his birthday too. Then I thought next week we might have a romantic weekend together to talk about it all, so I booked something.

From: Alice
To: Holly

Sounds perfect.

xxxx

wednesday

Subject: Special day

From: Holly
To: Toby

HAPPY BIRTHDAY !!!!!!!!

xxx

YIPPEEEEE

From: Toby
To: Holly

Thank you.

x

Subject: Pretty woman

From: Trisha
To: Holly

I wish I had a friend who could sort me out like that. You look gorgeous, you really do, a million dollars. You're a lucky girl.

X

From: Holly
To: Trisha

Thank you, Trishy, I am very lucky.

xx

Subject: TOBY

From: Jason
To: Holly

Tell me when he notices.

From: Holly
To: Jason

I will.

Subject: This morning

From: Marie
To: Holly

I want to tell you something important, Holly. Do you have a moment for me?

From: Holly
To: Marie

Yes, do you want me to come down here?

From: Marie
To: Holly

No, I just wanted to tell you that sometimes people are not nice on the phone. It isn't easy sometimes down here on my own and it can be very difficult you know.

From: Holly
To: Marie

I know. I'm sorry about that man's behaviour today on the phone. We are not here to be shouted at. It's not easy being happy all day when people are like that and if anyone swears at you, I want to know.

From: Marie
To: Holly

Richard came in to apologise to me himself. I know you told him to do that and I wanted to thank you. It made me feel special and appreciated you know.

From: Holly
To: Marie

No problem, you are.
X

From: Marie
To: Holly

Also how am I meant to do my job when someone is so rude? What do you think we should do?

From: Holly
To: Marie

Good point. I'll email everyone about it now.

Holly

Subject: To my team

From: Holly
To: Trisha; Claire; Aisha; Marie

A beautiful sunny afternoon to you all!!!

Marie just brought something up which I thought I'd just mention. I used to find it very difficult to deal with some of the clients coming through. Trisha used to tell me it was a challenge; that it would be so dull if everyone was nice. When you get a problem it breaks up the day; 'kill them with kindness' she'd say, but it isn't easy. If you end up making them feel embarrassed though—about their own behaviour—you've beaten them. I've watched people, who were rude to Trisha, come back down the next day with flowers and chocolates because they've realised they were wrong.

Hope this helps.

Holly

Subject: You remembered something then

From: Trisha
To: Holly

Kill em with kindness, I used to say, but if that don't work, tell your aunty Trisha and she'll lay into them with her boots.

From: Holly
To: Trisha

Yes, I left that bit out.

x

Subject: Battle plan for tonight

From: Jason
To: Holly

Come on, tell me? So you're as pretty as a picture, now what about the rest? Music?

From: Holly
To: Jason

Haven't thought about it yet, been too busy making myself edible.

From: Jason
To: Holly

What about Barry White?

From: Holly
To: Jason

Too obvious.

From: Jason
To: Holly

Barry Manilow?

From: Holly
To: Jason

Too cheesy.

From: Jason
To: Holly

Barry McGuigan?

From: Holly
To: Jason

He was a boxer, wasn't he?

From: Jason
To: Holly

OK, forget the music, what about the lighting?

From: Holly
To: Jason

Scented candles.

From: Jason
To: Holly

The sheets?

From: Holly
To: Jason

Clean, white with rose petals.

From: Jason
To: Holly

Nice. Clothes?

From: Holly
To: Jason

I'm going for Lindsay Lohan meets Paris Hilton.

From: Jason
To: Holly

They fought last time they met, didn't they?

From: Holly
To: Jason

They did.

From: Jason
To: Holly

So you're going for the beaten up look?

From: Holly
To: Jason

I could do, what do you think?

From: Jason
To: Holly

It's gutsy, just go easy on the black eyes and concentrate more on the rips.

From: Holly
To: Jason

OK.

From: Jason
To: Holly

And throw in some fur; try for classy slutty.

From: Holly
To: Jason

Fur bra?

From: Jason
To: Holly

Not scary-slutty, forget the fur.

From: Holly
To: Jason

I have fake-fur-trimmed boots?

From: Jason
To: Holly

They'll do. Now just move the washing off the side in the kitchen, the coats off the furniture, dirty plates in the sink, the rabbit in the cage, the cats out the door, throw in some perfume and away you go.

From: Holly
To: Jason

Why don't you come around to help, I'm nervous.

From: Jason
To: Holly

You'll be fine. I don't think he should find me hiding under the bed this week—he'll begin to question his own sanity.

From: Holly
To: Jason

True. Wish me luck.

From: Jason
To: Holly

Good luck.
X

Subject: Lunch Etiquette

From: Richard
To: Holly

Holly

I do believe it was one of your staff I saw pole dancing yesterday lunch time in the staff cafeteria. Luckily I don't think the incident was caught by anyone senior. Please can you explain to the team what is allowed and disallowed during lunch breaks.

Regards

Richard

Subject: Important

From: Holly
To: Aisha

I had an interesting email from Richard about someone putting on a show during lunch yesterday. Do you know anything about it?

From: Aisha
To: Holly

No, sorry.

From: Holly
To: Aisha

You don't know anything about someone dancing in the cafeteria?

From: Aisha
To: Holly

No, and I'm not telling tales but I don't think you should look further than the switchboard room.

From: Holly
To: Aisha

Marie?

From: Aisha
To: Holly

Yes.

From: Holly
To: Aisha

You are suggesting Marie was pole-dancing in the cafeteria yesterday.

From: Aisha
To: Holly

She might have been.

From: Holly
To: Aisha

ARE YOU TRYING TO GET ME THE SACK???? Richard
wants me to explain to you the company cafeteria rules, OK, so for
your information: Pole dancing is not allowed in the cafeteria, OK?

From: Aisha
To: Holly

I didn't know anyone had seen. It wasn't any kind of show—I was
explaining something.

From: Holly
To: Aisha

Well, can you not?

From: Aisha
To: Holly

Anyway it wasn't 'pole' dancing. He's such an idiot. Where would
I get a pole from???

From: Holly
To: Aisha

What were you doing then?

From: Aisha
To: Holly

Lap dancing.

From: Holly
To: Aisha

OK, that's worse, never do that again.

From: Aisha
To: Holly

Fine, is that it?

From: Holly
To: Aisha

No, just so there's no confusion, can you refrain from any kind of erotic dancing when you're taking your lunch.

From: Aisha
To: Holly

OK.

From: Holly
To: Aisha

Or in fact anywhere in the building.

From: Aisha
To: Holly

Fine, sorry, I didn't know, now I know.

thursday

Subject: Datacraft's Hospitality Suite

From: Tanya
To: Holly

Dear Holly

I got your message. You are so sweet, offering me help on the new software, but it's really not needed. You still seem to have this naïve understanding of what I do here. As Catering Manager I'm in charge of 20 staff and a budget which runs into millions, therefore I may sound stressed from time to time but I'm sure you can handle the odd difficulty you encounter there on your own. Sorry, just another thing, one of your receptionists was chewing gum today, can't remember which one, but this is where you can confidently step in.

Just trying to be helpful.

Tanya

From: Holly
To: Tanya

Tanya

Thank you for letting me know about the chewing gum. If you know how to use the system, then could you use it correctly. You should activate the auto-confirmation reply, so we know when meals are running late. If you need more training on it, I'll only be too happy to oblige.

Holly

Subject: Aisha

From: Holly
To: Jason

This whole managing Aisha thing—how do I do that then?

From: Jason
To: Holly

I used to compare her to a cute young fluffy tiger: lovable, but don't leave her on her own for long in case she eats someone.

From: Holly
To: Jason

Helpful.

From: Jason
To: Holly

How did it go last night????? I want to know all the gory details, just his gory details preferably.

From: Holly
To: Jason

Not great, I'll tell you later.

x

Subject: Worried

From: Aisha
To: Holly

I just want to make sure I don't upset you or get you in trouble. I was also wondering if I'm allowed to date a trader. I promise I won't do anything to get you into trouble or embarrass you or anything, but I thought I should check.

x

From: Holly
To: Aisha

Which one?

From: Aisha
To: Holly

The one from last week.

From: Holly
To: Aisha

The one I saw you pulling around by his tie?

From: Aisha
To: Holly

Yes, he likes that. I can get him to bark for me too.

From: Holly
To: Aisha

You can't.

From: Aisha
To: Holly

I can, I totally humiliate him in front of his sexist friends.

From: Holly
To: Aisha

And he likes that?

From: Aisha
To: Holly

Not sure. I do.

From: Holly
To: Aisha

OK, no dog leads, ties, or barking, and you can have my blessing.

From: Aisha
To: Holly

Can I slap his bottom in public?

From: Holly
To: Aisha

Definitely not!

From: Aisha
To: Holly

What about the others?

From: Holly
To: Aisha

One trader at a time.

From: Aisha
To: Holly

OK, love you sweetie.
X

Subject: Tanya

From: Aisha
To: Holly

Also I got a complaint.

I get on with this one guy who's been coming all week, he's really chatty, and he said he didn't want to moan, but every day during lunch times, although the food is great, the plates have been cold.

From: Holly
To: Aisha

Thanks, another chat with Tanya I won't enjoy. Here goes.

Subject: Tanya Mason

From: Holly
To: Richard

Richard

I feel sometimes that myself and Tanya don't quite see eye to eye. When I have to deal with her I don't look forward to our chats as I think there's a little friction between us. Is there a reason why I may have upset her? Sorry for bringing it up, it's not a huge problem, but just thought I'd ask.

Regards

Holly

From: Richard
To: Holly

Holly

Tanya, as you know, is the manager for the catering department which is run by the Ranixo Corporate Facilities Group. They also provide reception services to banks and law firms etc. Initially the idea was to put Tanya in charge of both divisions and outsource the reception to Ranixo. However it was decided to give you a chance first. Personally, I've found it a pleasure dealing with you and think you've done very well in such a short space of time. I hope you are rewarded for your efforts.

Because of this situation, I'm not saying this will have had a bearing on your relationship with Tanya, but you can see that she may have been disappointed not to be given the whole division to manage.

I do hope this won't impair your ability to work together?

Regards

Richard

From: Holly
To: Richard

Thank you.

No, it will be fine, I'm sure, but this is useful to know.

Regards

Holly

Subject: Classic!!!

From: Holly
To: Trisha

You won't believe this bit of information Richard conveniently forgot to mention to me. Can we go to lunch together?

From: Trisha
To: Holly

If you got gossip, I'm all yours, darling.

Subject: Important

From: Richard
To: Holly

Holly

Next Friday the Chief Financial Officer is due to meet with Financial B-TV to do a live broadcast. He is obviously extremely important. This is a great chance to show how front of house services operate as a well-oiled machine.

He is French, as you may be aware, and new to our building, therefore if you have anyone who can speak French on the team, I would give them the task of escorting him to the meeting room. They wish to use the Grand Boardroom Suite on the 40th so although this floor isn't open for any other clients yet, I wish to have a receptionist sitting opposite the lifts on this day to greet the CFO and take him down to meet the camera crews. If you think we'll need a temp, organise one yourself from www.frontrecruitment. co.uk as I don't want any mistakes.

Regards

Richard

Subject: Dying to know

From: Jason
To: Holly

Come on, tell me? Must have been good, your phone was off?

From: Holly
To: Jason

It wasn't good.

From: Jason
To: Holly

I couldn't get through to you. I thought you'd be having a wild time?

From: Holly
To: Jason

I didn't want to speak to anyone.

From: Jason
To: Holly

What were you doing?

From: Holly
To: Jason

Crying, mostly.

From: Jason
To: Holly

Holly kitten head, what happened?

From: Holly
To: Jason

He came home. I was lying on the bed, there were candles and rose petals everywhere, I was done up like a cheap whore. He definitely noticed me this time, so that was refreshing. He knelt down by the bed and found he'd put his suit knee in rabbit droppings, so he took his suit off and crawled onto the bed, but then Jessica (the rabbit) jumped through the cat flap to say hello. After he'd run around chasing her for a while and then had her back outside, we started again, but you could see he wasn't really in the mood. With everything else to do, I'd forgotten those boots so I told him to fish them out of the closet, while I rushed to the bathroom to check myself. He found them, but they looked like they'd been in a terrible fight. I'm guessing one of the cats attacked the fur, so to see what else had been attacked he grabbed the side lamp to shine it into the closet, flipped the socket on, there was an explosion, flames shot up the wall and all the electric went off.

Turns out the rabbit had eaten through the wiring and there were bare wires hanging out of the wall.

Toby starts shouting about how he was lucky to be alive and that was just about the end to my romantic evening.

From: Jason
To: Holly

I bet you were quite pleased when it finished?

From: Holly
To: Jason

I was. I went back to the bathroom feeling like lower than I've felt in a while, looking at myself in the mirror the way I was dressed and what an effort I'd made. I felt ridiculous.

From: Jason
To: Holly

You're not ridiculous, he is.

From: Holly
To: Jason

We argued until I fell asleep. I hate trying to sleep on an argument, it's horrible, I like to make up first; he usually does too. We haven't spoken since that moment. Things aren't good.

From: Jason
To: Holly

xxxx

Subject: Your reservation

From: SCOTTISHBREAKS.com
To: Holly

Reference number SCY2/2T988
You're reservation for two is confirmed on the ???? of ??? for two nights
Admin

friday

Subject: Any better?

From: Jason
To: Holly

Things a bit better today?

From: Holly
To: Jason

Not at all. I really wish he'd email me something nice and we'd make up. I keep checking my texts all the time too.

From: Jason
To: Holly

Why worry?

From: Holly
To: Jason

There was a look I saw on his face last night—like one you'd have if you'd been trying to do something tricky like thread a needle and then realised you had the wrong-sized needle or hole or thread.

From: Jason
To: Holly

Could be your imagination.

Subject: Reminder

From: Holly
To: Holly

Wk 3

UK Survey Program

We need your opinion to evaluate products, fill in this simple twenty-page survey for no reason.

Subject: us

From: Toby
To: Holly

I need to talk to you tonight.

From: Holly
To: Toby

What about?

From: Toby
To: Holly

Let's just wait till tonight, might be better.

Subject: Private and confidential

From: Marie
To: Holly

I know this is your private life, Holly, but we've all noticed how down you look today. We all just wanted you to know we're thinking of you, dear.

From: Holly
To: Marie

Thanks, Marie. By the way can you speak French?

From: Marie
To: Holly

No dear, only Spanish

Subject: Re the CFO's visit

From: Holly
To: Richard

Unfortunately no one in my team speaks French.

Regards

Holly

From: Richard
To: Holly

Don't worry, it was just a thought, as long as it all goes smoothly next Friday then no probs.

Richard

From: Holly
To: Richard

I'll organise a temp for that day just to make sure and put Claire up on the 40th to meet the CFO.

Regards

Holly

Subject: Late shift

From: Holly
To: Marie; Aisha; Trisha; Claire

Good news. I've just heard, we'll be getting free taxis from now on, for anyone doing the late shift.

Regards

Holly

Subject: Us

From: Holly
To: Toby

I don't want to wait till tonight.

From: Toby
To: Holly

Who is the receptionist on the 30th floor?

From: Holly
To: Toby

Why?

From: Toby
To: Holly

I think she's following me.

From: Holly
To: Toby

That sounds like you're being a little paranoid, if you ask me.

Subject: Team Alert

From: Holly
To: Claire; Aisha; Marie; Trisha

Are any of you following Toby?

From: Aisha
To: Holly; Marie; Trisha; Claire

We all are. Why? Where's he gone?

From: Holly
To: Claire; Aisha; Marie; Trisha

You are joking??? You're not really following him?

From: Aisha
To: Holly; Marie; Trisha; Claire

Not exactly following, but keeping an eye on him.

From: Holly
To: Claire; Aisha; Marie; Trisha

WHY????

From: Aisha
To: Holly; Marie; Claire; Trisha

Just to see who he's with, where he goes at lunch, that kind of thing. Find out what he's up to, it's fun.

From: Claire
To: Holly; Marie; Aisha; Trisha

We love you and we want to help.

From: Holly
To: Claire; Aisha; Trisha; Marie

CAN YOU STOP PLEASE?

From: Trisha
To: Holly; Aisha; Marie; Claire

I did tell them, Holly, but you know they never listen.

Subject: Following

From: Toby
To: Holly

Are you happy with how things are going?

From: Holly
To: Toby

No.

From: Toby
To: Holly

So what are you saying?

From: Holly
To: Toby

I'm not happy.

From: Toby
To: Holly

So are you saying you think we should have a break?

From: Holly
To: Toby

Why—is that what you think?

From: Toby
To: Holly

I'm not sure, but it's not good the way it is at the moment.

Subject: Help

From: Holly
To: Jason

Are you there? Going very bad with Toby, really really not good.

Subject: us

From: Holly
To: Toby

Really? Maybe it's not good because I never see you???

From: Toby
To: Holly

Maybe it's not good because I never see you sober?

From: Holly
To: Toby

If you were home more I wouldn't need to sit at home with a glass of wine.

From: Toby
To: Holly

No one needs to drink.

From: Holly
To: Toby

I never said they do! And if you'd notice me at all, you'd know I haven't had a glass of wine for two weeks now.

From: Toby
To: Holly

If you want to have fun all the time, you can, don't change for me, it's just not the way I want to live.

From: Holly
To: Toby

You think I've been having fun? It's not fun sitting at home alone drinking while you've been off in France without me, and maybe that's why my team want to follow you because they think you're having an affair????

From: Toby
To: Holly

Your team?

From: Holly
To: Toby

Yes.

From: Toby
To: Holly

You're the manager there now?

From: Holly
To: Toby

Yes.

From: Toby
To: Holly

When did that happen? You never said?

From: Holly
To: Toby

A while ago. I've been waiting for you to notice for weeks, I've been dropping huge hints.

From: Toby
To: Holly

That's incredible, that's brilliant, you should have just told me.

From: Holly
To: Toby

It's even been on my signature, Toby. I was so excited, but the longer it went on, the less exciting it seemed. You don't ever listen to anything I've got to say or do anyway, so what would be the point in telling you?

From: Toby
To: Holly

I do listen to you but I am busy thinking about work a lot of the time, and you do say a lot of crazy things which don't need my full attention, you must admit.

From: Holly
To: Toby

What crazy things?

From: Toby
To: Holly

You're always asking me strange questions, like do fish swim backwards. Waking me up and asking me why the moon doesn't affect the water in the bath????

From: Holly
To: Toby

Do you know why I ask these stupid questions???

From: Toby
To: Holly

No, tell me.

From: Holly
To: Toby

This is how sad it's all become. Mostly I ask you because I want to talk to you. I sit here sometimes thinking of something to talk to you about, anything, just so I can have an excuse to email you, so I can get an email BACK from you, because if I didn't we'd go the whole week without talking.

From: Toby
To: Holly

That's not true.

From: Holly
To: Toby

Why don't you check? Why don't you think of how many times you call me, text me or email me? The only time you recently have was to tell me you were going to the toilet or moan about rabbit droppings.

From: Toby
To: Holly

I don't like them, I like cats, I don't even mind rabbits and gerbils and all kinds of other creatures, but I don't want to live with them ALL and find their droppings everywhere. Is that so bad?

From: Holly
To: Toby

No.

From: Toby
To: Holly

Anyway if you want to talk, why don't you just talk to me normally?

From: Holly
To: Toby

I don't want to talk about anything serious with you.

From: Toby
To: Holly

Why?

From: Holly
To: Toby

Because.

From: Toby
To: Holly

Because what????

From: Holly
To: Toby

Because you might say something like, 'It's not good the way it is at the moment' so I bounce over it if it looks like a serious discussion.

From: Toby
To: Holly

Well, it's been on my mind.

Subject: Late

From: Jason
To: Holly

Sorry, been busy here, what's happened, fill me in????

Subject: Us

From: Holly
To: Toby

That's just fantastic that is. I can't believe you. If you hate living with me so much why don't you just move out? All the time I've been looking forward to having you home, you've been dreading it??? Is that what's been happening?

From: Toby
To: Holly

Not at all! I've just been wondering if it's working.

From: Holly
To: Toby

And you've only just thought to say something? I don't believe you????? Well I don't want to be just another Marco, SO GO IF YOU WANT TO.

From: Toby
To: Holly

Come on, we're discussing it.

From: Holly
To: Toby

So I've been on trial? You've been judging me, wondering whether I'm good enough for you have you??? Do you know how that makes me feel????

From: Toby
To: Holly

I haven't been judging you. If you are so concerned why don't you just make an effort to occasionally take a night off the wine?

From: Holly
To: Toby

I don't have a drink problem!!! I haven't touched a drop for two weeks!! But if you want to go—LEAVE ME—don't feel you have to make excuses.

From: Toby
To: Holly

Who? Look don't be silly, come on, I just don't want to carry on like this, that's all.

From: Holly
To: Toby

Just go.

From: Toby
To: Holly

Is that what you want?

From: Holly
To: Toby

I can live on my own, I've done it before. I don't want someone living with me who doesn't want to. You're making it so hard for me, it's obvious you're trying to push me away.

Subject: Help

From: Holly
To: Jason

Dying here, I just told him to leave if he's not happy. Didn't want to say it, just felt I had to stand up for myself.

From: Jason
To: Holly

I think you said the right thing. You've got to give him that option, show that you're strong. He won't want you if you're too wet, stay strong.

Subject: Argument

From: Jason
To: Holly

Has he emailed back yet?

From: Holly
To: Jason

No, it's been twenty minutes and I wish he would. Why is he leaving it this long? He must know what it's doing to me?

Subject: Argument

From: Jason
To: Holly

Any news?

From: Holly
To: Jason

No, I'm shaking, I want to puke. It's horrible, really horrible. Why doesn't he email back, he should say of course he doesn't want to move out, things aren't that bad, that's what he SHOULD SAY!

Subject: take a break

From: Trisha
To: Holly

Are you OK? You want a break?

From: Holly
To: Trisha

No.

From: Trisha
To: Holly

I can cover. Why don't you get some air? You don't look so good.

From: Holly
To: Trisha

I can't go, I'm waiting for an email.

Subject: The answer

From: Holly
To: Jason

I'm going to write and say something like—let's just calm down and meet up tonight and talk, work things out??

From: Jason
To: Holly

You really have to wait, just a bit longer.

From: Holly
To: Jason

All these games again, why does it always have to be like this? I can't wait, I'm dying, it's been two hours, can't work, can't speak. I've got to call him, no one should have to feel this, ever, I want to call him, why doesn't he call me?

From: Jason
To: Holly

Don't do it, Holly, it's time he learnt.

From: Holly
To: Jason

LEARNT WHAT???

From: Jason
To: Holly

Learnt you don't need him, good riddance if you ask me.

From: Holly
To: Jason

Jason, I'm pregnant, I'm fucking pregnant, I'm pregnant with his fucking baby, Jason.

From: Jason
To: Holly

What!!!!!????

From: Holly
To: Jason

I'm pregnant.

From: Jason
To: Holly

When, why didn't you tell me?

From: Holly
To: Jason

Found out last week.

From: Jason
To: Holly

Are you sure?

From: Holly
To: Jason

YES I AM SURE

From: Jason
To: Holly

Oh God, does he know?

From: Holly
To: Jason

No.

From: Jason
To: Holly

Call him, tell him. Maybe he's just been called away from his desk??? Maybe he's in a meeting?

From: Holly
To: Jason

He's not.

From: Jason
To: Holly

How do you know?

From: Holly
To: Jason

Because I just called him and he put the phone down, he's at his desk.

Subject: OK

From: Toby
To: Holly

I think it's best if I move out tonight then.

Subject: Help

From: Holly
To: Jason

Help me, Jason, help me.

From: Jason
To: Holly

What's happened?

From: Holly
To: Jason

Help me, Jason, I want to die. Help, please help.

From: Jason
To: Holly

Stay there, I'm coming now, right now, I'm just getting someone to cover, you should have told me before xxxxx

From: Holly
To: Jason

Hurry, help me Jason, please.

Subject: Why?

From: Holly
To: Toby

Why are you doing this to me? What have I done wrong?

From: Toby
To: Holly

Nothing, you've done nothing wrong.

From: Holly
To: Toby

I can change, tell me what I need to do to change, I'll do it straight away.

From: Toby
To: Holly

You don't need to change at all, Holly.

From: Holly
To: Toby

Then tell me, if it's drink, I won't drink again, I'll never ever ever have an alcoholic drink again, I'll even drink water the rest of my life if that's what you want?????? PLEASE!!!!

From: Toby
To: Holly

Don't, Holly, you don't need to.

From: Holly
To: Toby

Then you'll come home tonight and we'll talk about it.

From: Toby
To: Holly

No, I'm not coming back tonight. I'll go in tomorrow and get my things.

From: Holly
To: Toby

Please, Toby, don't do this, wait there for me, I'm coming up.

Subject: Us

From: Holly
To: Toby

Answer your phone.

Subject: Us

From: Holly
To: Toby

I need to tell you something, it's very important, something you need to know, please, Toby.

Subject: Holly, please

From: Trisha
To: Holly

Holly, leave the desk.

Subject: Come on

From: Trisha
To: Holly

I've called upstairs, Claire's coming down now. You have to leave the desk, you'll get in serious trouble if you stay there. You want me to come with you?

From: Holly
To: Trisha

No, thanks, Trish.

From: Trisha
To: Holly

Baby, go, I can't watch you do this xx

Subject: over

From: Holly
To: Jason

He doesn't even know I'm pregnant and we're over.

month 3

week 1

monday

Subject: Important

From: Richard
To: Holly

Holly

I have just had the pleasure of reviewing last week's stats. For your customer service figures—see below:

Previously Since you took over

Room reservations 10 15

Face to Face Contact 12 17

Telephone etiquette and techniques 12 15

In-house relationships 13 17

Beyond the call of duty 15 18

Amazing! Just brilliant. That gives you a figure of 82. This is astounding in the time you've been here. I'm very pleased for you obviously and, although I haven't had the official nod yet, I do believe it should just be a formality. By this time next week you should have heard the news you've been waiting for. Finally please remember we have the French CFO coming over on Friday. You need to begin getting things in place.

Regards

Richard

From: Holly
To: Marie; Trisha; Claire; Aisha

Hi

You've all done so well. We've hit our targets, so you get the bonus I mentioned. Really good.

Catch up soon.

Thank you, you've been great.

Holly

Subject: Morning

From: Aisha
To: Holly

Hope you're OK.

Love you.

Aisha

Subject: Morning

From: Trisha
To: Holly

Where did you stay?

From: Holly
To: Trisha

Been living with Jason.

From: Trisha
To: Holly

Has he moved out yet?

From: Holly
To: Trisha

Yes.

Subject: Toby

From: Alice
To: Holly

Hope you're OK today. If you want you can come out here and live with me for a bit?

xxx

From: Holly
To: Alice

Thanks, Alice. I'll be OK.

From: Alice
To: Holly

What are you going to do?

From: Holly
To: Alice

Don't know.

From: Alice
To: Holly

Has he moved out?

From: Holly
To: Alice

Yes.

From: Alice
To: Holly

Why don't you stay with Jason another few nights?

From: Holly
To: Alice

I'm OK.

From: Alice
To: Holly

I'm here if you need me, I'll even pay for your ticket.

From: Holly
To: Alice

Got to go, love you.

Subject: Don't look up, whatever you do

From: Trisha
To: Holly

You know why.

From: Holly
To: Trisha

Tell me when he's gone.

From: Trisha
To: Holly

All clear.

From: Holly
To: Trisha

Can you hold the desk for a bit? I need some air.

From: Trisha
To: Holly

Course I can x

Subject: Tonight

From: Jason
To: Holly

Not sure I want you on your own tonight.

From: Holly
To: Jason

I'll be OK.

From: Jason
To: Holly

I presume no contact still?

From: Holly
To: Jason

He walked past.

From: Jason
To: Holly

That must have been hard. Did he look at you?

From: Holly
To: Jason

I don't know, I didn't look up.

From: Jason
To: Holly

Nightmare.

From: Holly
To: Jason

I managed to keep myself from being sick on the desk.

From: Jason
To: Holly

You OK?

From: Holly
To: Jason

Trying not to start blubbering again.

From: Jason
To: Holly

Have you managed?

From: Holly
To: Jason

Just about.

You know since Friday I must have looked at my phone about every twenty seconds, just checking for a text or a missed call. This morning I got in this mad catch22 situation. Someone phoned me and when they'd gone I dialed 121 to check my messages, to see if he'd left one while I'd been engaged. He hadn't. Then, after a few minutes staring at the phone, I decided he might have left one while I was on the phone checking my messages, so I checked them again. This went on about 6 times before I realised I needed to stop before I was strapped to a stretcher and taken away.

From: Jason
To: Holly

I've been there. Horrible times.

From: Holly
To: Jason

I've been living on this fluffy white cloud for so long. Because I loved him so much, I thought he'd feel the same, like we were telepathically linked, thinking the same things about everything. We knew we'd never want anyone else again. When everyone was telling me things weren't as perfect as I thought they were, telling me he was having an affair, all I kept thinking was if they only knew what I knew, they'd know they were wrong.

From: Jason
To: Holly

They probably were wrong. He's just moved out, that's all.

From: Holly
To: Jason

I know and I spent all last night trying to work out why he did and how he could act like that and still be in love with me. I want him to still be in love with me, Jason, even if we've broken up. I worked out a hundred different reasons why he would break up but still be utterly in love with me. I know that sounds pathetic, but I really need to believe it.

From: Jason
To: Holly

I know.

From: Holly
To: Jason

The other thought is just too horrible to think about, and it makes me feel instantly sick when I begin. It's that, as much as I still love him—actually, he doesn't love me anymore, hasn't done for a while, if at all, and certainly won't ever ever ever love me again. I'm going to get some air.

x

From: Jason
To: Holly

Oh, honey, don't do this, it's not going to get you anywhere.

trisha's inbox

Subject: Holly

From: Trisha
To: Jason

She's OK, she's just about holding it together. So he's gone?

From: Jason
To: Trisha

Yes, we went back to check on Sunday and he'd taken all his things, left a short note.

From: Trisha
To: Jason

Nice, she's well shot of him, that's what I say.

From: Jason
To: Trisha

Don't tell her that.

From: Trisha
To: Jason

Why not? I think that's the best thing we can do for her.

From: Jason
To: Trisha

Just don't say that to her at the moment.

From: Trisha
To: Jason

Why?

From: Jason
To: Trisha

Trust me on this one, look after her for me, will you?

From: Trisha
To: Jason

Course I will.

Subject: Holly

From: Trisha
To: Aisha; Claire; Marie

Girls, go easy on me Holls today. Don't no one give her any problems, you all work your socks off.

Subject: Holly

From: Trisha Gillot
To: Les Gillot

She's not talking to me about it, wish she would.

From: Les Gillot
To: Trisha Gillot

Listen to you, you don't talk to no one when you're upset.

From: Trisha Gillot
To: Les Gillot

I do.

From: Les Gillot
To: Trisha Gillot

You don't.

From: Trisha Gillot
To: Les Gillot

What you talking about, Les? I do.

From: Les Gillot
To: Trisha Gillot

No, you never. You didn't tell me about your mole.

From: Trisha Gillot
To: Les Gillot

I would have if it had been a bad one.

From: Les Gillot
To: Trisha Gillot

And you never told Holly neither.

From: Trisha Gillot
To: Les Gillot

No point.

From: Les Gillot
To: Trisha Gillot

You should have told us both. I had no idea why you was being such a cow. You should have told Holly too when she was going through all those interviews, instead of just winding her up more.

From: Trisha Gillot
To: Les Gillot

Had me fun, kept me mind off it.

From: Les Gillot
To: Trisha Gillot

Daft cow.

From: Trisha Gillot
To: Les Gillot

Listen, Les, it's not funny having a mole tested, sitting around like a sparrow waiting to be shot, you try it.

From: Les Gillot
To: Trisha Gillot

No thanks.

From: Trisha Gillot
To: Les Gillot

I don't like being sick. You know I don't.

From: Les Gillot
To: Trisha Gillot

You weren't sick!!

From: Trisha Gillot
To: Les Gillot

Could have been.

From: Les Gillot
To: Trisha Gillot

But you weren't, were you!

From: Trisha Gillot
To: Les Gillot

I'm not having this with you, Les. What do you want? I'm busy.

From: Les Gillot
To: Trisha Gillot

We were talking about Holly!

From: Trisha Gillot
To: Les Gillot

I tell you she's done much better than I ever could anyways. She's made me right proud, the girls all love her here.

From: Les Gillot
To: Trisha Gillot

Course they do, we all love her. You should have her round she can sleep in Ant's room while he's away.

From: Trisha Gillot
To: Les Gillot

I asked her. She don't want to.

From: Les Gillot
To: Trisha Gillot

Poor thing, what we going to do then?

From: Trisha Gillot
To: Les Gillot

Nothing we can do.

From: Les Gillot
To: Trisha Gillot

Want to watch a film tonight?

From: Trisha Gillot
To: Les Gillot

The Nutty Professor's on?

From: Les Gillot
To: Trisha Gillot

Saw it at the cinema. I laughed twice, once when I farted and once when I smelt it.

From: Trisha Gillot
To: Les Gillot

You're a classy man, Les.

Subject: Snooping

From: Trisha
To: Jason

Would you think bad of me if I said we'd all been a bit sneaky?

From: Jason
To: Trisha

Sneakykaneeky, I love sneaky??? I live off sneaky pie while supping naughty snoop-soup. I'm the one you always see at the back of the restaurant; his eyes glowing with succulent secrets and cheeks half full of someone else's business!

From: Trisha
To: Jason

That sounds a bit rank.

From: Jason
To: Trisha

Does, doesn't it? So tell me, bad bad, bad bad bad Trisha, what fun have you been up to?

From: Trisha
To: Jason

We've been listening in to calls. You know what it's like, they phone in and you put them through to an extension and forget to hang up?

From: Jason
To: Trisha

No.

From: Trisha
To: Jason

Don't lie.

From: Jason
To: Trisha

I'm sorry, Trisha. I don't do that because our console won't let us and they can tell we're still on the line, it's pathetic.

From: Trisha
To: Jason

Well, we can, and before you know it, you're there, listening in, and you're on the edge of your seat because for once they're not rattling on about acquisitions, they're talking about an infected foot or some affair or something.

From: Jason
To: Trisha

So come on, tell all, what did you hear, you naughty eavesdropper?

From: Trisha
To: Jason

Not me, Claire this time and she didn't know who it was, but her ears pricked up when she hears Toby's name and realises it's his dad saying something about them meeting his new girlfriend. We reckon it's someone in the company.

From: Jason
To: Trisha

Bastard! When are they meeting this company slut???

From: Trisha
To: Jason

Two weeks' time.

From: Jason
To: Trisha

Where?

From: Trisha
To: Jason

Waterloo station.

From: Jason
To: Trisha

Are we going?

From: Trisha
To: Jason

Damn right we are.

From: Jason
To: Trisha

Right, he's in for it. I might even take a few of the boys with me!

From: Trisha
To: Jason

What? To lay into him?

From: Jason
To: Trisha

Verbally, Trisha, verbally, we don't fight. I was thinking a big group of us could stand a safe distance away, jeering and leering and gesticulating (I say boys, I mean more like girls really, from the bar).

From: Trisha
To: Jason

Wonder who she is then?

From: Jason
To: Trisha

My poor Holly, it's just not fair. I think I'm going to kidnap her and take her abroad and put her somewhere where she can miss all this, on a beach somewhere hot. Got any money?

From: Trisha
To: Jason

No.

From: Jason
To: Trisha

No me neither. Right, got to go.

x

holly's inbox

tuesday

Subject: Morning

From: Jason
To: Holly

You sleep much last night?

From: Holly
To: Jason

Between checking my phone and imagining I kept hearing his footsteps coming down and checking the window, not a lot. But I did.

From: Jason
To: Holly

What are you going to do then?

From: Holly
To: Jason

Don't know Jason. I'll think of something. It's a nice feeling you know.

From: Jason
To: Holly

What is?

From: Holly
To: Jason

Knowing there's someone tiny inside me, snuffled up, growing, needing me.

From: Jason
To: Holly

It must be wonderful. Have you decided what to do about Toby?

From: Holly
To: Jason

What do you mean?

From: Jason
To: Holly

Are you going to tell him?

From: Holly
To: Jason

Tried, can't do it now.

From: Jason
To: Holly

Have you seen him today?

From: Holly
To: Jason

Twice. Looked him in the eyes.

From: Jason
To: Holly

God. So when you ready to go out on the town—you don't have to drink?

From: Holly
To: Jason

I'm not going to go straight out and look for someone else. I don't think I need anyone.

From: Jason
To: Holly

OK.

From: Holly
To: Jason

I think I've always been too needy, I can imagine it's not a very attractive quality.

From: Jason
To: Holly

That's rubbish.

From: Holly
To: Jason

Sometimes I think Tanya is right, I have been childish, I need to grow up because I have another life relying on me now, and we'll be fine together, we really will, just fine because we have each other and that's perfect.

From: Jason
To: Holly

I know you will.

From: Holly
To: Jason

We'll be very very happy, we don't need anyone else in the world.

xxx

Apart from you xx

Thanx x

Subject: Interviews this week

From: Richard
To: Holly

The post room manager is interviewing for a new franking-machine operator. There may be a few who aren't as suited and booted as the people we usually get through the doors so don't be surprised, just send them along to the post room.

Regards

Richard

Subject: Toby

From: Alice
To: Holly

I want to ask you something and I don't want you getting upset.

From: Holly
To: Alice

What?

From: Alice
To: Holly

Can I ask how it happened?

From: Holly
To: Alice

Got drunk, forgot to take the pill, got drunk, forgot to take the second pill, had sex, got pregnant, in that order. I've decided I can't tell him. He'll think I did it on purpose.

From: Alice
To: Holly

Why would he? You told him you weren't interested in children.

From: Holly
To: Alice

I know, but I kept buying all those pets, which surely gives something away?

From: Alice
To: Holly

Believe me he won't have made any connection. Men don't understand the need to look after anything, apart from themselves, although Matt does care about his snakes.
Did you definitely forget?

From: Holly
To: Alice

OF COURSE!!!! What kind of person do you think I am????

From: Alice
To: Holly

Sorry, I just wanted to ask.

From: Holly
To: Alice

God, Alice, that's horrific, I'd never do that, God no. Anyway there's no really chance I'm telling him yet, not unless he comes back to me first.

From: Alice
To: Holly

Why?

From: Holly
To: Alice

Because I'll always think he just came back out of duty, not because he really wanted to. If he finds out that I'm pregnant and hasn't come back to me, then I don't think I could take him back. It's strange, but imagine all your life knowing someone's just with you because they felt obliged to.

From: Alice
To: Holly

I can understand.

xxxx

Subject: Afternoon

From: Jason
To: Holly

What's it like then?

From: Holly
To: Jason

What?

From: Jason
To: Holly

Being pregnant?

From: Holly
To: Jason

It would be the most wonderful thing in the world, if the father was in love with me, but as it is, it's like having something you've wanted all your life, but not being allowed to fully relax and enjoy it.

From: Jason
To: Holly

I'm still jealous.

From: Holly
To: Jason

xxx love you.

Subject: Excited

From: Mum
To: Holly

Holly
Has there been any news on your job yet? You're meant to be getting the permanent position this week, and we're all very excited, and so very proud of you.
Love Mum

Subject: Cancellation Ref 6790

From: Holly
To: SCOTTISH HOLIDAYS

I'm sorry I have to cancel my reservations please.

> **From:** Scottish Holidays
> **To:** Holly
>
> We have cancelled your booking. Unfortunately there is a cancellation fee of £100.
>
> Admin

Subject: Meeting

> **From:** UnknownAngel101@Yahoo.co.uk
> **To:** Holly
>
> We should meet. I want to talk to you, so very much.

wednesday

Subject: Morning

> **From:** Jason
> **To:** Holly
>
> Peanut pudding, where are you?

> **From:** Holly
> **To:** Jason
>
> Have you been emailing me from Unknown Angel?

> **From:** Jason
> **To:** Holly
>
> No?

> **From:** Holly
> **To:** Jason
>
> Promise?

> **From:** Jason
> **To:** Holly
>
> Promise, why?

From: Holly
To: Jason

Someone has, it's a bit spooky. I thought it was you and I've been waiting for the joke, some punch line, but there hasn't been one.

From: Jason
To: Holly

Definitely not me. You always know when I'm sending you rubbish. What do they say?

From: Holly
To: Jason

Saying stuff they know about my secrets or something.

From: Jason
To: Holly

Oh that's very weird. Yuck, creepy, you should report it.

From: Holly
To: Jason

I will do.

From: Jason
To: Holly

What secrets are you hiding anyway? Do you have secrets I don't know about?

From: Holly
To: Jason

Not many. Got to do something, email me later.

xx

From: Jason
To: Holly

I will.

Subject: Hotmail

From: Holly
To: Trisha

You haven't been emailing me from a set up yahoo account called unknownangel have you?

From: Trisha
To: Holly

No, darling, why would I want to do that?

From: Holly
To: Trisha

Don't know, someone is. I'm getting some kind of stalking spam coming through.

From: Trisha
To: Holly

You should tell the IT team.

From: Holly
To: Trisha

Thanks.

Subject: Spam

From: Holly
To: IT Admin

Jeff

I keep getting emails from someone called UnknownAngel101@ yahoo.co.uk and I don't know who they are and I don't think I want to read their emails.

Regards

Holly

From: IT Admin
To: Holly

Hi Holly

Do you want us to set something up for that address so their mail will go straight in the trash?

Jeff

Subject: Been thinking

From: Alice
To: Holly

Holly

I've been up all night, trying to work out whether I should say this to you or not and I've decided I should. Please don't get angry with me for sticking my nose in.

You know I'm not one to preach, but I think you need to tell Dad. I can understand you not wanting to tell Mum yet, but you'll be surprised, Dad has really become a lot more easy-going recently. He takes so much in his stride these days. He really has got some useful advice, and I think one of them should be told.

If you don't want to, I am happy to do it for you. It's your decision, but I thought I had to say this.

xxxx

Subject: Hello

From: Jason
To: Holly

How's the little 'un?

From: Holly
To: Jason

Fine. I spend all day just protecting her, or him, from getting knocked into by anyone on the train or in the lift even though there's no bump. Just stroking my tummy, picturing the little life inside, relying on me. I may not make a very good girlfriend, I might be a useless lover, but I'm going to make a good mother.

xxx

I mean it, Jason, you wait and see.

From: Jason
To: Holly

I believe you. I know you will, completely.

Subject: Spammer

From: Holly
To: IT Admin

Jeff

No, that's alright, don't cancel them.

Regards

Holly

Subject: Promotion

From: Holly
To: Jason

By the way, I think you-know-who might be getting the permanent manager's role.

From: Jason
To: Holly

That'll help with the little one and, just in time, you'll get more maternity leave too.

From: Holly
To: Jason

I know.

Subject: Girls night in

From: Aisha
To: Holly

You want to come around to mine tonight? It's not fair that Jason always gets to look after you, I want to, I'm responsible.

From: Holly
To: Aisha

I'd love to. I can come straight from work.

From: Aisha
To: Holly

Yippeee!! We'll have the best time. We can play with Shona and have a *Sex and the City* night or something (after she's gone to bed).

From: Holly
To: Aisha

Sounds perfect.

Subject: Your email

From: Holly
To: Alice

I'll call you in a few minutes. Don't go off feeding flies or anything.
Holly

thursday

Subject: Last night

From: Holly
To: Aisha

I felt very well looked after, it was fun, thanks.
X

Subject: Questions

From: Tanya Mason
To: Holly

Dear Holly

Your team still ask me basic company policy questions they should be asking you. You'll be pleased to know I tell them they should really try viewing you as their manager.

Hope this helps

All the best

Tanya

Subject: Tanya Mason

From: Holly
To: Claire; Aisha; Marie; Trisha

Dear everyone

Please remember in four weeks, on Friday the ? ? ? ? of ? ? ?, we have a charity evening on the 41st Floor, including a 'Party on the Roof Garden.'

Also, I've just had an email from Tanya Mason telling me my team is asking her questions they should be asking me. Please don't do this. If you want to make me feel an inch small, then this is the best way. I really have waded through mountains of DKH company policy info and have more useless DKH information rattling around inside my head than is seriously healthy, so just ask me.

Thanks

Holly

Subject: Bitch

From: Aisha
To: Holly

She's making it up, probably twisting someone's words. I wouldn't ask Tanya anything, unless it was to get out of my personal space - her perfume makes me want to puke.

From: Holly
To: Aisha

Thank you.

Subject: Strange

From: Holly
To: Tanya

Tanya

I think you must have misunderstood something one of them said, but I have spoken to them.

Thank you

Regards

Holly

From: Tanya
To: Holly

Maybe, like other people I know, they find you difficult to talk to?

Tanya

From: Holly
To: Tanya

What is that meant to mean?

From: Tanya
To: Holly

Nothing, I just think team spirit is key here.

Have a wonderful day.

Tanya

Subject: That woman!

From: Holly
To: Trisha

I think Tanya just made a sly dig about Toby, but I'm not sure. Do you think it's gone around yet that we've broken up?

From: Trisha
To: Holly

I'm sure Toby wouldn't say nothing, but you know what this place is like, full of gossips. You sit on the front desk, everyone walks past and you've been looking down, so yes I should think most of the PAs have been guessing.

Fuck her.

Subject: Tomorrow

From: Holly
To: Claire

Hi

This is just a reminder to say that from 11am tomorrow you'll be on the reception desk on the 40th Floor. Financial B-TV will be there from 9am to set things up in Grand Board Room. Michael Bertrand should be there around 1pm, apart from this no other people will be on that floor, so it will be very quiet, sorry.

Holly

From: Claire
To: Holly

I don't mind, I like it quiet. When is the 40th opening for everyone else?

From: Holly
To: Claire

Not for a few weeks.

Subject: Problem

From: Richard
To: Holly

Natasha, one of our traders, has been complaining that her PA changed her booking, because the day before they discovered there would be another four more people. But she still ended up with the same size room. Can you look into it?

Richard

From: Holly
To: Richard

Already have, with this software I can dig up the history of a booking and any changes made, because everyone needs a password to log in.

This booking was never altered by Natasha's PA, so her PA is just saying this to cover herself and shift the blame.

No one on our team was at fault.

Holly

From: Richard
To: Holly

Oh, that's good, I'm going to enjoy this call.

Much appreciated.

Richard

friday

Subject: From Frank Fraser your friendly upstairs neighbour

From: Frank
To: Holly

There's a strange smell coming from through my floorboards. Are you cooking something, Holly?

Frank

From: Holly
To: Frank

No, Frank, I'm at work.

From: Frank
To: Holly

Smells like death.

From: Holly
To: Frank

I can assure you it's not from my flat, and my cooking doesn't smell like that anyway.

Subject: Friday Mornings

From: William Duncan
To: Holly

My uncle has a saying, 'If you only have one leg to walk on, find yourself a crutch, until the other one grows back.' Doesn't make a lot of sense, but I'm here if you need someone to talk to.

From: Holly
To: William Duncan

Thanks.

From: William Duncan
To: Holly

My uncle has another saying: 'Stay away from bearded barbers and bald priests.' I have no idea why, but there it is in case that's useful too.

From: Holly
To: William Duncan

Thanks.

From: William Duncan
To: Holly

He's been divorced twice and wears a toupee, so maybe you should ignore all his sayings, thinking about it.

From: Holly
To: William Duncan

You've put a smile on my face, thanks. So why do I need sayings?

From: William Duncan
To: Holly

Just thought you looked like you needed some.

From: Holly
To: William Duncan

Have I been looking that awful?

From: William Duncan
To: Holly

NO, honestly, radiant, glowing, full of beans, in a good way, not in a 'do I really have to sit near them?' kind of way. Cartwright's doing his rounds, got to look like I'm working. Bye.

Subject: Heeeeeeelp

From: Holly
To: Trisha

Can you tell the CFO they're ready for him upstairs? I've got all this lot to check in.

xx

From: Trisha
To: Holly

No probs.

Subject: Lost Chief Financial Officer

From: Holly
To: Richard

Richard
We checked in Michael Bertrand and sent him up to the top floor.

However, he ended up in the post room—I just had a call from Dave saying Michael turned up down there and there was a bit of confusion before they realised who he was.

He's on his way back upstairs now.

Regards

Holly

From: Richard
To: Holly

I'm cringing, don't tell me Dave interviewed our CFO for a role in the post room???

From: Holly
To: Richard

He sat in a nice meeting room waiting for a half hour, and when Dave turned up he quickly realised the mistake. The CFO laughed about it all, promise.

Subject: Interesting

From: Frank
To: Holly

I knew someone who died once.

From: Holly
To: Frank

Really, Frank, that's awful.

From: Frank
To: Holly

Funny fellow, used to do impressions of Frank Spencer. I mean funny in the head, the impressions were awful, but no one told him, because he had bad hearing and he used to smell a bit too. So you didn't want to get to close to him.

So you say you're not cooking then?

> **From:** Holly
> **To:** Frank
>
> No, Frank.

> **From:** Frank
> **To:** Holly
>
> Is that man still living with you? Maybe it's him?

> **From:** Holly
> **To:** Frank
>
> No, he moved out, alive.

Subject: Mistake

> **From:** Richard
> **To:** Holly
>
> Holly
>
> I have just spoken to Financial B-TV. They say they've already got Michael up there with them and are just starting the interview. I think Dave must be losing his marbles. I've no idea who he thought he'd met.
>
> Richard

Subject: Important

> **From:** Holly
> **To:** Trisha
>
> I spoke to Dave and he thinks they had the CFO down stairs in the post room for the past half hour??

> **From:** Trisha
> **To:** Holly
>
> No, no, that's not my fault, I definitely told him to go up to the top in the lift. I did have another one for Dave though.

From: Holly
To: Trisha

Are you sure you sent the CFO upstairs? What was he wearing?

From: Trisha
To: Holly

A suit.

From: Holly
To: Trisha

No, the CFO had jeans on.

From: Trisha
To: Holly

It's so busy today. I went over to where everyone was sitting and I called out Miguel Berlanga and this man in jeans stood up. I asked if he was Miguel and he was and I asked if he was here for an interview and he said yes, so I told him to go down to the post room.

From: Holly
To: Trisha

You sent MICHAEL the French CFO down to the post room. Please Trisha, where did you send Miguel?

From: Trisha
To: Holly

Oh God, Holly.

From: Holly
To: Trisha

WHAT?

From: Trisha
To: Holly

I must have sent him upstairs.

From: Holly
To: Trisha

Shit.

From: Trisha
To: Holly

He was dressed in a suit.

From: Holly
To: Trisha

??

From: Trisha
To: Holly

You reckon our postie is being interviewed on telly?

From: Holly
To: Trisha

On live TV about his opinion of our share prices, possibly yes.

From: Trisha
To: Holly

Oh no, oh no, sorry, Holly.

Subject: Panic over

From: Mad Frank
To: Holly

I found some cheese in my beard.

Frank

saturday

POSTMAN'S BLUFF!

Cock-up bank puts mailman in front of camera.

In a case of mistaken identity a mailman was sensationally interviewed on live television instead of the Chief Financial Officer of a Bank.

Miguel Bertrand, 59, was on his way for a job interview at DK Huerst, the well-known City Investment bank in Canary Wharf. However, due to an internal cock-up and a confused receptionist, he was sent into a live press conference with Financial BTV. Thinking this was maybe a new strange British interview process, he struggled through the questions and after a while began to enjoy himself. When at last he realised their mistake, did he let on? Did he hell! On live TV, which was being fed to every major TV network, and shooting from the hip, Miguel Bertrand, our lovable Spanish postal worker gives it to you straight!

He says:

• What's wrong with economy?

• Who is Gordon Brown anyway?? Miguel certainly doesn't know, or care

• Are fish and chips on the menu? Not likely

• Why the Spanish football league is the best in the world

• How you get those fiddly little bits of dirt out of your nails after a hard day at work?

• And a million other things including how to bring up five children on 10 Euros an hour

It's all explained in Miguel's delightful Mediterranean accent and after 10 minutes of questioning and obviously not understanding much of his replies, the dozy reporter pressed on: what did he think of the recent rise in DK share prices? His response: don't put your money in shares, put your money in your pocket and then put your hand on your money in your pocket, and hold it there until you get home, then maybe send it to a relative who needs it more than you.

'What about house prices?' 'What about them?' he asked. 'You ask me about house price, I ask you about cigarette prices, about petrol prices, about everything prices, unless you are Mr Richman from Richmond you have a problem in London, no?'

Does he like it here? 'London is incredible, I love London, you have the culture, you have the art, the music and many many people, but you don't have the most important thing in the world, my wife, and she hates it, so until you have my wife, I think you have a problem, for me.'

We don't have a problem with him, we love him.

Next up, see how the BBC mistook a taxi driver for an IT expert

http://uk.youtube.com/watch?v=zG9hZ66TA4E

week 2

tuesday

Subject: Important help

From: Mum
To: Alice; Holly

We've been telling the rector for the parish all about Charlie's charity work in Brazil and he wants us all to help, so we're planning a fundraising event. Does anyone know the name of the village?

Love Mum

Subject: Urgent

From: Richard
To: Holly

Dear Holly

I'm sure you are aware of the seriousness of the situation we are now in.

I have been requested by the CEO to present a report piecing together the series of events which led the wrong people arriving at the wrong interviews on Friday.

I need to present this by 2pm today. Also the CEO wishes to then have a meeting with us at 4pm.

Can you spend the morning compiling a report that shows your version of how the events unfolded in chronological order, names of everyone involved, times of incidents etc with a great attention to accuracy and detail, which I will need by 11.30am.

Kind Regards

Richard

Subject: Rules

From: Jason
To: Holly

I have one for you… you're not allowed to get stressed about all this. It's not good for you, or for small and scrumptious.

From: Holly
To: Jason

I'm trying to cope with it all, but I'll be honest it's so hard. What with Toby's face wanting to appear every time I close my eyes, I barely know what I'm doing and all I really want to do is just bury my head in a pillow and cry. Sorry to sound so pathetic, but I really do, Jason.

From: Jason
To: Holly

Keep working, and it'll keep your mind off things. And keep calm, whatever you do. I know it's easy for me to say.

xxx

Subject: Look at them

From: Trisha
To: Holly

You do anything fun at the weekend?

From: Holly
To: Trisha

Nothing, stayed in.

From: Trisha
To: Holly

I thought you'd be out with Jason partying.

From: Holly
To: Trisha

No.

From: Trisha
To: Holly

See this lot coming in now?

From: Holly
To: Trisha

I saw.

From: Trisha
To: Holly

Looks like all the company mafia's flying in.

From: Holly
To: Trisha

I don't like the way they look at me when they come past. It's like they know something I don't.

From: Trisha
To: Holly

I'm sure this one here's been on the cover of our company brochure.

From: Holly
To: Trisha

You always wonder what they look like and now we know. I have to leave you soon—there's a report for Richard I need to hand in. I'll be back in the afternoon. I've got someone coming down to cover. Will you be OK?
Holly

From: Trisha
To: Holly

Course I will. I keep saying I'm sorry, but I can't think of what else to say. I really am sorry.

From: Holly
To: Trisha

Don't worry, it really could have happened to anyone.

From: Trisha
To: Holly

I messed up and I spoke to Richard earlier and told him if anyone goes it should be me, so I don't want you worrying.

From: Holly
To: Trisha

We haven't killed anyone, no one's been injured. We've done nothing more than point the wrong person through the wrong door. People all over the City are being sent to the wrong room all the time, it happens. In this case it led to a little more controversy than the usual, but that's still all we've done wrong.

x

Subject: A thought

From: Granny
To: Holly

Holly
Do you think I'm too old for male company? Now be honest with me, I need you to tell me truthfully.
Granny.

From: Holly
To: Granny

Of course not, you look amazing. What male company were you thinking about?
Holly

From: Richard
To: Holly

Holly

Also, can you make sure the guys from security are even more aware of unwanted guests than usual; the last thing we want would be reporters sneaking into the building.

Regards

Richard

From: Holly
To: Richard

Of course, I'll talk to them now.

Subject: Up here

From: Claire
To: Holly

Oh dear, we're all so very glum today.

From: Holly
To: Claire

I'm sorry to hear that.

From: Claire
To: Holly

Do you think the bank will go bust?

From: Holly
To: Claire

I don't know.

From: Claire
To: Holly

Banks go bust though, don't they?

From: Holly
To: Claire

They do, Claire.

From: Claire
To: Holly

You think your money's safe then whoosh it's all gone. Look what happened to that Rolling Rock.

From: Holly
To: Claire

Northern Rock, Claire.

Subject: Us

From: Marie
To: Holly

Holly dear, we all want you to know we are right behind you, you know, and if you think it would help we can all talk to Richard for you?

From: Holly
To: Marie

Thank you, but that's OK.

From: Marie
To: Holly

Do you think they will sack you, dear?

From: Holly
To: Marie

I don't know.

From: Marie
To: Holly

What about Trisha? Will they sack her?

From: Holly
To: Marie

I don't know, Marie, they haven't told us anything, but the positive approach from my team is truly refreshing.

Subject: Question

From: Rubber Ron
To: Holly

Now the cat's out of the bag, do you want me to tell your parents Charlie's in prison too?

From: Holly
To: Rubber Ron

No, Ron, I don't!

Subject: Things there

From: Jason
To: Holly

How's it going?

From: Holly
To: Jason

It's kind of irritating at the moment. How's it going with you?

From: Jason
To: Holly

OK, when do you find out the damage?

From: Holly
To: Jason

I'm meeting the big boss this afternoon.

From: Jason
To: Holly

Lordy! Is he called that because he's important/fat/or has a big knob?

From: Holly
To: Jason

Important.

From: Jason
To: Holly

If you want me to, I·could go in first and talk to Mr Big myself.

From: Holly
To: Jason

He doesn't look anything like Mr Big off *Sex and the City*, so stop fantasizing.

From: Jason
To: Holly

I'll stop. Just tell them they should really be thanking you—you put them firmly on the map. Before you came along no one had even heard of DK Huerst, now they're a household name.

From: Holly
To: Jason

I think that's what's upset them.

From: Jason
To: Holly

Well I think it's a piece of television gold as Kate said this morning on GMTV.

From: Holly
To: Jason

It was on GMTV?

From: Jason
To: Holly

And most other channels. You can't turn around without seeing Miguel's face. If you have any more postroom jobs going, I'm your man.

xx

From: Holly
To: Jason

I had this dream last night where I was looking up at the DK Tower and it was like one of those parades you see happening in America where everyone from every window is showering the place with confetti and torn up paper and things and everyone is hanging out of the window, but this time they were all screaming abuse at me, and then I was taken out in front of the building and had my head chopped off.

From: Jason
To: Holly

God, I don't think that will happen.

From: Holly
To: Jason

I hope not. Right, here goes.

wednesday

Subject: I just had another thought

From: Granny
To: Holly

Dear Holly
Please don't think bad of your silly old gran. I don't want a new husband, I think far too much of your dear departed granddad for that. I do though believe that a lady, even in her twilight years, should still be able to enjoy some attention in the way of a meal or nice chat.
Granny

From: Holly
To: Granny

Dear Granny

I think it would be rude not to, and a total waste of your charm and beauty! Do be careful though. Why don't you just invite them over for a glass of wine and a seat in the garden there?

Lots of love

Holly

From: Granny
To: Holly

Oh you are full of good ideas, I think that sounds just great. I'll invite him over next week and let's hope it's not too hot and we get some proper English weather. Let's pray for some thunder, I miss it so much.

Love Granny

Subject: Morning

From: Aisha
To: Holly

Hope you're OK. Will you come to mine one night this week again?

From: Holly
To: Aisha

Sounds good, sweetie, thanks.

xxx

Subject: From Southern Finance

From: Southern Finance
To: Holly

Claimant:

Southern Finance Ltd, PO BOX 339802T, FELTHAM TW

Defendant:

Holly Denham

Flat 8, 121 Springfield Avenue, Maida Vale

COURT DATE JUNE 2008

Do not ignore this claim form. A judgement may be entered against you without further notice.

Claim details and form attached.

Subject: Party next Friday

From: Trisha
To: Holly

You going to this thing Friday?

From: Holly
To: Trisha

You've got to be joking. If I see Toby walking around hand in hand with someone new… no, I feel sick already.

From: Trisha
To: Holly

Well I'm not going if you're not.

Subject: Re Mum's email yesterday

From: Alice
To: Holly

Did you read that from Mum?

From: Holly
To: Alice

Yes, I did.

From: Alice
To: Holly

What are we doing to do?

From: Holly
To: Alice

I have no idea. I've run out of ideas these days.

From: Alice
To: Holly

I keep wondering when she's going to realise this is just rubbish, but she's totally gone for it. I know you have enough problems of your own at the moment and I've been sending you Zaps every day, but I think she's serious about this fundraising thing.

From: Holly
To: Alice

Oh dear.

From: Alice
To: Holly

It's amazing, we've fought all our lives for Mum to notice us, rarely had any praise or recognition. Mum thinks her daughters are usually an embarrassment, whereas Charlie is generally perfect if not a little warped, and get this—yesterday I heard her talking to someone at church and comparing Charlie to one of the African missionaries.

From: Holly
To: Alice

Oh dear.

From: Alice
To: Holly

I wish one day she'd tell me what an amazing job I've done bringing up two wonderful children on my own (before I met Matt) but I won't hold my breath.

From: Holly
To: Alice

So what are we going to do about Charlie?

From: Alice
To: Holly

Even though Charlie obviously doesn't give a shit about them and doesn't care whether they know or not, and thinks it's hysterical that he's locked up, I'm not going to tell them. I think it's kinder to let them have this fantasy about their son than spoil it for them. I've no idea what we're going to do about this village thing, the next thing I read they'll be recommending him for sainthood.

From: Holly
To: Alice

I did tell him to stop emailing about strippers, but I didn't expect this. I'm hoping he'll call me tonight. If he does I'll talk to him about this mess.

From: Alice
To: Holly

OK, and I'll try and figure out a way to stop Mum fundraising.

xxx

PS send him a kiss from me.

From: Holly
To: Alice

I will. x

Subject: Statement

From: Richard
To: Holly

Dear Holly

I need to confirm with you that the statement you have submitted covering the events last Friday is the one you wish us to proceed with. Management wishes to take some action following a press conference earlier. This should happen tomorrow morning at the latest.

Regards

Richard

From: Holly
To: Richard

Hi Richard

Yes, this is how it happened.

Regards

Holly

Subject: Question for you

From: Claire
To: Holly

Do you think she likes men or women?

From: Holly
To: Claire

Who??

From: Claire
To: Holly

Aisha, because she talks about both of them, A LOT.

From: Holly
To: Claire

Then I guess both. Is it busy up there, Claire?

From: Claire
To: Holly

No, not really. I'm building a pyramid using only a biro and a pile of pins. Aisha showed me how. Only mine keeps falling down.

From: Holly
To: Claire

Please don't build anything on the desk.

Subject: Excuse me

From: Holly
To: Aisha

Behave yourself.

From: Aisha
To: Holly

What? Do you have cameras up here?

From: Holly
To: Aisha

Of course I do, so stop it.

From: Aisha
To: Holly

OK. Sorry.

Subject: Statement

From: Richard
To: Holly

Are you 100% certain that is what happened?

From: Holly
To: Richard

Yes, absolutely.

From: Richard
To: Holly

I imagine you are aware the statement conflicts a little with the information I have already gathered, having personally spoken with those involved.

Subject: Holiday

From: Holly
To: Jason

I haven't had a holiday for a while. I think the sun must be very good for a baby. I'll do some research on the web.

Subject: Not received a reply?

From: Richard
To: Holly

Holly

Having worked alongside various reception managers over the years at a number of other blue chip companies, I have had a opportunity to see various management styles and how they each approach a situation.

I would say yours has been the most creative, fun and forward-thinking I've had the pleasure of witnessing. This brings me to your statement; if you insist on going ahead with this I need you to be absolutely clear of the consequences. You will carry the sole blame for Friday's mistake squarely on your shoulders, bringing with it the full force of the company's justified retribution, financial and otherwise.

I just want you to be absolutely clear on what this means.

Richard.

From: Holly
To: Richard

Thank you, Richard, for the compliments and yes I do realise.

Subject: Your email

From: Jason
To: Holly

Where are you going to do then?

From: Holly
To: Jason

Not sure, but I think I might go away some place nice.

xxx

Subject: Meeting

From: CEO
To: Holly; Richard

Dear Holly Denham

On Friday I had decided to take some business associates for a round of golf. We were relaxing in the club house afterwards when it was pointed out we were about to see my Chief Financial Officer give his opinions on the state of the economy and the welcome rise in DK Huerst share prices.

At this point you can imagine my surprise at not recognising my own CFO but instead watching in horror as this bumbling fool took his seat. Realising there had been a mistake I imagined this man would politely inform the interviewer and apologise. However, I believe this may have been the first time anyone had asked his opinion on anything, and nothing was going to stop him now.

The resulting scandal could have seriously hurt our reputation with our investors and share holders. Fortunately I believe they have seen it simply for what it was: a terrible case of mistaken identity.

During your brief reign as our Front of House manager I believe the standards of excellence have actually improved slightly. Your terrible mistakes which resulted in Friday's debacle have, however, left us in a very difficult situation, and after a great deal of consideration we have come to a decision.

Your presence is requested tomorrow at 10am for a meeting with myself, Richard Mosley and Nigel Thorn.

Yours sincerely

Timothy Cartwright

CEO, DK Huerst, 50 Cabot Square, Canary Wharf, London

thursday

Subject: Post swap

From: Jason
To: Holly

Who else knows about it? Have you heard from your Mum yet?

From: Holly
To: Jason

No, I don't think anyone in my family watches the news over there.

From: Jason
To: Holly

Lucky you.

From: Holly
To: Jason

I know.

From: Jason
To: Holly

So to the big question…

From: Holly
To: Jason

Still don't know yet, going to see them any moment.

Subject: Did you know

From: Trisha
To: Holly

I said good afternoon twice so far this morning, and both times I had to suffer the hilarious reply—oh dear, wishing your life away.

From: Holly
To: Trisha

It's a classic.

From: Trisha
To: Holly

So you going for your meeting then?

From: Holly
To: Trisha

Right now. See you later.

x

Subject: Baby

From: Trisha
To: Holly

This can't be good, what they done to you?

From: Holly
To: Trisha

Wasn't good, really not good at all.

xxx

Subject: Your meeting

From: Richard Mosley
To: Holly

Dear Holly

I am sorry this has happened. They have asked that when you email the team about all this you copy me in, so I have an official record of it.

Kind regards

Richard

Subject: Changes

From: Holly
To: Trisha; Marie; Claire; Aisha; Richard Mosley

Dear Team

I have discovered today my position as manager has been terminated. I am allowed to carry on as a receptionist here with limited responsibilities excluding the booking of rooms pending their full investigation, which I've decided to accept. So from tomorrow, I'm back as one of the team. Hope you accept me with open arms.

xxx (I know kisses are totally unprofessional, but I'm not a manager now, so I guess it doesn't matter)

Holly

From: Trisha
To: Holly; Marie; Claire; Aisha; Richard

Richard

That isn't right, I'm not having it. I don't see why Holly's made to suffer from my mistake. If I hand in my notice, will you keep Holly on as manager?

Trisha

From: Richard
To: Trisha; Holly; Marie; Claire; Aisha

Trisha, nothing you do will change this decision and it's not one I have authority to overturn anyway.

I understand everyone will be feeling upset at the moment and this is understandable, but we will have to move on and business will need to continue as normal.

Regards

Richard

Subject: Men

From: Granny
To: Holly

I've invited a man over. He sounds ever so nice. He's coming around next week for tea and maybe a drop of wine, who knows.

xxxx

Love Granny

Subject: Not right

From: Trisha
To: Holly; Marie; Claire; Aisha

I can't believe they've done that, what with all you've done for them too.

From: Claire
To: Holly; Trisha; Marie; Aisha

Will they let you keep the badge, or do you have to give it back?

From: Holly
To: Trisha; Marie; Claire; Aisha

What?

From: Claire
To: Holly; Trisha; Claire; Aisha

I like working for Holly though. I don't want anyone else.

From: Aisha
To: Holly; Trisha; Claire; Marie

Nor me.

From: Marie
To: Holly; Trisha; Claire; Aisha

What is happening, Holly? Do you know who is managing us?

From: Holly
To: Trisha; Marie; Claire; Aisha

No, I don't.

From: Marie
To: Holly; Trisha; Claire; Aisha

Why don't they make Trisha manager?

From: Trisha
To: Holly; Marie; Claire; Aisha

Managing isn't for me.

From: Aisha
To: Holly; Trisha; Claire; Marie

Would you tell us if they had asked you?

From: Trisha
To: Holly; Marie; Claire; Aisha

Yes, and no, I haven' t been asked.

From: Claire
To: Holly; Trisha; Marie; Aisha

I haven't been asked either

From: Aisha
To: Holly; Trisha; Claire; Marie

I was asked yesterday to close my legs while on reception—
apparently you can be seen from the couches at the end through
the glass.

From: Holly
To: Trisha; Marie; Claire; Aisha

No, you can't.

From: Aisha
To: Holly; Trisha; Claire; Marie

You can if you stretch your leg out sideways.

From: Holly
To: Trisha; Marie; Claire; Aisha

Who sits like that? ? ? ?

From: Aisha
To: Holly; Trisha; Claire; Marie

I do.

From: Holly
To: Trisha; Marie; Claire; Aisha

I'm going to miss managing you, Aisha. Good luck to the next victim. (meant in the nicest possible way)

From: Aisha
To: Holly; Trisha; Claire; Marie

I'll make their life hell.

From: Claire
To: Holly; Trisha; Marie; Aisha

Maybe we should have a protest, like a sit in?

From: Trisha
To: Claire; Holly; Trisha; Marie; Aisha

That's actually what we're paid to do, Claire, they wouldn't notice the difference.

Subject: Ranixo

From: Nigel Thorn
To: Claire; Holly; Trisha; Marie; Aisha; Tanya Mason

To the Team

I am pleased to announce with immediate effect outsourcing of our reception client services to Ranixo Corporate Facilities Group.

This will mean you no longer work directly for DK Huerst but work instead for the Catering and Facilities company Ranixo on site at DK Huerst. Ranixo have a great deal of expertise in Client

Services and we are pleased they have won the reception contract here for the next five years.

A full information pack will be sent out to you to explain the changes, however I must stress to you that very little will be different in your day to day duties. Of course salaries and benefits will remain the same for existing staff.

If you have any queries or questions please first visit their website where there is a FAQ section.

Yours sincerely

HR Director

Subject: Ranixo

From: Tanya Mason
To: Holly; Trisha; Marie; Claire; Aisha; Richard

Dear Team

As the new Client Services Director, I will be overseeing Ranixo's contractual operations here on a day to day basis, and welcome you to our company. I hope you enjoy working for Ranixo. My management style is fair but firm. If we are to hit our expected targets over the coming weeks, we will need to pull together and work as a unit.

I intend to introduce some tough new measures which, if you embrace them, will help you improve yourself in the long term, but for now I would just like to say I am looking forward to working with you all and feel together we will make an unbeatable team.

Tanya Mason

Subject: Formal Handover

From: Tanya Mason
To: Holly

Dear Holly

I request a meeting with you for tomorrow and I would spend the evening preparing your handover notes.

Please bring with you a disk with every form, file, and document used during your time as manager.

I expect a full break down of all stats and an updated journal of how things ran.

Yours sincerely

Tanya Mason

Subject: Tanya

From: Trisha
To: Holly

Worst nightmare. You going to quit?

From: Holly
To: Trisha

Don't know, I'm in shock.

From: Trisha
To: Holly

You and us the same.

friday

Subject: PARTY

From: William Duncan
To: Holly

Fancy accompanying me to this DK party on the roof thing next week? Thought I could prove myself the nice guy I really am?

William

Subject: Tanya Mason

From: Holly
To: Jason

I've just come out of meeting with Tanya.

She told me as sweet as pie that, in the circumstances, she could understand if I felt unable to carry on and that the company would accept my notice if I wished to leave immediately.

From: Jason
To: Holly

Bitch. I hate her.

From: Holly
To: Jason

However, if I decided to stay, off the record, this would embarrass the company, and that it may be best for all concerned if I did leave.

From: Jason
To: Holly

Oh my god, I am going to start a website right now called 'Tanya Mason is a slut bag bitch' and invite people to put imaginary pins in her, or blow her up with a puffer pump or just slap her with a bit wet paddle.

From: Holly
To: Jason

She wants me to think about it and let her know.

From: Jason
To: Holly

What are you going to do?

From: Holly
To: Jason

Still deciding. I really think I'd be happier if I left. Working here since Toby finished with me has been hell. My heart keeps breaking each time he walks past. He looks sad too, and I don't know if it's because he feels guilty about something, or because he regrets it or because he's just had something bad for lunch. I just want it all to go away, I wish I could go back in time.

I HATE IT ALL.

From: Jason
To: Holly

Calm down, but please don't give in to that smirking cow. Women like that should never win. Whatever you do you have to tell them about your maternity leave.

From: Holly
To: Jason

How can I?

From: Jason
To: Holly

But if you don't, you could end up with nothing.

From: Holly
To: Jason

You know I can't do it yet.

Subject: Training

From: Tanya Mason
To: Trisha; Aisha; Marie; Claire; Holly

The mistakes from last week cannot be repeated and therefore I will be spending the coming days updating our procedures and systems to ensure nothing like this can happen again. I will spend the week sitting with each of you to see what areas you can improve on.

Yours sincerely

Tanya Mason

Subject: Our meeting

From: Holly
To: Tanya

Thank you for your kind offer of accepting my immediate resignation. I feel my experience and skills are best suited here though and I still feel I have a lot to offer the team.

So I'm staying. :)

Holly

From: Tanya
To: Holly

Dear Holly

This is your decision but I must warn you that I will not stand for a slack attitude just because you used to manage here. In fact, in light of your recent mistakes I would say you would have to try harder than the others in the team. Finally I abhor the use of smiley faces in emails. I do not expect to see any on professional communication again; this is your first warning in this matter.

Tanya Mason

Subject: PARTY

From: Holly
To: William Duncan

That sounds nice, thank you.

Subject: Firm Management Style

From: Holly
To: Tanya

Tanya

Is this one of those tough new measure's you wish to introduce, the removal of smiley faces from emails?

Gosh, whatever next? This sweeping regime is both exciting and enlightening.

Holly

From: Tanya
To: Holly

You'll discover what's next, when I email all my staff.

Tanya

Subject: Improvements

From: Tanya
To: Holly; Marie; Trisha; Claire; Aisha

Dear receptionist team

I have spent the afternoon reading through all the reports and references which have been given to me, and on the whole, I feel that you have been doing well. There are, of course, many areas that we may be able to improve upon. Being in charge of both catering and reception I have been given an office on the 22nd floor and I want you to feel free to come in whenever you want (as long as your station is covered) should you have the need to discuss something. As Holly is currently on minimized duties and cannot book rooms, she will be ferried off to another one of our sites for a few days where we are short staffed.

Have a wonderful weekend

Tanya Mason

PS Details for you Holly—9am. P. Simms & Sons, 28 Harriford Way, Wandsworth.

Don't be late, sweetie.

trisha's
inbox

week 3

monday

From: Trisha
To: Holly

You in there yet?

Subject: Girls

From: Marie
To: Aisha, Trisha, Claire

Did anyone talk to Holly at the weekend? Do we think she will go today?

From: Aisha
To: Marie, Trisha, Claire

I spoke to her briefly. She hadn't made up her mind.

From: Trisha
To: Marie, Aisha, Claire

I hope she doesn't, I wouldn't do it. Now you sure you're going to be alright on Friday, Aisha?

From: Aisha
To: Marie, Trisha, Claire

No, I'm going to be sick.

From: Trisha
To: Marie, Aisha, Claire

You know what I mean. Don't go out Thursday night thinking you've got Friday to lay in bed, because you won't make it to Waterloo in time, I know you.

From: Aisha
To: Marie; Trisha; Claire

Aunty Trisha, I'm a responsible adult, trust me.

From: Trisha
To: Marie; Aisha; Claire

OK, well you just make sure you don't miss him. He's meeting her at Waterloo and the train's arriving at 10am. I want you there an hour early, OK?

From: Aisha
To: Marie; Trisha; Claire

Hassle hassle hassle, Aunty.

From: Trisha
To: Marie; Aisha; Claire

And less of the Aunty. If you were my niece you wouldn't be working around dressed like that, I'm telling you.

From: Claire
To: Trisha; Marie; Aisha

I think she always looks nice.

From: Trisha
To: Marie; Aisha; Claire

This isn't a dating line, Claire, and don't think you should start with Aisha.

From: Marie
To: Claire; Trisha; Aisha

No, I must agree I don't think Aisha is the one for you. We'll find you a nice girl, wont we, girls?

From: Aisha
To: Marie; Trisha; Claire

I am reading these emails you know!

From: Trisha
To: Marie; Aisha; Claire

WE KNOW!

Subject: Morning

From: Trisha
To: Holly

You there, girl?

Subject: Holly

From: Trisha
To: Jason; Les

Jason, you'll keep me informed when you know something, won't you?

From: Jason
To: Trisha; Les

Of course, Trisha, I am your eyes and ears, my lovely, and I want to know as soon as Aisha sees something on Friday. Is she taking photos too?

From: Trisha
To: Jason; Les

She'll try. I don't want her getting seen though.

From: Les
To: Trisha; Jason

Hey, it makes a change, don't it, Trisha? We hear nothing from Jason for months, no calls, no emails, no nothing, it takes Holly to have a problem for us to hear from him.

From: Jason
To: Les, Trisha

Oh, you're such a bitch, Les!!!!

From: Les
To: Trisha, Jason

True though init.

From: Jason
To: Les, Trisha

I asked you both loads of times to come out for drinks, I gave up asking. And Les, is it cause I'm gay? Is that it???

From: Les
To: Trisha, Jason

Didn't know you was—you don't have one of those funny walks?

From: Jason
To: Les, Trisha

Oh, take that back. I'm as gay as a pink penguin and I'll walk like one too if that's what you like, Les?

From: Les
To: Trisha, Jason

Anyway, you just don't like me cause I'm from the Wharf, is that it? Not posh enough for you?

From: Trisha
To: Jason, Les

Les, have you finished flirting with him?

From: Les
To: Trisha, Jason

Listen to her—flirting! He started it.

From: Jason
To: Trisha, Les

He was flirting, Trisha, I felt a definite flirt.

From: Les
To: Trisha, Jason

Trisha, tell him!

From: Trisha
To: Jason, Les

Both of you shut up. It's like sitting on a train between two ten year olds. Les, haven't you got some work to do?

From: Les
To: Trisha, Jason

No!

From: Trisha
To: Jason, Les

Well I have. I'll catch up later, Jason.

Subject: Hi

From: Holly
To: Trisha

I'm here.

From: Trisha
To: Holly

What's it like?

From: Holly
To: Trisha

Grubby and everyone keeps calling me 'the temp'.

From: Trisha
To: Holly

You can't stay down there.

From: Holly
To: Trisha

What other choice do I have? I can't exactly refuse Tanya, can I? I'm here, I'm a receptionist here, that's all I know. I'm just getting through.

From: Trisha
To: Holly

OK, good, honey.

Subject: Holly

From: Jason
To: Trisha

So why has Tanya put Holly on another site? What's that for?

From: Trisha
To: Jason

Gets her out of the way.

From: Jason
To: Trisha

What for?

From: Trisha
To: Jason

We think it's so she can get her claws into Toby. You know he just pulled off some big deal, made himself a big bonus. They reckon it could have been anything up to a million.

From: Jason
To: Trisha

NO!!!!

From: Trisha
To: Jason

I know, big time init.

From: Jason
To: Trisha

So he leaves Holly and a week later makes a fortune?

From: Trisha
To: Jason

Doesn't look good, does it. Tanya's always liked him, and now she's like a fly on shit and she's put Holly in some solicitors in Wandsworth to get her out the way.

From: Jason
To: Trisha

Holly really shouldn't be on her own.

From: Trisha
To: Jason

I know, what with what she's going through, I want her here with me.

From: Jason
To: Trisha

She's told you then?

From: Trisha
To: Jason

Course she has, I'm her Aunty Trisha, she tells me everything.

From: Jason
To: Trisha

Do you think this much stress could be damaging then?

From: Trisha
To: Jason

Course it could.

From: Jason
To: Trisha

She's got to be careful then, she'd fall apart if she had a miscarriage.

> **From:** Trisha
> **To:** Jason

Jason, anyone would fall apart if they had a miscarriage, so are you telling me she's pregnant?

Subject: Don't you be going nowhere

> **From:** Trisha
> **To:** Jason

Answer me???

Subject: OI!!!!

> **From:** Trisha
> **To:** Jason

I said answer me! You telling me she's pregnant???

> **From:** Jason
> **To:** Trisha

I thought you knew.

> **From:** Trisha
> **To:** Jason

No I didn't know she was pregnant. My baby's pregnant???

> **From:** Jason
> **To:** Trisha

Yes.

> **From:** Trisha
> **To:** Jason

Oh God, what, how?

> **From:** Jason
> **To:** Trisha

The usual way.

From: Trisha
To: Jason

Toby?

From: Jason
To: Trisha

Of course.

From: Trisha
To: Jason

Does he know?

From: Jason
To: Trisha

No.

From: Trisha
To: Jason

And she's over there on her lonesome, sitting on her own without her friends?

From: Jason
To: Trisha

I know, not good is it.

From: Trisha
To: Jason

Oh my poor little girl, oh Holly.

holly's
inbox

From: Holly
To: Trisha

They've realised I'm not a temp now, but my boss here keeps referring to me as 'Polly or whoever'.

From: Trisha
To: Holly

Nice.

Subject: Expenses

From: Tanya
To: Holly

I noticed you put in a claim for a taxi last night? Can you explain this?

From: Holly
To: Tanya

Yes we have a taxi allowance for getting home after a late shift. My shift finished at 11pm.

From: Tanya
To: Holly

This is a privilege for the contract at DK Huerst, you are not at DK Huerst. There is no such agreement with the client you are stationed at. So tonight you will have to get the bus back or pay for a taxi yourself, is that clear?
Tanya

Subject: Hey

From: Trisha
To: Holly

You just look after yourself, and none of that stressing, you hear me?

From: Holly
To: Trisha

I hear you.

From: Trisha
To: Holly

You just stay put, I don't want you moving around too much, you get them to get run around after you. You're not too close to the door are you?

From: Holly
To: Trisha

No, Trisha.

From: Trisha
To: Holly

You eating OK?

From: Holly
To: Trisha

Why?

From: Trisha
To: Holly

Just making sure you're OK.

From: Holly
To: Trisha

Have you been speaking to Jason?

From: Trisha
To: Holly

Yes.

From: Holly
To: Trisha

He tell you?

From: Trisha
To: Holly

By mistake.

From: Holly
To: Trisha

I couldn't get hold of him this morning, it makes sense now. Tell him to stop hiding from me, I like speaking to him.

From: Trisha
To: Holly

I will, you know you should put in for maternity leave quick though, I'd put in for it now.

From: Holly
To: Trisha

I can't, Toby doesn't know, and I don't want him hearing it from Tanya.

From: Trisha
To: Holly

Why don't you just tell him then?

From: Holly
To: Trisha

Because I still have some tiny hope I'm clinging to that he comes back to me before he hears it. I would always wonder if he did it out of sympathy otherwise.

From: Trisha
To: Holly

If you don't put in for maternity leave soon, Tanya will get you fired for one reason or another then you'll lose it all.

From: Holly
To: Trisha

Why doesn't he call me, Trisha?

From: Trisha
To: Holly

I thought you'd decided to move on.

From: Holly
To: Trisha

I tried.

From: Trisha
To: Holly

Not easy is it.

From: Holly
To: Trisha

I'm not getting very far.

From: Trisha
To: Holly

Wish I was there with ya.

From: Holly
To: Trisha

What's going to happen Trisha?

From: Trisha
To: Holly

Can't tell you.

From: Holly
To: Trisha

Each night, when I turn the corner into my road, I always imagine I'll see him there outside my flat, with his bags. But even when I don't I then decide there's a chance he's found a way in, maybe he's putting on the kettle about to surprise me with flowers.

From: Trisha
To: Holly

What's the place there like?

From: Holly
To: Trisha

Alright, I've been cleaning the fridge all morning. The other girls here are using me for any jobs they've been putting off.

From: Trisha
To: Holly

Tell them to get lost.

From: Holly
To: Trisha

I'm feeling a bit lost, Trisha.

From: Trisha
To: Holly

I know you are.

From: Holly
To: Trisha

I keep thinking about Toby. Can I tell you some things? Do you have time?

From: Trisha
To: Holly

Always got time for you darling.

From: Holly
To: Trisha

Every time I open a email, I get one of those lurches, the ones you get when you feel your ankle go in heels and you know you're about to fall and you get that rush. Every time the phone buzzes, even if it's the bloody alarm, I'm hoping the phone's malfunctioning and it's a call from him. I miss his voice, his touch, his smell, even when he was away I used to sleep on his side of the bed. I know people think he's serious, but he's not. He was always making me laugh; he'd make complete strangers laugh and feel good about themselves. I miss having someone to answer the door to strange-looking salesmen and even miss being told off for leaving my CDs in a pile on the floor.

Now he's gone I keep forgetting to put a glass of water by the bed, because he always did it for me. I miss being forced to watch the occasional thriller instead of a comedy or romance and I miss sleeping on his chest, I'm sorry, I drifted off there. Writing about him was nice, and bad.

I really miss him, Trisha.

From: Trisha
To: Holly

You just keep positive over there and don't take no sh*t from them.

From: Holly
To: Trisha

I want to go back to DK Huerst. I feel like I'm stuck in a foreign country here.

Subject: Brazil

From: Mum
To: Holly

We're thinking of booking some flights to go out and see Charlie. Do you know what airport he's nearest?

From: Holly
To: Mum

No, Mum.

From: Mum
To: Holly

OK, do you know where we can send the money?

From: Holly
To: Mum

No, Mum, I don't, sorry.

From: Mum
To: Holly

You're not being very helpful.

From: Holly
To: Mum

Sorry.

From: Mum
To: Holly

You'd think you'd make an effort. Your brother is doing something really inspiring out there and needs all our support. Your lack of enthusiasm is concerning me.

Love Mum

From: Holly
To: Mum

By the way, I didn't get the promotion full time in case you wondered.

From: Mum
To: Holly

Oh, was it this week?

From: Holly
To: Mum

Yes.

From: Mum
To: Holly

Oh, Holly, why not? At last you do something I can really tell people about and within a month you've lost it. Really, darling, what did you do wrong this time?

From: Holly
To: Mum

I nearly bankrupted the bank by wiping millions off their share price.

From: Mum
To: Holly

What?

From: Holly
To: Mum

Yes, also, I'm not with Toby anymore, we split up.

From: Mum
To: Holly

Holly, you poor thing, that's awful for you. Slightly relieving though, I never liked him.

From: Holly
To: Mum

You always said he'd break my heart, and he did, you were right.

From: Mum
To: Holly

Oh no. I don't want to say I told you so, but maybe you'll listen to me in future?

From: Holly
To: Mum

I will, also I'm pregnant with his child.

From: Mum
To: Holly

WHAT?

From: Holly
To: Mum

Oh and Charlie's in prison.

Hope you're well.

Lots of love

Holly

PS next time you see Alice do mention how well she's done, all those years bringing up two children on her own.

wednesday

Subject: Float Receptionist

From: Tanya
To: Holly

Holly

Would you like to come back and work at DK Huerst?

From: Holly
To: Tanya

Yes, Tanya.

From: Tanya
To: Holly

Then do you think you can improve your attitude?

From: Holly
To: Tanya

Yes, Tanya.

From: Tanya
To: Holly

I want you to behave as well as my other little receptionists? Is this going to be possible?

From: Holly
To: Tanya

Yes, Tanya.

From: Tanya
To: Holly

Good girl, I'll see you at 9am sharp.

Subject: Your news

From: Dad
To: Holly

I don't like using this thing. I have never used it before and would prefer to write to you, but with the post these days it will take too long and I want to tell you this now. I'm going to keep this brief, I hit one letter and two come out, my fingers are getting worse. It's just typical of your granny that while I sit here with arthritis, a bad liver and glaucoma she can still thread a needle with a bottle of Gin in one hand.

I had a chat with Alice last week and she told me your situation.

It's taken me a while to work out how to put things into words and now of course you've told your mother so once again I'm slow off the starting blocks.

I'm afraid my views on this kind of thing have always been black and white. You should never have a child out of wedlock and you should always stick by your man, no matter what he does and so on.

These aren't just my views, these are the views of most people of my age.

When you had that terrible time with Sebastian during your turbulent marriage, I knew he was bad news from the start, but you married him and so I said nothing.

I rarely regret things. I think you make mistakes so you can learn from them, but not letting you know what I thought of Sebastian at the time will always be something I regret. You probably wouldn't have listened to me anyway, but at least I would have done what a father is supposed to do, give good advice. I regret that, I regret it deeply and I'll tell you now, it still haunts me.

Now I hear you are pregnant. If you tell me you are in love with a good man and he loves you back then I would be over the moon, but it's better to have no man at all, than a bad one.

So I think you will make the best mother there is.

You do it, if that's what you want and I'll be the best grandpa there is too.

Love

Dad

PS Don't reply to this, I am switching it off now before your mother gets home.

Subject: Pass

From: Holly
To: Tanya

Shall I give them back my pass here, or will I be working back here again?

Holly

From: Tanya
To: Holly

Holly

No, you can hand it back for the moment. Also tomorrow afternoon, can you report to my office where you will pick up a different uniform as the catering team are severely short staffed and need an extra waitress.

Regards

Tanya

thursday

Subject: Events

From: Natasha
To: Holly

I'm sure the champagne for my event was over-ordered. Is this something you can help me with?

From: Holly
To: Natasha

No, Natasha, I'm no longer manager here.

From: Natasha
To: Holly

Oh yes, I forgot, sorry.

Natasha

Subject: Company event

From: William Duncan
To: Holly

Don't forget you're my date tomorrow night. Hope you've got yourself a party frock.

From: Holly
To: William Duncan

I'm not sure I'm up to it, Will.

From: William Duncan
To: Holly

You need to relax and have fun and I need to have the most beautiful woman in the company on my arm.

You'll have fun really, I promise.

From: Holly
To: William Duncan

Thanks.

Subject: Party

From: Holly
To: Jason

I'm thinking about going to a company do on Friday.

From: Jason
To: Holly

WHY???

From: Holly
To: Jason

Because I've been asked to go.

From: Jason
To: Holly

By who???

From: Holly
To: Jason

Some guy who's been sending me emails.

From: Jason
To: Holly

What kind of emails? Flirtatious sexual ones?

From: Holly
To: Jason

Just flirtatious.

From: Jason
To: Holly

You secretive little fox, you do keep things from me then!??

From: Holly
To: Jason

Not really, didn't think much of it, but maybe it would be nice to go. I really don't know what would be nice any more. Do you think it's a good idea? You decide.

From: Jason
To: Holly

No, don't be doing that, don't be collapsing on me, stand back up, come on.

From: Holly
To: Jason

Don't want to.

From: Jason
To: Holly

Get up, Private Denham!

From: Holly
To: Jason

No.

From: Jason
To: Holly

You have to. If you don't fight, who's going to, hmmm????! What are you made of?

From: Holly
To: Jason

Pudding.

From: Jason
To: Holly

No, you're not.

From: Holly
To: Jason

Pudding, jelly and custard.

From: Jason
To: Holly

No you're making me hungry. Keep your wits about you, young lady. Little urchin needs someone strong, OK.

X

From: Holly
To: Jason

OK.

trisha's
inbox

Subject: the bitch

From: Trisha
To: Jason

She's trying to force Holly out, she's got her waitressing today.

From: Jason
To: Trisha

Oh God, she never told me that.

From: Trisha
To: Jason

Don't think she'd want to talk about it.

From: Jason
To: Trisha

Oh how could she be so mean? Why are there people like that? They shouldn't exist.

From: Trisha
To: Jason

Also she had a bit of hassle on the night bus the other night. Tanya wouldn't let her get a cab. I wish Holly'd just put in for maternity leave.

From: Jason
To: Trisha

She's been sounding very strange to me this week.

From: Trisha
To: Jason

Me too, it's all becoming too much for her I reckon.

Subject: Waterloo

From: Trisha
To: Aisha

I can't think of nothing else today except finding out who he's meeting.

From: Aisha
To: Trisha

I know.

From: Trisha
To: Aisha

Another thing: tomorrow put some shades on or something and a hat if you've got one. Last thing we want is Toby recognising you, he'll probably get a restraining order on us all.

Subject: Hello from up here.

From: Claire
To: Trisha

Why's Holly dressed like a waitress?

From: Trisha
To: Claire

Tanya's got her helping out up there with the catering staff.

From: Claire
To: Trisha

Oh no, you know that lunch meeting booked under Tanya's name?

From: Trisha
To: Claire

Yes.

From: Claire
To: Trisha

Look who her guest is.

From: Trisha
To: Claire

Oh my God, no, go grab her, that's enough. Tell her to come down and see me here.

From: Claire
To: Trisha

I think it's too late, she's coming back, looks as white as a ghost.

Subject: Holly

From: Aisha
To: Trisha

Trisha, I think Holly's in a bad way, she just walked past me mumbling something about Toby and Tanya, grabbed her coat from the cloakroom and she's gone back in the lift.

From: Trisha
To: Aisha

She just had to serve them in the meeting room.

From: Aisha
To: Trisha

No.

From: Aisha
To: Trisha

The lift isn't doing down.

From: Trisha
To: Aisha

Where's she off to then?

From: Aisha
To: Trisha

It's heading up.

From: Trisha
To: Aisha

Where to?

From: Aisha
To: Trisha

All the way to the top, it's stopped at the roof garden.

From: Trisha
To: Aisha

Oh shit, get in THAT LIFT NOW AND GO GET HER!

From: Trisha
To: Aisha, Claire

TELL ME HAS SOMEONE FOUND MY BABES, PLEASE TELL ME????

friday

Subject: Holly

From: Trisha
To: Jason

We've had no news yet from Aisha. How was Holly this morning?

From: Jason
To: Trisha

She was sleeping when I left.

From: Trisha
To: Jason

I told them she was sick, I really wanted to say she was pregnant too, but I held it back. Hope you gave her a kiss from me, I thought she was a gonna yesterday, I really thought she would do it, you know. My heart nearly stopped.

From: Jason
To: Trisha

She says she was just going up to be on her own, fresh air, think about things, that kind of thing.

From: Trisha
To: Jason

Scared the life out of me, you read about people doing it.

From: Jason
To: Trisha

Tanya and Toby, well there's a surprise. I think it's time you got in touch with some of those bad people you know, Trisha

From: Trisha
To: Jason

Init. I don't believe it though, she's not his type.

From: Jason
To: Trisha

She said Tanya was leaning in close with her hand on his shoulder.

From: Trisha
To: Jason

Means nothing, tell her it means nothing.

From: Jason
To: Trisha

By the way, she doesn't want to go to your company party tonight. She was meant to be meeting someone called Will Duncan.

From: Trisha
To: Jason

I heard about him, I think that's best. He sounds like trouble to me. You think Holly will come back?

From: Jason
To: Trisha

Don't think so.

X

Subject: Urgent

From: Claire
To: Trisha; Marie

I have Aisha on the phone, she says not to shout at her, but Toby still hasn't turned up and she promises she wasn't late.

From: Trisha
To: Claire; Marie

It's nearly eleven, he'd be there by now. What time did she get there?

From: Claire
To: Trisha; Marie

She says around 10am.

From: Trisha
To: Claire; Marie

Tell her to go and check out the Eurostar entrance.

From: Claire
To: Trisha; Marie

OK.

From: Marie
To: Trisha; Claire

Trisha, you think his girlfriend went to France?

From: Trisha
To: Claire; Marie

Marie, all you really heard was he's meeting someone he loves in Waterloo. Really it could be his favourite flaming parakeet for all we know?

From: Marie
To: Trisha; Claire

Yes but that isn't a someone, Trisha, that's a something.

From: Trisha
To: Claire; Marie

Are you sure it weren't Waterloo underground?

From: Marie
To: Trisha; Claire

It could be but I really don't think it's so romantic to meet someone from the underground?

Subject: Found him!

From: Claire
To: Trisha; Marie

She's found him. The Eurostar is late in, should be there any moment though.

From: Marie
To: Trisha; Claire

Oh girls, here we go.

william
duncan's
inbox

Subject: I missed a call from you, fluffins?

From: William Duncan
To: Cheryl Waters

What is it?

From: Cheryl Waters
To: William Duncan

What you talking about, Will? You're mad you are, really mad, you know that?

From: William Duncan
To: Cheryl Waters

Oh come on, I know you have a secret fascination with me, you probably even have a photo of me somewhere.

From: Cheryl Waters
To: William Duncan

You must be joking, why would I have a photo of you?

From: William Duncan
To: Cheryl Waters

To remind yourself of what your future husband looks like. Don't worry, I'll send you one, would you like Will relaxing by the pool or holding up his school boxing medals? Or even Will at home cooking, do you like Lobtherhoop?

From: Cheryl Waters
To: William Duncan

You what?

From: William Duncan
To: Cheryl Waters

Lobster Soup, sorry I was eating when I wrote that, I'm a great cook, so how about it, sexy? Want to know what makes a young Duncan really tick?

From: Cheryl Waters
To: William Duncan

Where would we go then?

From: William Duncan
To: Cheryl Waters

I'm thinking pasta, good wine, maybe some dancing, could be on the river…

From: Cheryl Waters
To: William Duncan

Go on then, when? Tonight?

From: William Duncan
To: Cheryl Waters

I can't tonight, I'm going to that company thing, very dull probably spend the night talking work. What about tomorrow?

From: Cheryl Waters
To: William Duncan

I'm going to the Maldives for a couple of weeks on Sunday, so it looks like you missed your chance, Will.

x

Subject: Tonight

From: Peter Candid-Smith
To: William Duncan

So do you still think you'll get anywhere tonight with Holly?

From: William Duncan
To: Peter Candid-Smith

Don't know, but I just got in there with Cheryl Waters.

From: Peter Candid-Smith
To: William Duncan

No! Tell me what happened?

From: William Duncan
To: Peter Candid-Smith

She sounded like she would play tonight, but I'll be with Holly, and then she's off on holiday for two weeks, very bad timing.

From: Peter Candid-Smith
To: William Duncan

Surely you're not going to blow Holly out, after hounding her for so long?

From: William Duncan
To: Peter Candid-Smith

No, that wouldn't be good, and the poor thing's been miserable ever since that idiot left her, miserable and a tad ropey. I hope she gets herself together tonight.

From: Peter Candid-Smith
To: William Duncan

Whatever you do, don't get pissed and end up kissing her at the party, wait till you're someplace else. I did that last year and blew it for myself with two other PAs that I didn't know were interested. Also I don't think you should wind Toby up, he's not over her at all.

From: William Duncan
To: Peter Candid-Smith

That's because Toby's a big girl's blouse.

From: Peter Candid-Smith
To: William Duncan

I don't think he is, Will, to be honest, I think that's just his way.

From: William Duncan
To: Peter Candid-Smith

OK, I'll try not to rub his face in it too much, but to be honest Pete I really don't care, NOW ENOUGH!!! TONIGHT IS THE BIG ONE, YOU BIG GAY QUEEN, LAST ONE THERE BUYS THE ROUND.

Subject: Tonight

From: William Duncan
To: Holly

See you at 8pm

xx

Will

trisha's
inbox

Subject: She's called

From: Trisha
To: Marie; Claire

I just got a call from Aisha, you ready for this?

From: Marie
To: Trisha; Claire

Tell us?

From: Trisha
To: Aisha; Claire

Toby goes to the gates to wait, Aisha follows, she's standing not too close, but close enough to see everyone as they come through. She sees some snotty cow with Gucci sunglasses and thinks that'll be HER. But no, she walks on passed him. A bit later there's this old man who shouts out to Toby, and they hug, must be Toby's dad

From: Marie
To: Trisha; Claire

So that's it, he just met his father?

From: Trisha
To: Aisha; Claire

No get this, alongside his Dad is some girl who runs out and into Toby's arms. This weren't a girlfriend, or wife. It was his daughter, Toby's got a fucking daughter.

toby's inbox

week 4
monday

Subject: My witless brother

From: Georgia
To: Toby

Got your message. You've really made a mess of all this, haven't you?

From: Toby
To: Georgia

Total shambles.

From: Georgia
To: Toby

If you'd told her at the start…

From: Toby
To: Georgia

I would have told her all about Bonnie if Bonnie hadn't been in boarding school at the time, and if we'd been living together. Of course I would have, there wouldn't have been a choice. But for the first six months we were living in separate countries.

From: Georgia
To: Toby

Still…

From: Toby
To: Georgia

OK, but it's not completely my fault. If Holly had shown even the slightest interest in children I would have rushed to tell her. But all she did was moan about children and get drunk.

From: Georgia
To: Toby

I thought we were discussing her positives.

From: Toby
To: Georgia

You know a few times towards the end I discovered she'd been taking complete strangers back to our flat.

From: Georgia
To: Toby

Men?

From: Toby
To: Georgia

Just people she'd met, I'm not saying she'd done anything with them, God no, but she just invites whole parties back to the flat, complete strangers all drunk falling around the place, then she would try and hide it from me. You can't bring a child into that? And I couldn't have Bonnie getting to know her then have it finish for one reason or another.

From: Georgia
To: Toby

You should have given her a chance.

From: Toby
To: Georgia

What for? So she can go the same way Helen did, in a pile of drink??? What kind of dad would let his daughter see that twice?

From: Georgia
To: Toby

You're going to have to try though, you're going to have to introduce her to Bonnie and you'll have to give her a little trust.

From: Toby
To: Georgia

OK, two weeks ago, Holly was meant to meet me outside the theatre. I'd arranged for her to meet the cast of Mamma Mia. I was there with special tickets, huge surprise, big night, the works. She'd been going on to me about how we never went out so there I was waiting. I knew she was low on phone charge so we were keeping calls to a minimum. After an hour of standing around worrying, I get a call from her, drunk as a skunk, crying, barely able to speak. She's in London—somewhere.

From: Georgia
To: Toby

Where was she?

From: Toby
To: Georgia

You tell me! She was so drunk all she could say was 'Eros, Toby, Eros'! I could hear men's voices trying to talk to her, then her phone went dead. Eros, Toby, Eros???

From: Georgia
To: Toby

Eros statue?

From: Toby
To: Georgia

She's in the middle of London somewhere, about to pass out, without any credit on her phone. I'm so worried about her, I'm so worried, I just can't go through all this again with another woman, Georgie, I can't.

From: Georgia
To: Toby

Tell me what happened.

From: Toby
To: Georgia

I jump in a rickshaw and race off towards the Eros statue in Piccadilly Circus, my heart's going so fast because I've seen her like this many times and I know she would be about to collapse. I arrive and across the road I can see a group of teenagers huddled around something.

It's Holly, unconscious by the statue. I don't know if they were about to mug her or help her. I can't do it again, and neither can Bonnie.

From: Georgia
To: Toby

Then talk to her. Tell her all this and for God's sake introduce her to Bonnie. Bonnie is adorable, she'll love her.

From: Toby
To: Georgia

The madness of it all is that Holly would be an incredible mother. She's funny, kind, caring and creative.

From: Georgia
To: Toby

And you love her still.

From: Toby
To: Georgia

And I still love her, Georgie, completely.

From: Georgia
To: Toby

So it's time you called her, isn't it?

From: Toby
To: Georgia

You know she keeps her bills in the freezer?

From: Georgia
To: Toby

Not a bad place to keep them. At least you know where they are.

From: Toby
To: Georgia

And once I found a bag under her bed full of hair. I've no idea what it was for. She's mad, so mad, you never know what you're going to get when you arrive home. You could open a door and find her in a cupboard, once she even put all my clothes into a rainbow, no idea why. I love her, I miss her, I really really do, Georgie.

From: Georgia
To: Toby

The last thing you told me Holly said was that she'd stopped drinking, so what's stopping you?

Subject: Drinks last Friday

From: Brian Jones
To: Toby

Toby

I'm hearing reports back that you had a bit of a row with William Duncan on Friday. I don't know the full details, but I want to know if I should be concerned about the two of you?

Brian

European Head of Corporate Finance. DK Huerst, 50 Cabot Square, Canary Wharf, London

From: Toby
To: Brian Jones

No, we're fine. It's all sorted, Brian, sorry about that, mate.

From: Brian Jones
To: Toby

Good.

Oh and well done with the structured finance deal. Didn't think you were ever going to close that one, keep going.

Brian

holly 's
inbox

Subject: Morning

From: Trisha
To: Holly

You alright?

From: Holly
To: Trisha

Yes, Trisha, absolutely fine, sorry I'm late.

x

From: Trisha
To: Holly

Tanya didn't think you were coming back. Told me to get all your stuff together to post onto you. You might want to give her the good news. Glad you made it. You know I can't sit here on me own.

xxxx

Subject: LATE

From: Tanya
To: Holly

I see you have now arrived. I actually presumed you had decided it best to leave the company, having not heard from you this morning.

From: Holly
To: Tanya

No, I love my job, and I think I can speak for the whole team when I say what really makes it so enjoyable is the communication we receive each day from such an inspired leader whom we respect so much.

Holly :)

From: Tanya
To: Holly

Explain why you are over an hour late?

From: Holly
To: Tanya

Traffic.

Subject: Friday night

From: Marie
To: Holly; Trisha; Claire; Aisha

Oh girls, you all missed so much excitement on Friday night, you should have seen it. Why didn't you come?

From: Trisha
To: Marie; Holly; Claire; Aisha

Wasn't really in the right mood to be honest, Marie, did you find yourself a man then?

From: Marie
To: Holly; Trisha; Claire

No, but what do you think about what happened with Toby?

From: Trisha
To: Marie; Holly; Claire; Aisha

What happened?

From: Aisha
To: Holly; Marie; Claire; Trisha

I missed this. What is Marie talking about?

From: Marie
To: Holly; Trisha; Claire

So tell me you don't know what happened on Friday? Do you know, Claire?

From: Claire
To: Marie; Trisha; Holly; Aisha

No.

From: Trisha
To: Marie; Holly; Claire; Aisha

What you talking about?

From: Marie
To: Holly; Trisha; Claire

None of you know yet?

From: Trisha
To: Marie; Holly; Claire; Aisha

WHAT HAPPENED, MARIE?

From: Holly
To: Marie; Trisha; Claire; Aisha

If you're going to tell her he was with Tanya all night, I really don't think I could handle it.

From: Marie
To: Holly; Trisha; Claire

No, no, you will love this, I'm sure. Your man William, the handsome man with the nice bottom, was so angry because you didn't show, and he says all these bad things about you, about you being not good enough for him anyway, this is what I heard, and he's angry and saying these things and none of it is nice at all, Holly.

From: Holly
To: Marie; Trisha; Claire; Aisha

Is this going to get better, Marie?

From: Marie
To: Holly; Trisha; Claire; Aisha

Of course, I am working, you know. OK, so he's saying these things and then Toby comes over and says something and no one's knows what he says, but then it all goes crazy and suddenly Will is being held over the balcony by Toby and he says something to him and then lets him go. On the floor, not over the balcony.

> **From:** Holly
> **To:** Marie; Trisha; Claire; Aisha
>
> NO!

> **From:** Marie
> **To:** Holly; Trisha; Claire
>
> Yes, girls, it's true.

> **From:** Trisha
> **To:** Marie; Holly; Claire; Aisha
>
> Did you see this with your own eyes?

> **From:** Marie
> **To:** Holly; Trisha; Claire; Aisha
>
> No, I was talking to a very nice young boy and didn't see this, but everyone is talking about it.

Subject: Stalker

> **From:** Trisha
> **To:** Holly
>
> Can you forward me one of those emails you kept getting, Holl?

> **From:** Holly
> **To:** Trisha
>
> From UnknownAngel101@hotmail.com
> To Holly
> I am coming to see you on Wednesday, please be nice to me.

Subject: Your answer

> **From:** Tanya
> **To:** Holly
>
> What about the traffic????

From: Holly
To: Tanya

It got in the way. Between me leaving my house and getting to work there was traffic which was moving slower than I wished to move, therefore causing my unavoidable lateness. Short of me leaving my car and walking around the traffic, I had no option but to wait for said traffic to resume motion.

Very very unfortunate, sorry.

Regards

Holly

From: Tanya
To: Holly

Is this negative attitude still related to the time when you were desperate to be my friend? It was so very sweet. But surely you must be happier now knowing at least you can achieve my approval if you work hard? And you get to talk to me every day!

From: Holly
To: Tanya

Dear Tanya

Having arrived so regrettably late, I am very busy. Did you have anything important to say to me?

Holly

From: Tanya
To: Holly

Yes this morning I noticed some white flakes around the shoulders of your jacket. It's not quite the corporate image we're striving for anymore here, clients will notice this kind of thing. Does your jacket need dry cleaning or is this simply a continual problem that needs looking at?

Regards

Tanya

Subject: Plans?

From: Trisha
To: Holly

So what you up to then?

From: Holly
To: Trisha

Not sure.

From: Trisha
To: Holly

You OK?

From: Holly
To: Trisha

Battling, Trisha, battling.

Subject: My jacket

From: Holly
To: Tanya

Are you running a dry-cleaning service here then, Tanya?

From: Tanya
To: Holly

Not yet. Please see attached the rotas for this week. I've given you the late shifts again this week. I just thought now that you're obviously not house-hunting with Toby anymore in your evenings, you wouldn't mind.

Oh and sorry you had to interrupt us on Thursday, I hope our relationship won't affect your ability to carry out your duties for me in a professional capacity.

Regards

Tanya

Subject: Got to leave the desk

From: Holly
To: Trisha

Oh God, Trisha, I want to be on my own for a bit, will you cover me?

From: Trisha
To: Holly

Of course darling, you go have a nice walk, get some fresh air.

X

From: Holly
To: Trisha

No, I'm going into one of the hot-desk business suites.

From: Trisha
To: Holly

OK, just want to be on your own, do you?

From: Holly
To: Trisha

That kind of thing.

xx

From: Trisha
To: Holly

Don't you get caught. You know they're out of bounds. You know what will happen if anyone catches you, just make sure you're online so we can let you know if Tanya notices you're not around.

From: Holly
To: Trisha

Thanks.

trisha's
inbox

Subject: Emails

From: Trisha
To: IT Admin

Can you trace an email for me, Jeff?

From: IT Admin
To: Admin

No problem, just forward the email to me and I should be able to give you a location, possibly even a name.
I'll do my best.

From: Trisha
To: IT Admin

It's attached.
[ATTACHMENT]

Subject: Everyone

From: Tanya
To: Trisha; Marie; Aisha; Claire

Dear Team
Regards to Holly, firstly she's late, letting you all down, then she disappears completely, can anyone tell me where she is now?
Tanya

From: Trisha
To: Tanya; Marie; Aisha; Claire

She's been with me all day, but I think she went on a floor walk, checking the rooms, making sure they got everything they should have.

From: Tanya
To: Trisha; Marie; Aisha; Claire

Did she now?

From: Trisha
To: Tanya; Marie; Aisha; Claire

A few chairs were missing from the conference suite, I think.

From: Marie
To: Tanya; Trisha; Claire; Aisha

Oh Tanya, can you be a dear and cover my desk for a moment. I need to take my break.

From: Tanya
To: Trisha; Marie; Aisha; Claire

What do you mean cover you?

From: Marie
To: Tanya; Trisha; Claire; Aisha

I mean use the switchboard, Tanya dear, answering the calls.

From: Tanya
To: Trisha; Marie; Aisha; Claire

Yes, Marie I get it, but I am not a switchboard operator and I don't have the time. Sorry but I am not just managing the reception team, I am in charge of catering too.

From: Marie
To: Tanya; Trisha; Claire; Aisha

But I thought they had found you a supervisor in the kitchens, Tanya?

From: Tanya
To: Trisha; Marie; Aisha; Claire

What has that got to do with anything? Why can't one of the others do it like usual?

From: Marie
To: Tanya; Trisha; Claire; Aisha

Because I have to take my break now and that will mean two of us off the desks at the same time which we aren't allowed to do.

From: Tanya
To: Trisha; Marie; Aisha; Claire

What usually happens then?

From: Marie
To: Tanya; Trisha; Claire; Aisha

Holly used to cover me. You see I have my yoga class, Tanya. I can't miss a yoga class. I explained this before to everyone, this was one condition of me working here. I really do have to go, I cannot miss a yoga class, Tanya.

From: Tanya
To: Trisha; Marie; Aisha; Claire

OK, don't get worked up, Marie, it is not a problem.
I'll be down now.
Tanya

Subject: Alert

From: Trisha
To: Holly

Holly, you should come back now. Tanya's knows you're missing.

Subject: Hello

From: Claire
To: Trisha; Aisha

I thought Marie's class was tomorrow?

From: Trisha
To: Claire; Aisha

It is, she's lying her arse off. Don't let Tanya go looking for Holly. Not sure what she's doing, but she's in one of the business suites.

From: Aisha
To: Trisha; Claire

So when are we going to tell Holly about Toby's daughter and who's going to tell her?

From: Trisha
To: Claire; Aisha

I don't know, I'm lost with that one. You definitely heard her say Daddy?

From: Aisha
To: Trisha; Claire

Couldn't miss it, she was so happy to see him.

From: Trisha
To: Claire; Aisha

OK, well I think we leave it down to Jason and I know he's stressing over it now.

Subject: IMPORTANT, READ THIS

From: Trisha
To: Holly

URGENT, come back, she's going mad looking for you.

Subject: Back

From: Marie
To: Trisha; Holly; Claire; Aisha

I'm back. Sorry, girls, I stayed away as long as I could. She's left here and is going to the IT floor.

From: Aisha
To: Trisha; Marie; Claire

She's coming towards us now. I'll say I need a toilet break then I'll leave before she can say anything.

From: Trisha
To: Aisha; Marie; Claire

OK, see if you can find Holly.

Subject: Spam

From: IT Admin
To: Trisha

I am presuming there's no point in sending you the report it's come back with, it's a bit technical.

From: Trisha
To: IT Admin

No point at all, what, is it all figures and things?

From: IT Admin
To: Trisha

Mainly, it gives things like the IP address and various other bit and pieces.

From: Trisha
To: IT Admin

No you lost me already, is there anything like a name?

From: IT Admin
To: Trisha

No unfortunately it was sent from an internet café.

From: Trisha
To: IT Admin

There are hundreds in London, so that's a waste of time then.

From: IT Admin
To: Trisha

It wasn't sent from London, it's registered at a server in a place called Douville, in France.

Subject: STOP

From: Tanya
To: TEAM

Can everyone stop moving around the building and just stay at their desks, no more breaks, no more jumping into lifts, do not move from your stations. I can see from the system that there are six of us logged into the reservations system so Holly is using a computer somewhere. Can someone tell me WHERE IS HOLLY!!!?

holly's
inbox

Subject: NO

From: Holly
To: Toby

I'm busy doing something, I don't have time.

From: Toby
To: Holly

Please talk to me.

From: Holly
To: Toby

Why? Why on earth should I???

From: Toby
To: Holly

I can understand you never wanting to talk to me again, but I need to at least explain things. I still love you.

From: Holly
To: Toby

Go away, Toby.

Subject: Doc 1

From: Holly
To: Holly.Denham@Yahoo.co.uk

[Attached Document] Excel Spread sheet.

Subject: Important

From: Toby
To: Holly

There's something I never told you. We need to discuss it, please, Holly.

From: Holly
To: Toby

If you loved me so much why have you put me through so much pain???

From: Toby
To: Holly

I didn't mean to put you through any pain, I have been suffering too. I just had to do what I thought was right, and I got it wrong. I can tell you everything tonight?

Subject: Move it

From: Trisha
To: Holly

Tanya knows where you are, she's on her way there now. Whatever you're doing be aware she'll be there any moment.

Subject: Go away

From: Holly
To: Toby

There won't be a tonight, Toby, I don't want to see you, ever. Remember—you're with Tanya now—or has that slipped your mind???

From: Toby
To: Holly

What?

From: Holly
To: Toby

YOU ARE WITH TANYA, REMEMBER??????!

From: Toby
To: Holly

I'm not 'with' her, I have an event coming up that I had to speak to her about, that's all?

From: Holly
To: Toby

When I walked in, she was all over you, can you imagine how that made me feel????

From: Toby
To: Holly

She was leaning very close to me but I have no idea why.

From: Holly
To: Toby

She's told me you're together!

From: Toby
To: Holly

What? I've never been near her? I've been ducking her calls for ages. I told my secretary to deal with her, but she kept insisting I personally go through the final bits of this thing. I kept putting her off but in the end I agreed to give her ten minutes. You came in and then ran out. I went after you, but you'd gone.

From: Holly
To: Toby

Well she's made my life hell here, absolute hell, and I thought you were together?

From: Toby
To: Holly

Together???? Not even been on a date with her, she's not my type at all. In fact the few times I have talked to her recently I've found her thoroughly unpleasant.

From: Holly
To: Toby

Look I have to go, I've got to carry on, I'm not interested, Toby, OK.

Shit, talk of the devil.

Subject: Announcement

From: Tanya
To: Trisha; Marie; Claire; Aisha; Holly

Dear Team

As you are well aware the use of those computers in the business suites is restricted to clients and senior management, and support staff found using them will be up for a disciplinary. I'm sure you're all aware by now, that I caught Holly using them. She was also late today and I noticed a tear in her tights, which brings everyone's scores down. This means as it stands your bonuses will now be cancelled for this month.

Regards

Tanya

Subject: Confusion

From: Toby
To: Holly; Tanya

Dear Tanya

I fear there's been a misunderstanding between us. I just heard you told Holly we are dating. We are not and this couldn't be further than the truth. I would prefer it if you didn't make up what is frankly a solicitous rumour and stopped hounding me. Can you confirm to me by return email that you are clear on this otherwise I will be forced to take further action.

Toby Williams

From: Tanya
To: Toby, Holly

Dear Toby

I don't know where you heard this, I have never said we were together. I think, as you are aware, Holly has been going through a difficult period and this may have affected her judgement somewhat. We all feel for her during this difficult time.

Tanya

From: Toby
To: Holly, Tanya

I don't think she has any problems at all. I believe she was telling the truth and that it is you who have had the impaired judgement.

However, I will accept your email as confirmation that you will not be continuing with your incorrect assumption of any type of relationship.

In future please communicate through my secretary, as instructed.

Toby

tuesday

Subject: Morning

From: Holly
To: Alice

I've just booked my flight, thanks for this.

From: Alice
To: Holly

Oh I'm so excited, you can stay for as long as you want. What about your flat?

From: Holly
To: Alice

The agreement was rolling and they could fill it easily, and get more than I was paying.

You promise Matt's OK about it?

From: Alice
To: Holly

He's very excited. He said you can help him feed the family.

From: Holly
To: Alice

Oh, God, I so know he's not talking about Ophelia and Joseph.

From: Alice
To: Holly

He's not. By the way did you hear what happened to Granny last week?

xxx

From: Holly
To: Alice

No, tell me?

From: Alice
To: Holly

Granny and Cecilia found a man on one of these ex-pat meeting places on the web. He arrived on their doorstep last week because she had told him if he wanted to have a cup of tea with her he had to come right away. He'd travelled down from Madrid, by car, took him six hours just to have a cup of tea with Granny. She's still got it.

x

Subject: Meeting

From: Holly
To: Tanya

I have a meeting with HR at 10am. Can you arrange for someone to cover my desk.
Holly

From: Tanya
To: Holly

Of course, I must let you know that after you arrived late, disappeared early and were caught using the hot desks I told them you had become unmanageable. I have just been on the phone to Ranixo head office who have decided your behaviour amounts to gross misconduct. Therefore you will be leaving us at the end of the week.

Such a shame as I really thought you had potential. Do you have any idea of what you might do next?

Whenever one of my staff has left the company in the past, I have always attempted to help their career path, so may I suggest waitressing? I noticed how spirited you were scurrying my plates around and thought at the time this was an area you were particularly skilled in. You took to it so quickly, it was as if you were born to do it and, although things haven't worked out for you here, I do have a contact at a local pizza place who may need staff, just let me know. I only want to be helpful.

Thanks again for your time here. We hope you go on to be successful in anything you do.

Yours sincerely
Tanya Mason

Subject: Meeting

From: Holly
To: Trisha

Right, I'm off.

From: Trisha
To: Holly

Who's going to be in the meeting?

From: Holly
To: Trisha

I think everyone.

From: Trisha
To: Holly

What do you mean?

From: Holly
To: Trisha

HR, CEO and Richard.

From: Trisha
To: Holly

Heaven help you. You'd think HR could have handled it themselves.

From: Holly
To: Trisha

No, I wanted everyone to be there.

From: Trisha
To: Holly

What do you mean you wanted them??

From: Holly
To: Trisha

They haven't called the meeting, I have.

From: Trisha
To: Holly

What? Don't get it???

From: Holly
To: Trisha

Got to go.

Subject: Today

From: Jason
To: Holly

Tell me tell me tell me tell me tell me?!!??

Subject: Meeting

From: Trisha
To: Holly

How did it go?

From: Holly
To: Trisha

Fine.

From: Trisha
To: Holly

Why you grinning so much, you thinking about that email Toby sent Tanya?

From: Holly
To: Trisha

No, although that was good.

From: Trisha
To: Holly

I bet it was darling, she must have been screaming in her little office. So why you look so happy?

From: Holly
To: Trisha

Didn't know I was, Trisha.

From: Trisha
To: Holly

Liar! Tell me.

From: Holly
To: Trisha

No.

From: Trisha
To: Holly

Tell me!!!!

From: Holly
To: Trisha

Just a moment.

x

Subject: News

From: Holly
To: Jason

Yes.

From: Jason
To: Holly

Yes what?

From: Holly
To: Jason

Yes, I was right.

From: Jason
To: Holly

NO!

From: Holly
To: Jason

Completely, I'll fill you in any moment, sorry, got to dash.

From: Jason
To: Holly

Holly!!!

Subject: Look out

From: Trisha
To: Holly

What d'you think they want?

From: Holly
To: Trisha

I think they want to talk to Tanya.

From: Trisha
To: Holly

Why?

From: Holly
To: Trisha

You'll see.
X

Subject: Arrivals

From: Holly
To: Tanya; Marie; Claire; Trisha; Aisha

Tanya
There's some gentlemen here to see you.

From: Tanya
To: Holly; Marie; Claire; Trisha; Aisha

No one's booked into the diary. Are you sure they're for me and not for someone who sounds like me? ? ?

From: Holly
To: Tanya; Marie; Trisha; Claire; Aisha

Ha ha, that's so funny, your sense of humour is 1st class.

From: Tanya
To: Holly; Marie; Trisha; Claire; Aisha

I am not in the mood. I believe you're trying to be a disruptive influence in front of the others. Do you want me to forward your emails to HR?

From: Holly
To: Tanya; Marie; Trisha; Claire; Aisha

Sorry, no they're definitely for you, Tanya.

From: Tanya
To: Holly; Marie; Trisha; Claire; Aisha

Who are they?

From: Holly
To: Tanya; Marie; Trisha; Claire; Aisha

Sorry, can't say, but they're already on their way up.

From: Tanya
To: Holly; Marie; Trisha; Claire; Aisha

Didn't you ask them? If they're salesmen and you've sent them up, I won't be happy.

From: Holly
To: Tanya; Marie; Trisha; Claire; Aisha

You misunderstood me, I said I can't say, not that I don't know.

From: Tanya
To: Holly; Marie; Trisha; Claire; Aisha

If you don't explain what you' re going on about soon, I'll have to admit to HR you are being a disruption on your final day and you will be escorted off site. Is this what you want?

From: Holly
To: Tanya; Marie; Trisha; Claire; Aisha

Oh, don't think this is my final day. However, as you are still the manager... I believe it's something to do with the discrepancies on the meeting room system.

From: Tanya
To: Holly; Marie; Trisha; Claire; Aisha

Patience, Holly, patience wearing thin.

From: Holly
To: Tanya; Marie; Trisha; Claire; Aisha

I'll explain quickly. I noticed you shutting something down on your screen when I went to see you last week, and looking very flushed, so I thought it's either illegal sites, hmmm, or something else. We've been having problems on the system for months, things seem to be changing on their own, lots of over-ordering.

Do you remember when I offered you training on the reservations system?

From: Tanya
To: Holly; Marie; Trisha; Claire; Aisha

What about it?

From: Holly
To: Tanya; Marie; Trisha; Claire; Aisha

Well if you'd taken it up my offer back then, you may have discovered there's now a way of monitoring the purchasing of food and beverage more closely and where it all disappears to.

So I've been through the whole system and compiled a report which I sent to HR, the CEO and Richard. It looks like that huge budget you always go on about was disappearing into your pockets (via backhanders from suppliers). That's called fraud, dear, and very naughty it is too. You know what happens to naughty girls, don't you?

They get taken away. Looks like you lasted less time in the role than me.

: (

So if I am waitressing in some pizza place, I'll be thinking of you, locked away somewhere, scrubbing dishes, it's a tough life.

xxxx

PS shame about Toby, it did make me laugh though, you really do live in a dream world... he's way out of your league.

From: EASYJET
To: Holly

Your flight to Spain is confirmed for Wednesday at 8pm. Please ensure you arrive two hours before the flat is due to take off.

Subject: SO?

From: Jason
To: Holly

Tell me what they said in that meeting?

From: Holly
To: Jason

They had studied my report and agreed with my assumptions (and huge accusations) which was a relief, because if I had got it wrong... can you imagine?

From: Jason
To: Holly

They'd have probably taken you away for false somethings.

From: Holly
To: Jason

False somethings, Jason, exactly. Anyway it was nice to see them as nervous. They were all jittery, shocked, unsure of exactly what to say.

From: Jason
To: Holly

Ha, serves them right.

From: Holly
To: Jason

The CEO told me off the record he was sorry the way things had gone, but he'd just had to please investors etc.

From: Jason
To: Holly

So he should.

From: Holly
To: Jason

They said they're cancelling the contract with Ranixo, because they broke their terms and conditions (about their staff not stealing from them I presume) which means we would all be back on their books.

I told him I wanted absolute assurances that what I was going to tell them wouldn't go any further for another week, but that I wanted to formally take maternity leave. He said they needed to get someone new in to wipe the slate clean and show a fresh image for the company. He offered me full manager's pay for the entire time, if I agreed not to come back.

From: Jason
To: Holly

NO! That's dodgy!

From: Holly
To: Jason

I don't care, I agreed. So, now for the good part, it just happened.

From: Jason
To: Holly

When? What?

From: Holly
To: Jason

About two minutes ago, some plain clothes CID took her away for questioning, quietly, no fuss.

From: Jason
To: Holly

Oh my God!!!! I wanted to be there, did you take pictures????

From: Holly
To: Jason

No, Jason, strangely I didn't.

xx

Yay, one for the home side.

wednesday

Subject: Final Day in Work

From: Holly
To: Trisha; Marie; Aisha; Claire

Thanks, it's been great. Time to move on. Everyone has agreed it's time to turn over a new leaf here, I'm taking my maternity leave early too.

From: Marie
To: Holly; Trisha; Aisha; Claire

You're pregnant, Holly??

From: Holly
To: Marie; Trisha; Aisha; Claire

Don't pretend you don't know. I know there are no secrets from you lot.

From: Marie
To: Holly; Trisha; Aisha; Claire

We didn't know until very recently we promise.

From: Aisha
To: Holly; Trisha; Marie; Claire

What about Toby?

From: Holly
To: Marie; Trisha; Aisha; Claire

What about him?

From: Aisha
To: Holly; Trisha; Marie; Claire

Aren't you going to tell him you're pregnant?

From: Holly
To: Marie; Trisha; Aisha; Claire

I'm going to write from Spain and tell him everything. Some things are maybe just not meant to be. If you see him

From: Trisha
To: Holly; Aisha; Marie; Claire

What?

From: Holly
To: Marie; Trisha; Aisha; Claire

Tell him I will miss him, very much, always.

It's been nice knowing you all, I'll stay in touch.

xx

Subject: I keep trying to speak to you

From: Toby
To: Holly

Why did you slam the phone down again???

From: Holly
To: Toby

I didn't want to speak to you. Don't you remember doing that to me, when you didn't want to talk to me anymore?

From: Toby
To: Holly

Please, Holly.

Subject: Phones

From: Toby
To: Holly

I'm sorry I put the phone down on you then. But I couldn't talk to you because I knew if I did once I heard your voice, I wouldn't be able to break up.

From: Holly
To: Toby

Why did you break up? I didn't turn out to be all you'd hoped for, was that it?

From: Toby
To: Holly

No, you turned out to be the most amazing person in the world, it broke my heart to do what I did.

From: Holly
To: Toby

So, why did you do it Toby, why did you put me through all this pain?!

From: Toby
To: Holly

I have a daughter.

From: Holly
To: Toby

What?

From: Toby
To: Holly

That's what I've been doing. I go to see her, she's been in a private boarding school in France and she goes home at the weekends to live with my dad.

From: Holly
To: Toby

Why didn't you tell me?

From: Toby
To: Holly

It's not something you say straight away, when you're trying to win a woman's heart, especially when she keeps saying 'children yuk' every time you bring them up.

From: Holly
To: Toby

What's her name?

From: Toby
To: Holly

Bonnie, and she's wonderful.

From: Holly
To: Toby

Where's her mother?

From: Toby
To: Holly

She died, of pneumonia. She'd been up for three days drinking and taking cocaine, she complained about some chest pains and she died in hospital the next day.

From: Holly
To: Toby

I'm sorry.

From: Toby
To: Holly

She started out a fantastic person, but over time she changed. She was either happy and drunk or angry and hung over, and the binges got worse. She used to disappear for days. I couldn't stop her and the more I tried, the more she thought I was trying to control her, so the more she did.

From: Holly
To: Toby

No, no, you shouldn't have lied to me, Toby, you put me through hell. I got through it, I did, I got through it, it was hard, and you've changed me forever, but no you can't do this to me, Toby.

From: Toby
To: Holly

Holly, I love you.

From: Holly
To: Toby

No, you can't take me back now it's over, you should have said these things before.

From: Toby
To: Holly

I just couldn't work out what to do, I was barely sleeping with work, I had my daughter crying on the phone every night, I had you drunk, I had no idea what to do, but I needed to do something.

From: Holly
To: Toby

So you got rid of me.

From: Toby
To: Holly

I wanted you, I just couldn't go through it again, Holly, please.

From: Holly
To: Toby

No, Toby, you can't have me back and, for your information, I don't hate children, you idiot. I love them.
I'm going now, it's too late for all this, Toby.
Goodbye.

From: Toby
To: Holly

No wait there, don't leave.

trisha's inbox

Subject: Leaving

From: Trisha
To: Holly

Where you going?

From: Holly
To: Trisha

I'm going to get my coat. I'll call you from Spain.

xxx

Subject: Wake up!

From: Trisha
To: Aisha; Claire; Marie

Aisha, Holly's about to go up to see you lot, getting her coat. I'm calling Toby.

From: Aisha
To: Trisha; Claire; Marie

OK.

From: Trisha
To: Aisha; Claire; Marie

He's not answering.

From: Marie
To: Trisha; Aisha; Claire

Try one of the other people in his office Trisha??

From: Trisha
To: Aisha; Claire; Marie

Toby's come out of the lift down here. He's coming over, she hasn't seen him yet.

From: Aisha
To: Trisha; Claire; Marie

What's happening now?

From: Trisha
To: Aisha; Claire; Marie

He's trying to talk to her and she's scrabbling with bits of paper and trying to look for things. She's picked up her keys and her handbag, telling him it's too late.

He's following her over to the lift.

But some annoying client has just spotted them. She's marched over and is yabbering to them both about all kinds of rubbish.

They're trying to be polite, but it's obvious they just want her to leave. Oh no, she's just asked Holly how many months she is.

From: Marie
To: Trisha; Aisha; Claire

What? Who?

From: Trisha
To: Aisha; Claire; Marie

The client asked Holly! She's just staring back in shock and the client is saying she may be wrong, but there just seems something different about her and Holly's saying about a month.

Toby looks dumbstruck, she's stroking her tummy, her eyes have drifted to his, she tries to smile and steps into the lift with that sad half-smile.

From: Aisha
To: Trisha; Claire; Marie

Say something Toby you jerk!!!!

From: Trisha
To: Aisha; Claire; Marie

Too late, the doors have closed and he's hit his head against the lift.

He's looking up and is pressing the button for the other lift.

Stop her when she gets up there someone.

From: Claire
To: Trisha; Aisha; Marie

We'll try.

From: Trisha
To: Aisha; Claire; Marie

He's jumped in a lift. But he's grabbed one going down, the moron.

From: Aisha
To: Trisha; Claire; Marie

God, how that guy made so much money I'll never know.

From: Trisha
To: Aisha; Claire; Marie

Guess who's just walked in.

From: Marie
To: Trisha; Claire; Marie

Who? Trisha, tell us!

From: Aisha
To: Trisha; Claire; Marie

Tanya??? More police????

From: Trisha
To: Aisha; Claire; Marie

No, but I reckon it's the person who's been sending Holly all those emails.

From: Aisha
To: Trisha; Claire; Marie

Who?

From: Trisha
To: Aisha; Claire; Marie

You'll see, I'm sending her up—JUST TRY AND KEEP THEM ALL THERE.

Subject: Here

From: Claire
To: Trisha; Aisha; Marie

Holly's up here, she's taking her coat, she won't wait. The lift doors have opened and there's a young girl standing there. What does she want?

From: Aisha
To: Trisha; Claire; Marie

That's her, that's his daughter.

From: Trisha
To: Aisha; Claire; Marie

She weren't emailing about Holly's secrets, she was talking about Toby's, and she's the secret, the Unknown Angel. Bless her, she wants to be known.

From: Aisha
To: Trisha; Claire; Marie

Let me carry on telling you now.

From: Marie
To: Aisha; Trisha; Claire

Oh, I wish I was up there, I want to see.

From: Trisha
To: Aisha; Claire; Marie

Go on then, Aisha, tell us.

From: Aisha
To: Trisha; Claire; Marie

She's come out of the lift and Holly's just looking at her, mouth open. Are you Holly? she just asked.

Holly is nodding now with her hand over her mouth, eyes watering and the girl is saying she's Toby's daughter.

Holly's opened her arms and Bonnie's given her a hug.

The lift doors have pinged, Toby's standing there. The girls have drawn back from each other, Toby's saying 'Holly, I love you, I love you so much, please, will you m—'

From: Trisha
To: Aisha; Claire; Marie

WHAT???

From: Aisha
To: Trisha; Claire; Marie

That's as far as he got, the lift doors shut, someone must have called it on another floor. Are we sure Holly's picked the right guy? He's so dim!

From: Trisha
To: Aisha; Claire; Marie

Not the brightest of sparks is he. I can see it's coming back down to me.

From: Claire
To: Trisha; Aisha; Marie

Stopping at all the floors.

From: Aisha
To: Trisha; Claire; Marie

The girls are still standing here waiting. Bonnie's looked up at Holly, Holly's looked down and shrugged then around at us, face covered in tears, eyes like some puppy waiting to be fed.

From: Trisha
To: Aisha; Claire; Marie

It's arrived back down here, loads of people are getting out, he's left standing there looking awkwardly at me. He's pointed up as if to tell me he's going back up. Good boy, that's it.

From: Aisha
To: Trisha; Claire; Marie

Here we go, it's coming up and, and, bingo, he's launched himself out of the lift, they're all over each other.

From: Claire
To: Trisha; Aisha; Marie

They're kissing.

From: Aisha
To: Trisha; Claire; Marie

His daughter looks happy, now a bit revolted, and now looking at me because I'm trying to get her over here so I can tell her about life.

From: Trisha
To: Aisha; Claire; Marie

NO!!!!!!

From: Marie
To: Aisha; Trisha; Claire

No, Aisha!

From: Aisha
To: Trisha; Claire; Marie

Just kidding. Oh there we go, will you marry me, I love you… She's nodding and put out her hand to the girl's to hold too.
That's nice.

From: Trisha
To: Aisha, Claire, Marie

Right, I'm going for a fag.

holly's
inbox

Subject: News

From: Richard
To: Holly

Dear Holly

I wanted to say congratulations on your pregnancy and I wish you all the best for the future. Make sure you send through some pictures of the little one later in the year!

Although I couldn't tell you in the meeting, I am also leaving. I have enjoyed my time here, however, in the last few months I have felt a distinct lack of support from my own immediate superiors.

Without going into the details, I felt their lack of faith in my judgement on various matters was something I could not accept.

During your time as manager you proved yourself a fabulous people manager and motivator and an excellent strategic planner, introducing new ideas at every corner. Talking of which, you may be interested to know the room-space software search function we now use will have saved the company millions in wasted floor space by the end of the year. So I am leaving, and I have accepted a position as the Head of UK Facilities for Tamworth O'Brien, the largest or the second largest law firm in the world (these things change so quickly these days). They have around 40 receptionists and are in need of a communications manager. I have already talked to them about you and they are very interested in a chat, if you are thinking of a return to work.

Give it some thought, and get in touch if you're interested.

Have a great time off.

Richard

Subject: OUT

From: Charlie
To: Holly

Out at last! Thanks for your support, sis. I hear Mum knows the truth now, but I've called her and told her I just didn't want her worrying and the courts misunderstood my attempt to help improve corporate communications. She's fine. Am a bit miffed you didn't let her continue with the charity, I'm sure that money could have come in handy.

Just pulling your leg, don't be growling at me, I've told you before it's not ladylike.

xxx

PS On a serious note, it did actually give me time to think a lot about how I've been, and I will change, you just wait and see.

Love Charlie

X

Subject: Away

From: Charlie
To: WHOLE CLIENT LIST, FRIENDS LIST, Holly

Dear valued client/friend

As you know from my partner, Rubber Ron, I have been away. The real reason I went was to find myself but, as it happens instead I found JUNGLEJUICE (developed by tribal doctor Medicine Sam). It cures, it relieves, it medicates and, for £24.99, it can be yours!!!

Details attached, all major credit cards accepted. See our full catalogue online including bringing the authentic jungle experience directly to your home with this set of realistic/plastic jungle spears (not suitable for under fives). Buy all and get a missionary cooking pot free!!

If you liked *Scandal in the City*,
you'll love the original

Holly's inbox

sourcebooks
casablanca

week 1

monday

Subject: To Holly—New Job

From: Mum and Dad
To: Holly

Holly,

Exciting news about the job. Are you enjoying it?

Your sister has a parcel (books or something) that needs bringing out with you, when you come to see us. Alice says it's very important and 'Ferret,' a friend of hers, is passing by Maida Vale next week to drop it off.

Love, Mum

PS Send us your flight details!

From: Holly
To: Mum and Dad

Job—I don't know yet, only been here an hour, very busy.

Ferret—what? How does anyone get to make a friend called Ferret?

Parcel—no problem, as long as it's not too heavy.

xxxx

Subject: Welcome

From: Roger Lipton
To: Holly

Dear Holly,

Glad to have you on board.

I hear everything went well with your induction on Friday and you are now familiarising yourself with our systems and policies.

It's a shame the reception area is so separated from the rest of us here, but you know where we are if you need anything.

I hope you'll be very happy here.

Roger Lipton, Director of Human Resources, H&W, High Holborn WC2 6NP

From: Holly
To: Roger Lipton

Dear Mr Lipton,

Thank you for your email. I'm sure I'll be very happy; everyone has been so welcoming.

Kindest regards,

Holly

Receptionist, H&W, High Holborn WC2 6NP

Subject: Reception experience

From: Patricia Gillot
To: Holly

Holly,

I told them to get me a receptionist I could work with, like the one I had before with lots of experience. Not having a go at you on your first day, but I feel like giving up, I really do. Where've you worked again?

Trish

Patricia Gillot, Senior Receptionist, H&W, Holborn WC2 6NP

From: Holly
To: Patricia Gillot

Hi Patricia,

In 5* Hotels—on reception.

Holly

From: Patricia Gillot
To: Holly

Great.

From: Holly
To: Patricia Gillot

It was really busy there.   ·

From: Patricia Gillot
To: Holly

That's nice for you, darlin. Just keep grinning at people for today, and I'll do the rest. Hopefully by the end of the month you might know your arse from your elbow.
Trish
PS Stop trying to talk to me; this is a corporate bank. If you wanted to natter; you should've taken a job in a salon. Email me when you have a problem.

Subject: A good luck message

From: Alice and Matt
To: Holly

Holls,
Glad things are going so well again. It sounds wonderful there, and you've got yourself a new start. Just what you wanted.
Love,
Alice & Matt

From: Holly
To: Alice and Matt

I hate the job and everyone's awful.

From: Alice and Matt
To: Holly

Oh dear, by the way, thanks for agreeing to bring out our parcel. It's really nice of you.
xxxxxx

From: Holly
To: Alice and Matt

No problem. What's in it?

From: Alice and Matt
To: Holly

Oh, nothing, just a box of essentials.

From: Holly
To: Alice and Matt

What—books and things?

From: Alice and Matt
To: Holly

Yes, all that. I've given Ferret your number.
xxx

From: Holly
To: Alice and Matt

Oh good

tuesday

Subject: A little advice from your Mum

From: Mum and Dad
To: Holly

Holly,

Sorry to bother you again, dear. Glad to hear you bumped into Jennie from school. You were always very fond of her. Sounds like she's doing so well there.

I've given it some thought, and the only way you're going to get as far as she has done is by using any contacts you come across. My advice is: take her out for lunch as fast as possible. You never know what doors she could open for you.

What are you doing there at the moment again, PA work?

Mum xxx

From: Holly
To: Mum and Dad

Mum,

Jennie has been nice on the couple of occasions I've seen her, but I'm fine doing what I'm doing, which is RECEPTION work.

x

Holly

From: Mum and Dad
To: Holly

That's what I said, darling, it's the same thing.

Just make sure you eat properly, especially if you're going to be greeting all those people. You could pick up an infection from one of them.

Mum

Subject: A few pointers

From: Patricia Gillot
To: Holly

Stop standing up when people come to the desk!

I'm off for a fag. I'll be on the other side of the glass doors, and I'll be keeping an eye on you.

Got any problems—don't shout whatever you do. Just think you're working in a library, and you'll be halfway there.

From: Holly
To: Patricia Gillot

OK, Patricia. What time are toilet breaks?

From: Patricia Gillot
To: Holly

Any time you can't hold on, darlin—also, it's just Trish. No one calls me Patricia.

Subject: School Friend!!!

From: Jennie Pithwait
To: Holly

Hi Holly,

You went off the map for a few years. Where've you been??

So glad you're working here; sorry about the misunderstanding yesterday. I should have told you what Mr Huerst looked like; lucky he was so forgiving, even when you told him he needed an appointment.

Jennie

Jennie Pithwait, Associate, Corporate Finance, H&W, High Holborn WC2 6NP

From: Holly
To: Jennie Pithwait

Hi Jennie,

I felt like a real idiot. I even chased after him with his security pass.

Holly

From: Jennie Pithwait
To: Holly

He was fine. I said it was your first day.

What's it like sitting with Trisha?

From: Holly
To: Jennie Pithwait

Awful, rude, I can't stand her.

From: Jennie Pithwait
To: Holly

Tough old girl, probably doesn't get laid much. Great with clients, but that's about it.

Jennie

From: Holly
To: Jennie Pithwait

xxxx

Thanks Jennie.

Subject: Pretty P'Holly

From: Jason GrangerRM
To: Holly

Hiya,

How's the job going? Is it OK to email you?

Jason Granger, Reception Team Leader, LHS Hotels, London, W1V 6TT

From: Holly
To: Jason GrangerRM

Emailing is good, the job stinks, and I'm about to take a contract out on my mum.

How are you?

xx

From: Jason GrangerRM
To: Holly

I'm good.

Talking of stinky, guess what smelly celeb we've got staying here?

From: Holly
To: Jason GrangerRM

Smelly?

From: Jason GrangerRM
To: Holly

(Housekeeping told me she's got a few personal hygiene problems.)
Who cares though—she's famous!!!

From: Holly
To: Jason GrangerRM

That makes it OK then, does it?

From: Jason GrangerRM
To: Holly

Of course! You don't like her though (she's a bit of a marriage breaker)—can't tell you who it is. If you were still working here, I could, but I can't. It's a trust thing.

Enjoy your nasty bank.

From: Holly
To: Jason GrangerRM

JASON!!!

An Offer You Can't Refuse
Jill Mansell

"The perfect read for hopeless romantics who like happily-ever-after endings."—*Booklist*

Nothing could tear Lola and Dougie apart... except his mother...

When Dougie's mother offers young Lola a £10,000 bribe to break up with him, she takes it to save her family. Now, ten years later, a twist of fate has brought Dougie and Lola together again, and her feelings for him are as strong as ever.

But how can she win him back without telling him why she broke his heart in the first place?

"Mansell knows her craft and delivers a finely tuned romantic comedy." — *Kirkus Reviews*

"A fast pace and fun writing make the story fly by." —*Publisher's Weekly*

"Endearingly optimistic and full of attitude." —*Saturday Telegraph*

978-1-4022-1833-0 • $14.00 US